D1010519

DEVIL'S HARBOR

ALEX GILLY

DEVIL'S HARBOR

FORGE®

A TOM DOHERTY ASSOCIATES BOOK
NEW YORK

This is a work of fiction. All of the characters, organizations, and events portrayed in this novel are either products of the author's imagination or are used fictitiously.

DEVIL'S HARBOR

Copyright © 2015 by Alexander Gilly

All rights reserved.

A Forge Book
Published by Tom Doherty Associates, LLC
175 Fifth Avenue
New York, NY 10010

www.tor-forge.com

Forge® is a registered trademark of Tom Doherty Associates, LLC.

The Library of Congress Cataloging-in-Publication Data is available upon request.

ISBN 978-0-7653-7732-6 (hardcover)
ISBN 978-1-4668-5513-7 (e-book)

Forge books may be purchased for educational, business, or promotional use. For information on bulk purchases, please contact the Macmillan Corporate and Premium Sales Department at 1-800-221-7945, extension 5442, or write to specialmarkets@macmillan.com.

First Edition: June 2015

Printed in the United States of America

0 9 8 7 6 5 4 3 2 1

FOR KAREN,
AND FOR OSKAR

ACKNOWLEDGMENTS

First, sincere thanks to my agents, Charlie Campbell at Kingsford Campbell in London and Farley Chase at Chase Literary in New York, for seeing this book all the way through.

Next, a huge thank-you to Kristin Sevick, acquiring editor at Forge in New York, to her wonderful assistant, Bess Cozby, and to all the team at Forge who made this happen.

Thank you to everyone at the Writers' Studio in Sydney, most particularly Roland Fishman. For anyone who wants to develop a practice of writing, I know of no better place to do it than the Writers' Studio.

I'm deeply grateful to all those who read drafts and gave me feedback, particularly Marie-Hélène Gilly-Claudel as well as Laetitia Rutherford and Mark Milln.

Thank you to Aurelie-Anne Gilly and Ashley Underwood for answering my legal questions, and to Dr. Georgina Clark for answering my medical ones.

Thank you also to Dr. Victoire de Lastours, who at the final draft stage helped me distinguish the medically impossible from the merely improbable.

Thank you to Keley Hill, director of marine operations, and Marine Interdiction Agent Tony Williams from the U.S. Customs and Border Protection Office of Air and Marine in San Diego, for taking the time to talk me through the realities of the difficult work they do. Thank you also to Jackie Wasiluk from the CBP Public Affairs department in San Diego, for facilitating the interviews.

Finally and most important, thank you to my wife, Karen, without whom this novel never would have been finished. Karen, you told me to finish the book or you'd cancel the wedding. Well, now you're married to an author and have only yourself to blame. Thank you for believing. I couldn't be more blessed.

Consider the subtleness of the sea; how its most dreaded creatures glide under water, unapparent for the most part, and treacherously hidden beneath the loveliest tints of azure. Consider also the devilish brilliance and beauty of many of its most remorseless tribes, as the dainty embellished shape of many species of sharks. Consider, once more, the universal cannibalism of the sea; all whose creatures prey upon each other, carrying on eternal war since the world began.

—Herman Melville, *Moby-Dick*

DEVIL'S HARBOR

PROLOGUE

Marine Interdiction Agent Nick Finn peered at the suspect boat, his night-vision goggles tinting her insect-green against the black sea. She was a sport fisher around fifty to fifty-five feet long, with a flybridge and two long spindles sweeping back from her superstructure like antennae from the head of a praying mantis. It was a half hour before sunrise on a cold Thursday in October. The moon was waning. The praying mantis was treading water; she had just enough way on her to keep her nose pointed into the breeze. And she had her navigation lights switched off, which was why Finn was interested in her.

He was standing in the cockpit of a thirty-nine-foot Customs and Border Protection Interceptor about a mile northeast of the tiny hamlet of Two Harbors, on Catalina Island. He lowered the goggles. The air against his cheeks was cold; the sea looked colder. There was a light breeze out of the west. He looked up at the sky. A thin light the color of weak tea was creeping over the eastern horizon. Everywhere else, it was still dark.

He turned to his patrol partner and brother-in-law, Marine Interdiction Agent Diego Jimenez, and said, "It's officially night until the sun rises, right?" Finn saw Diego's silhouette against the lightening eastern horizon: thick stocking cap pulled down to his brow, collar up against the cold. The silhouette nodded and said, "Definitely."

Finn snorted cold, salty air. "So let's go tell this dope to turn his lights on," he said.

They arced around the unidentified boat and approached her from the west, where it was darkest. Then they swung in behind her and Finn scanned her again through the goggles. No one was visible aboard. The tinted-glass door leading from her stern deck to her cabin was shut, and he couldn't see any interior lights spilling from its edges. He figured whoever was inside hadn't yet noticed the Customs and Border Protection vessel approaching.

When they were within hailing distance, he switched on the wailer and the blue lights, then shone the spotlight on the boat's transom. The praying mantis had a name scrolled in gold letters: *La Catrina*. Finn swept the spotlight across her stern deck, and the beam reflected back at him from the glass door, an angry yellow eye dazzling his own. He pressed the spotlight's signal button and the orb in the glass blinked at him three times, then stayed lit.

La Catrina responded by taking off, her inboard roaring, her prop kicking up a rooster tail of white water. Finn caught a face full of exhaust, rubbed his stinging eyes with the back of his hand.

"I think we spooked her," said Diego, dry as sand.

"Jesus, she stinks. Get us out of her fumes," said Finn.

The Interceptor darted forward, jumping over her quarry's wake, and came up alongside her. Finn aimed the spotlight at *La Catrina*'s port-side window, but it, too, was tinted.

He frowned. "Let's give her the warning shot," he said, shouting over the noise of the outboards and rushing air. Diego nodded and pushed the Interceptor about twenty feet ahead of *La Catrina*. Finn pulled the Remington 870 from its holder and racked the action. The shotgun was loaded with a flash bang shell—harmless but intimidating. He aimed at a spot about ten feet ahead of the sport fisher.

"On target," he said loudly enough for Diego to hear. Then he thumbed down the safety, drew breath, and pulled the trigger.

A violent flash of white light tore up the darkness just ahead of *La Catrina*. The sound cracked through Finn's skull; he felt it in his teeth.

La Catrina responded by accelerating right through the cloud of smoke from the shotgun.

"Son of a bitch," said Finn, and he glanced in Diego's direction.

His younger friend was waiting for him to call their next move. Finn was vessel commander, so it was his call. He looked at the eastern horizon. Sunrise wasn't far off. He put the shotgun back in its holder, picked up the radio mic, and called the Air and Marine Operations Center. He gave their position, their course, their speed, and a description of the praying mantis. He said that she'd been running with her lights out and hadn't responded to their signals to heave to or to their warning shot.

Then he said, "I intend to board the vessel while under way. Over."

"While she's moving?" said Diego.

Finn heard the surprise in Diego's voice. He signed off and hung up the mic.

"Sure. We practiced it plenty in Saint Augustine," he said, referring to the CBP's National Marine Training Center in Saint Augustine, Florida.

"Yeah. But that was training. And we don't know who's in there," said Diego, pointing at the sport fisher.

Finn turned to look at their quarry.

"So let's go find out," he said.

The two boats were running no more than six feet apart, a narrowing channel of water rushing between them. Dawn was unfurling quickly and Finn could now see *La Catrina*'s teak deck with his naked eye, though he still couldn't see through the tinted windows into her cabin. He had the uncomfortable feeling of being watched.

He put a foot up on the Interceptor's gunwale and prepared to leap across.

Just then *La Catrina* veered left, hard. Diego reacted quickly enough to avoid slamming the Interceptor into her, but not quickly enough to prevent the two boats' sides grinding against each other. The impact threw Finn backward. He landed hard on the deck, right on his tailbone.

Diego eased off the throttle and the Interceptor drifted to a stop. He yelled to see if Finn was all right. Finn ignored him and made a show of bending over the side of the boat to check for damage. Turned out that only his pride and maybe his coccyx were bruised.

Making a supreme effort to ignore the pain in his backside, he walked stiffly back toward the console.

"Well, don't just stand there," he said, sounding sharper than he intended. "Go after him."

Diego closed the gap with *La Catrina*. Finn's knees and spine shuddered each time the Interceptor slapped down on the face of the sea, sending up a spray of salt water.

Soon they were running thirty feet or so behind the fleeing boat. Of the two boats, Finn knew, the Interceptor was the faster. He figured thirty knots was the sport fisher's top speed, whereas the Interceptor still had at least twenty more in her. No way the suspect boat could outrun them.

Trouble was, he and Diego were at the end of a six-hour shift. They had enough left in the tank to get back to the dock at Long Beach, but not enough to chase this bozo for miles across the sea. He had a choice: either figure out how to force *La Catrina* to stop now or call it in and let the guys in San Diego make the intercept.

Finn's pride was bruised enough as it was. He wasn't going to let someone else catch his prey.

He thought for a moment.

Then he went forward and grabbed a mooring line and two fenders. He pulled out his knife, cut off a fifteen-foot length of mooring line, and tied a fender to each end. Then he went back to the console and told Diego his plan.

Diego smiled. "That's even dumber than your last idea," he said. "I like it."

It was a tricky maneuver at any speed, let alone at thirty knots. Both men knew that Finn was by far the better helmsman, and anyway it was his idea, so it was only natural that he should handle it. Diego had ceded his place at the helm and was now in the stern, holding the fenders that Finn had tied to the length of line. Finn was now at the controls. His eyes were fixed on the praying mantis; his grip tightened on the wheel.

Both boats were running parallel on a southeast track. When he judged the distance to be right, Finn threw the Interceptor into a tight, torquey turn. The boat leaned toward the water. Now she was heading east-southeast, into the rising sun, with *La Catrina* on her left side about a hundred feet away and rapidly getting closer. The two boats were heading toward the same point, the Interceptor like a cowboy heading off a steer split from the herd. If neither vessel changed course or speed, they would slam into each other at a combined velocity of seventy knots. Finn's heart beat in overdrive. Adrenaline surged through him. If he'd timed it right, he figured he'd cross the sport fisher's bow with ten feet to spare. He felt 80 percent certain he'd timed it right.

Seventy, maybe.

"We gonna make it?" shouted Diego over the roar of the outboards.

"A hundred percent!" shouted Finn.

Just when collision seemed inevitable, Finn pushed the throttles all the way down, giving the Interceptor her last bit of thrust. She slingshotted ahead and launched clear off a wave. The blades of all four outboards cleared the air. For a moment, Finn felt weightless, his stomach rising. The praying mantis appeared so close, he could almost have reached out and grabbed the rail on her bow walk. Then the Interceptor slammed back down with a bone-shattering shudder.

"Now!" he screamed back at Diego.

Diego flung one of the fenders off the stern. It landed in the water a few feet ahead of *La Catrina,* on her starboard side. The line ran out after it. Diego made sure the fender attached to the other end cleared the outboards. It splashed down on *La Catrina*'s port side.

They'd managed to string fifteen feet of thick rope across the surface of the water right in front of *La Catrina*'s track, like a seaborne tripwire. And Finn had timed it so that there was no way she could avoid running over the line.

He carved the Interceptor around in a big turn, came up behind the praying mantis, and watched what happened.

La Catrina made it another fifty feet or so. Then she lost all her momentum, abruptly came off the plane, and drifted to a halt.

Finn smiled. He couldn't see it, but he could imagine how tightly the rope had wound around the sport fisher's propeller shaft. He could imagine gears grinding, shear pins snapping, oil leaking, rubber hoses melting as the engine overheated.

Just then, he saw a whiff of black smoke rise from what he figured was *La Catrina*'s engine room beneath her stern deck.

Still no one appeared from the cabin. That disturbed him. Almost all the traffickers he intercepted, when they realized there was no way out, turned meek—especially if their boats were about to sink or catch fire. Usually what they did was show themselves, put their hands in the air, make it clear that they were unarmed and surrendering. Most of them knew they were just going to get shipped home anyway.

Finn sensed that this guy was different. There was something all-or-nothing about this guy.

It was an attribute Finn shared.

He went to the gun locker and pulled out an M4 carbine. He clipped it into its mount on the starboard rail. Then he put a bead on the glass door and waited.

A minute passed. *La Catrina* bobbed serenely up and down, a thin stream of smoke rising from her stern. After all the commotion, the silence was eerie. Plus, Finn sensed that the M4 had changed the atmosphere, darkened the mood. Unlike the shotgun, the M4 was a battlefield weapon, and he knew Diego wasn't comfortable with it. Neither man spoke. Finn kept the rifle sighted on the glass door. He saw the Interceptor's blue lights flashing in the sport fisher's darkened windows.

"He coming out or what?" said Diego finally. He sounded nervous.

Finn thought he saw movement through the glass—with the tint, he couldn't be 100 percent sure. His finger tightened slightly on the trigger.

The door slid open.

A man stepped out.

One guy, dressed all in black.

"Manos arribas!" shouted Diego.

The guy gave him a blank look. He had black hair, a black mustache. The black smoke rising from the engine bay was thickening.

"You see a weapon?" asked Finn, his finger tightening a little more. He had a bead on the guy's chest. He was deliberate with his breathing.

"No. No weapon," said Diego, still sounding nervous. He shouted at the guy some more in Spanish.

The guy kept staring at them. His arms hung at his side.

"Put your hands up!" Finn shouted in English.

The guy's hands didn't move.

He started shuffling toward the stairs leading to the flybridge.

Then he started climbing the stairs.

"Where the fuck does he think he's going?" said Finn.

Diego kept yelling in Spanish. Finn didn't understand what Diego was saying, but whatever it was clearly wasn't working. The guy ignored them both and kept going up the stairs. When he got to the flybridge, he disappeared from view.

Finn realized the guy now had the height advantage. If he came out with a weapon, he'd be shooting downward. Letting him get up there had been a tactical mistake.

The guy reappeared.

He had something in his hands. Finn thought it looked like an AK-47, but before he could be sure, the breeze pushed the plume of smoke in front of the guy, obscuring him.

Then he heard what sounded like machine-gun fire.

The smoke cleared.

He saw the guy firing at them. Shells spat from the gun, going over the flybridge rail.

Finn had the M4 set on semiautomatic. He fired a single three-round burst.

Two of the rounds blew holes through the fiberglass canopy above the guy. The third caught him in the chest. His arms flew up and he lost hold of his weapon. He stumbled back, flipped over the rail, and fell into the sea.

CHAPTER ONE

Twelve days after Finn had shot and killed Rafael Aparición Perez, he was back on patrol, looking out over the Interceptor's stern. It was the end of a cool autumn day, with the Santa Anas blowing exhaust fumes inboard and shreds of cloud off the San Gabriel Mountains, across Los Angeles and out over the dirty, wind-chopped sea. Night was falling, and in the two minutes since they'd left the dock, the water's color had changed from police-uniform blue to slate.

Diego was slouched in the helmsman's seat, one leg dangling, as he helmed the Interceptor at no-wake speed toward the gap in the breakwater that protected the vast Terminal Island port complex from the Pacific's swells. He was wearing a pair of blue Customs and Border Protection overalls, a low-profile life jacket over that. The black grip of a Heckler & Koch P2000 stuck out from the holster on his utility belt. He was arguing that Finn shouldn't have shot Perez, enumerating the reasons it had been a bad idea.

Finn, wearing the same CBP uniform and carrying the same service-issue handgun on his hip, was only half listening to his young patrol partner. He felt the low-rev shudder of the four 300-horsepower Mercury outboards passing through the floor and up through his legs. After more than a week of mandatory leave, it felt good to be back on the water.

"You shouldn't have shot him," Diego said again.

"He was shooting at us."

"I'm telling you, it's gonna be a giant headache for the both of us," said Diego, not hearing Finn.

"It'll blow over," said Finn.

Diego didn't look convinced. They were nearing the breakwater.

"What did Mona say about it?" said Diego.

Finn turned to face him and said, "She's glad I wasn't the one who got killed."

"She say it like that?"

"Her words exactly."

"What about me? She say she was glad I wasn't killed, either?"

"She didn't say."

Among other things, Finn had missed the shipboard banter during his furlough. Moping around the house hadn't been good for him. It had darkened his mood.

"If one of us was killed, who do you think she'd be more upset about, you or me?" said Diego.

"I'm her husband."

"Yeah, but she's my sister. What's worse, a dead husband or a dead brother?"

"A dead husband, no question."

Diego shook his head. "Your husband gets killed, you can always get another. But you only get one brother."

"Maybe. But when I asked, she said she'd choose me over you."

They were passing the breakwater now. The gulls on the rocks squawked.

"You actually asked that?" said Diego.

"Yup," lied Finn.

"Really? And that's what she said?"

"Her words exactly."

Diego shook his head. "Dude. That's fucked up."

Finn turned back toward the stern to hide his grin. The sun was setting and he watched the fading light gild the playing fields and gardens of the Terminal Island Federal Correctional Institution, its

garden plots a glade amid the mesas of container stacks and forests
of giant cranes in the port behind it. The stacks and prison buildings
protected the water in the channels at either side of the island from
the wind, and the low-slung light now gave it a lacquered look, like
the surface of a newly waxed car. The sheen made the water look
clean, but Finn knew better. He'd seen what dregs the city flushed
out through its sewers and overflow outlets.

He knew what drifted in the depths.

The outboards roared to life and sent him lurching toward the
stern. They had passed into open water, and Diego had opened the
throttles.

He'd neglected to warn Finn.

An hour later, Finn took the helm from Diego. He leaned against
the chair and pulled back the throttles, leaving just enough thrust
to give the Interceptor way. The Santa Anas and the chop had died
down. Now the sea was dark and quiet. They were five miles off
Santa Catalina Island, about midway between Two Harbors and
the resort town of Avalon.

Not far from where he'd shot Perez.

Finn rested his hands on the wheel, the boat drifting ahead, his
fingers reading her slightest movements, his whole body in its element. He sensed the effect that the current streaming alongside
Catalina was having on the boat, how the waves refracting off the
island were nudging her bow eastward, toward Newport. Instinctively he held the wheel a quarter inch off-center so that she tracked
true. He gazed out at the starlight reflecting off the sea and, though
he couldn't see it, he knew the flow was slackening, that the tide
was reaching its peak, and that, when it started ebbing, it would
travel at least two knots.

He let go of the wheel and scanned the darkness through the
night-vision binoculars. The thirty-nine-foot Midnight Express

Interceptor was a state-of-the-art boat fitted with state-of-the-art navigation electronics, and Finn loved it dearly. But he'd served in the Gulf, aboard inshore boats patrolling the waters around the Al-Basrah Oil Terminal, keeping it, the contractors rebuilding it, and the supertankers docking at it safe from insurgents, and he'd seen the damage that blind faith in marine electronics could cause. He took advice from the machines, but he trusted only his own eyes.

And then, there was the phantom. Over the last four months, Finn and Diego had picked up a signal off Catalina three times on the radar, had gone looking for it three times, and three times had come up empty-handed. The last time it had happened was the night he'd shot Perez.

He let the binoculars hang around his neck and killed the engines. He planned to drift awhile, wait for the tide to turn, and enjoy being out on the dark, quiet sea. He heard Diego snap shut his Zippo lighter and saw the orange glow of the cigarette's ember brighten. Finn stared into the darkness and retreated into his thoughts.

When Perez had opened fire, maybe what he should've done was drop back to a safe distance and called for backup. Instead of returning fire, maybe he should've ensured the safety of himself and his crew first. There'd been no reason to get into a firefight. "You're not in a war zone anymore," Mona had said. Her words had been looping in his head ever since, and he hadn't been sleeping right. For the first time in a year and a half, he'd felt like a drink—another reason to get back on the water.

On the other hand, the guy had been shooting at him; all he'd done was return fire and hit his target. It seemed simple enough, and part of him resented Mona for not seeing it like that. He thought he'd just been unlucky, that when his shot had hit his target, Perez and his weapon had splashed into the sea. They'd recovered Perez's body, but his gun had gone straight to the bottom.

Out in the patch of night into which he was staring, he saw something shift. He raised the binoculars to his eyes.

"What?" said Diego.

"Thought I saw something."

He stared through the glasses for a full minute before looking down at the radar. Dozens of green dots to the east of their position revealed all the vessels plying the channel into the Port of Los Angeles. Most were tracking north or south, heading into or leaving Long Beach. He checked his watch. The glow-in-the-dark face told him that it was close to midnight. He pointed at a dot tracking eastward from the island.

"There," he said, looking up from the screen in time to see Diego flick his cigarette butt into the sea.

Finn got behind the wheel and pushed down the throttles. The nose tilted up and the boat gathered speed, lifting until it was on the plane. Wind blasted through the cockpit. Diego held fast to the handles on the console, the instruments' green glow lighting his face so that he looked like a creepy magician Finn had once seen on a fun-park poster as a boy.

"Moving slow like that, might be just a fishing boat," said Diego, shouting against the roar of the engines.

"No. She's the phantom," said Finn.

At the intercept point, he pulled her back into neutral. The roar died, the way fell off her, and her knifelike bow dropped. He looked down at the display. Half a mile of water separated the two vessels, according to the radar. Diego stepped onto the aft deck and scanned the darkness through the night-vision binoculars.

"You see it?" said Finn.

"I don't see anything," said Diego.

"It's right there," said Finn.

"Yeah, well, I don't see it. She's got her lights out, that's for sure."

"Give me the binoculars."

Diego was right. The binoculars revealed nothing. Yet there she was, on the radar.

"Kill the lights," said Finn.

Diego switched off their navigation and interior lights and dimmed the display, blacking out the boat. Water splashed against the hull. It sounded louder in the dark.

"I don't like it," said Diego.

Finn didn't, either. "Better get the M4," he said.

He switched the lights back on. Diego hadn't moved.

"Did you hear me?"

"Why? We got nothing to shoot at."

"We got an unidentified boat blacked out right under our nose, Diego. I don't want to get shot."

"Let's find it first, see who it is. Could be nothing, Finn. Could be some bozo on a Sunseeker he bought last week, looking for Avalon." Then, more quietly, he added, "I don't need you shooting another Mexican."

Finn stared at his friend. "You're an idiot, you know that?" he said. "Fine, I'll get it myself."

He started moving toward the forward cubby where they kept the M4 carbine.

Diego pointed at the screen. "Don't bother," he said.

Finn looked at the radar.

The green dot was gone.

Finn pushed the twelve hundred horses wide open and sent the boat straight into the blackness at forty knots, the boat leaping from the crests of unseen waves, the whine of her spinning blades rising an octave each time they broke free from the surface. He knew what he was risking. The quarter moon wasn't giving much light; driftwood, migrating whales, and containers floating just below the surface were not uncommon in the channel.

He didn't care.

They reached the point where the phantom had been when her echo had disappeared. He slowed down, looped the boat across her own wake, and idled the engines.

Nothing but cold air and dark sea.

"How does a boat just disappear like that?" said Diego, turning 360 degrees with the binoculars. Finn looked at the compass dome and speculated on which direction the phantom might have gone. North, toward Oxnard or Santa Rosa Island? West, back to Catalina? Southwest, to the naval base on San Clemente?

The naval base brought to Finn's mind another axis. "Maybe she's a sub," he said, "one of those narco-subs."

Diego lowered the goggles. "Seems weird how she didn't dive till she's this far north of the line," he said.

"Maybe she's too small, a custom job with a limited amount of air, built in some guy's backyard," said Finn. "So she stays on the surface as long as possible, till she sees us or the Coast Guard."

Diego nodded. "That would explain her vanishing act."

Finn switched on the sounder and turned the beam-width knob to its maximum so that the sounder revealed the widest possible wedge of water beneath them. Schools of fish at different depths appeared as bright green arcs.

"Jesus, look at that," said Diego, pointing at a slow-moving, inch-long block of solid green.

"Whale?" said Finn.

"Not on its own. A big shark, more likely. *Real* big."

A swarm of butterflies took flight in Finn's gut. He hated sharks.

He nudged the throttle forward and set the Interceptor on a course to follow the phantom's projected track. If the phantom was a sub and she hadn't changed course, the sounder would pick her up.

By five A.M. they were back at their original intercept point for the tenth time. They'd sounded the depths of a large patch of water north, east, and south of Two Harbors and had found nothing but fish. The radar had not picked up the phantom again.

The two CBP marine interdiction agents gave up the search and resumed their patrol. An hour passed without incident and in silence before Finn said, "About Perez . . . have we got a problem there, Diego?"

Diego lit a cigarette. "If you mean for the incident report, no. The guy opened fire and you returned it. That's what happened and that's what I told them. If you mean out here . . ." He dragged on the cigarette and searched for words. "You were a sniper in the navy, right?"

"I was the designated marksman on our patrol boat."

"And for that you had sniper training, right?"

Finn nodded in the dark. "Sure, I had a bit of training," he said. In fact, Finn had served with the navy's Maritime Expeditionary Security Force, and had been trained to shoot accurately from one moving boat at another. Finn was a very good shot.

"And you were in Iraq, so, you know, you've probably been in firefights before," said Diego. "Me, I've never been shot at, or seen anyone get killed before. I'm not too proud to say, it shook me up."

Finn got where Diego was coming from. The CBP Office of Air and Marine was nominally a civilian organization, not a military one, but the fact was that 90 percent of the guys serving in it were ex-military. Diego was one of the 10 percent. He'd started out in a booth at San Ysidro, waving through cars.

"You've seen bodies before," he said. "How many floaters have you and I pulled out?"

"I don't mean Perez. I mean *you*. I'd never seen someone kill another human being. You were just so *cold*. It shook me up, man, after knowing you all these years."

The sun was rising. Finn stared into the blackness to the west, screwing up his eyes.

"You get used to it."

He realized he'd said the exact same thing to Mona. He was speaking the words without believing them.

An irregular shape in the near water caught his eye. He grabbed the handheld marine spotlight and aimed its beam at it.

The beam passed over something matte and gray floating on the sea's shimmering, blue-black surface. Phlegm caught in his throat. He jerked the beam back to the object.

"Over there . . ."

"I see it," said Diego. He took the wheel and drove the boat toward it.

They drew nearer. Both men recognized it long before they drew alongside. Over the years, they'd pulled dozens of floaters from the water—freighter-crew suicides, murder victims dumped from boats, rank, fish-eaten John Does. It was almost a routine part of their jobs, yet neither man had ever managed to formulate the right thing to say. So they did what they always did and said nothing. Diego handed Finn a set of latex gloves and pulled on a pair himself. Finn passed him the handheld spotlight and took out the boat hook from under the rail. He was nervous. A dead body in the water was like a beacon to sharks. Diego used one hand to keep the spotlight shining on the body, the other to steer the boat toward it. Finn leaned far out, with his thighs pressed against the rail, holding the gaff pole in both hands, his torso bent forward, just a couple of feet above the water. He sensed a presence beneath him and looked down. A huge black shape glided beneath the hull. He jerked back into an upright position.

"Jesus," he said, sweating cold.

"What?" said Diego.

"Shark."

"Well, hurry up, then."

Finn leaned out again, not so far this time. He kept one hand on the rail and with the other gaffed the body and pulled it aboard as quickly as he could. He was surprised at how light it was.

Then he saw why.

The shark had taken the man's legs.

He laid the body down on the stern deck.

The sweetish, sickening stench told Finn that the bloated corpse had started to putrefy. He made a point of not looking at the stubs where the man's legs should've been and instead concentrated on his face.

The floater was a young Latino man. He had on a blue-and-white Dallas Cowboys jersey, the hem black with blood. There was peach fuzz on his upper lip. Rust-colored liquid streamed out of his mouth. His hazel eyes pointed at the lightening sky.

Finn went forward to fetch the body bag from the cubby. When he came out, he saw Diego looking at the GPS, fixing their position. Diego took the white plastic bag from him and wrote their coordinates and the time on it with a Sharpie. They laid the bag down next to the body and unzipped it.

Once they'd bagged the body, Diego turned to Finn as though he wanted to say something. But whatever it was slipped away unsaid. Instead, he picked up the mic and radioed in what they'd found.

Finn turned toward the eastern horizon. He heard his own shallow breathing and the sound of the water slapping against the fiberglass hull. In the far distance, first light was creeping over the endless sprawl of Los Angeles.

CHAPTER TWO

The emergency workers were waiting on the dock, one of them sitting on the gurney, looking relaxed, the sun behind them filling the world with gold.

After they'd trolleyed the body away, Finn slipped off his life jacket and got to work scrubbing the floater's blood out of the deck with a hard-bristle broom. Diego hosed it down after him. Finn tried to steer his mind away from the image of the legless young man, but it kept coming back at him like a tetherball.

He heard steps, looked up, and saw a pair of boots on the dock at eye level. He looked up some more and saw Garcia, a short, very overweight man in a CBP dress uniform—midnight-blue shirt, black tie. He had a rolled-up newspaper tucked under his arm. Finn had never seen Garcia in work overalls.

"I heard you guys picked up half a floater," said Garcia, grinning down at them.

Finn frowned and went back to scrubbing. Garcia picked up on the vibe.

"Seriously, though, how far were you from Catalina when you found the body?" Garcia said, the humor gone from his tone.

Finn stopped scrubbing and looked up. "Few miles. Why?"

"I saw on the TV this report about how there's been a bunch of shark sightings off the island lately," said Garcia, "way more than usual."

Diego cut the hose. "Every time anyone sees a shark, the TV people make like it's a big deal," he said. "It's the ocean and there are sharks in it. Period."

Garcia shrugged. "Just telling you what I heard. Also, the DMO wants to see you in his office, Finn, A-sap."

"Where'd they say they've been seeing the sharks?" said Finn.

"Out off Catalina."

"Channel side or ocean side?"

"Channel side."

"The DMO say what he wants to see me about?"

"No, but I think I got an idea," said Garcia. He handed down the newspaper.

"Page three, metro."

Finn leaned the broom against the rail and watched Diego open the paper.

Diego read in silence and started shaking his head.

"Holy fuck," he said finally.

"Gimme that," said Finn.

FAMILY OF CBP SHOOTING VICTIM SUES U.S. GOVERNMENT

by Garrett Smith

In the early hours of October 8, a U.S. Customs and Border Protection Marine Interdiction agent fatally shot a 46-year-old man some two miles east of Catalina Island.

Rafael Aparición Perez, a citizen of Mexico and the father of four, was aboard a fifty-five-foot Hatteras Sport Fisherman called *La Catrina*. After allegedly failing to respond to the CBP agent's order to heave to, he allegedly opened fire at the CBP Midnight Express Interceptor with an automatic rifle. Marine Interdiction Agent Nicholas Peter Finn (pictured) then allegedly shot him dead.

The law firm Edsall, Luna, Cheng of Los Angeles has confirmed that it is representing the family of Mr. Perez and that it intends to file a civil lawsuit against the U.S. government for wrongful death.

"The best-case scenario is that Mr. Perez is dead because he didn't understand English," said Jim Edsall, lead counsel for the Perez family. "The worst case? He's dead because of endemic bias and racism within the CBP. The agent saw an Hispanic man driving an expensive boat and assumed he was a drug dealer, when in fact Mr. Perez, a businessman who owned three gas stations in the Tijuana area, was simply out fishing. This is yet another example of the total failure of our border policies."

In a statement released to the press, the CBP said it regrets the loss of life and is conducting an internal investigation. A source within the CBP confirmed that Agent Finn remains on active duty.

Finn folded the paper and handed it back to Garcia.

"There's an editorial, too. The DMO is pissed, Finn," said Garcia, before walking off.

When they were alone, Diego said, "Edsall fucking Luna Cheng. They've got themselves the best law firm drug money can buy. You need a lawyer, Finn."

Finn forced a grin. "Good thing I'm married to one," he said.

He went back to scrubbing. He knew he should've been worrying about the lawsuit, but he couldn't stop thinking about the sharks.

Heading up from the dock to the Long Beach Air and Marine Station, Finn saw *La Catrina* sitting in a cradle at the top of the launching ramp. He hadn't seen her since she'd been lifted out of the water. He figured Immigration and Customs Enforcement had their forensics guys combing over her. Finn wasn't a forensics guy, but he knew boats, so he figured he'd take another quick look. The director, Marine Operations would just have to wait.

La Catrina was fifty-five feet of gleaming white freeboard, superstructure, and deck. Her tinted windows were set at a raked angle, which, along with her flared, Carolina-style bow, gave her an aggressive, raptorlike look. A week after the fire in the engine bay, she still smelled of burned fiberglass. After he'd shot Perez, Finn had boarded *La Catrina,* found her fire extinguisher, and tried to put out the fire, but the extinguisher had failed. Diego had had to throw one over to him from the Interceptor.

Finn looked at the boat and wondered what her secret was. There had to be a reason why Perez had opened fire, he reasoned; if Perez had had nothing to hide, why had he opened fire?

Nor could Finn make sense of what the man had been doing off Catalina. As far as he knew, the cartels had no people on the island; all the action was on the mainland.

Then he thought that maybe *La Catrina* hadn't been going anywhere when they found her; maybe she'd been treading water because she was waiting to meet another boat. . . .

The phantom.

Finn felt a rush of excitement. Maybe if he and Diego had shown up half an hour later . . .

Finn was more convinced than ever that the narcotics were still somewhere onboard.

Find the drugs, he thought, and suddenly Perez wasn't a nice family man out fishing anymore.

The day was heating up. He unzipped the top part of his overalls and banged on the hull. A man in oil-stained coveralls, the letters ICE just visible under the stains, appeared from the engine bay.

"Found the stash yet?" said Finn.

The man wiped his hands on a rag. "Not even a single joint," he said. Then he said, "You're Finn, right? The MIA that shot the guy?"

Finn frowned. He was getting famous for all the wrong reasons. "What about shells from an AK-47?" he asked.

The forensics guy shook his head.

"Not one? You put a dog on it?"

The man nodded. "Yep. No dice."

"Check the fuel tanks?"

"I'm telling you, there's nothing here."

Finn started scanning for cuts in the resin-infused fiberglass hull.

"Where's the rest of the forensics team?"

"You're looking at it."

Finn looked up, furious. It must've shown, because the guy said, "Hey, don't look at me. That's the order from the boss. Said we couldn't afford the manpower."

"But it's going to take you all week!"

The guy raised his hands in the universal gesture of helpless frustration and said, "You don't think I know that?"

"Keep looking," muttered Finn. "It's there, I know it. He didn't want to get stopped, and there's a reason for it."

"Well, if there are narcotics here, they've been real clever about hiding it, is all I can say."

Finn tapped the hull.

"They're drug traffickers. They're not that smart."

The director of Marine Operations' secretary told Finn that the boss was busy and he'd have to wait. He passed the time looking at photos of past directors, of the commissioner of the Customs and Border Protection Agency, of the secretary of Homeland Security, and of the president of the United States, each and every one of them posed before a background of the Stars and Stripes.

Finally he was invited in.

DMO Glenn didn't look like he'd been busy. Without getting up from the high-backed leather throne behind his vast, glass desk, he waved Finn toward a seat. Finn's mood blackened. First the floater, now this.

There was nothing on Glenn's desk except a near-empty in-box, a severe-looking desk lamp, a framed photo facing out toward his visitors, a whiff of Windex, and a copy of the day's *Times*. A leafy potted plant drooped in the corner near the door, far from the morning sunlight streaming through the window. A flag hung from a pole in the other corner.

DMO Glenn was a small man with a small, round, close-cropped head. His eyes darted around behind small, round glasses perched on a pug nose, and he had a rash-colored mustache. His small, womanish hands were clasped over the copy of the *Times*. He wore a blue uniform shirt, meticulously pressed, and a gold badge on the left side of his chest, his name embroidered on the right. The framed photo facing out, which was meant to be seen by visitors, showed Glenn in shorts and a singlet, standing by a striped marlin hanging from its tail on a dock. The chief had the thin white legs and flabby triceps of a man who worked all year behind a glass-and-metal desk. The marlin was as long as Glenn was tall, not counting its bill, and Finn figured it to be at least 180 pounds. He wondered how Glenn had landed it and decided he hadn't. Then he wondered how the Long Beach Air and Marine Station had ended up with a civilian DMO, one who'd been parachuted into the position from Miami, which meant that nobody knew anything about him, other than that he was an asshole.

Finn held Glenn's gaze, waiting for the man to get to the point. Glenn looked away, taking a long moment to look out his window, which Finn figured he was doing for effect, since the view was of the windowless wall of another building.

Then Glenn turned, swept away an imaginary speck of dust from his spotless desk, and said, "A hundred miles from the border and you managed to create a border incident. This is a terrible mess, Agent Finn."

"If you mean Perez, the guy opened fire on us. I just—"

Glenn pushed his glasses back up his nose. "I don't care about Perez. I mean this!" he said, bringing his finger down on the copy of the *Los Angeles Times*. "Have you read the editorial? No? Here's a summary: they're saying you're a cowboy, with your lasso trick. They make it look like we're *all* a bunch of cowboys who shoot first and ask questions later. It's a PR disaster. We're in full damage control. You got a lawyer or you want a union one?"

"I didn't shoot first. And you're worried about what the newspapers are saying?" said Finn.

The pitch of Glenn's voice jumped a couple of notes. "*Of course* I'm worried about what the newspapers are saying. There's a bigger picture, Agent Finn. There's more at stake here than a few pangas landing on the beach. This could go national. We have to fix this." Glenn's face was flushed the color of sunburn.

"Fix it how?" said Finn.

With thumb and forefinger, Glenn stroked his mustache. "I called the paper, said I wanted to make a statement. And I spoke to the assistant commissioner in Washington. He suggested we conduct a proper inquiry, and I agreed."

Finn looked quizzical. "A proper inquiry?" he said.

Glenn leaned forward. "The Office of Internal Affairs in Washington is sending out two of their guys. Guys with no connection to this station or even to Air and Marine. We need to make it clear to the media that we're doing things thoroughly. That we're not hiding anything."

"Wait—I *do* get it. You're hanging me out to dry."

"I'm not 'hanging you,'" said Glenn, making air quotes, but saying it like he wished he were. "I'm establishing a proper, multichannel internal investigation that will get to the truth—"

"We already had our own investigation—"

"That was before the family sued and the *Times* got the story."

"What difference does that make?"

"A statement from you and a statement from Agent Jimenez is not a proper investigation—"

"You planning to get a statement from Perez?"

Finn heard the squeak as Glenn shifted in his leather chair.

"This isn't a joke, Agent Finn. The government's being sued. People in Washington are asking questions. Worse than that, the media's having a field day. They'll say there was a cover-up. Customs and Border Protection gets enough bad press as it is."

It had been a long night. Finn was tired. He wasn't in the mood to argue. But he pushed back because he knew it mattered.

"Doesn't matter whether they say there was a cover-up or not, so long as there wasn't one. He was shooting at us. I did my job. That's it."

"It's more complicated than that."

"You mean it's ruining your chance of promotion?"

"You're forgetting that I'm your boss."

"Exactly. You're meant to be on my side."

"Of course I'm on your side," said Glenn, "But let's not make it about who's on whose side. Don't be so black-and-white."

Finn fumed. This was what it meant to have a civilian for a boss. No sense of corps.

"What about *La Catrina*?" he said.

"What about her?"

"You've only got one forensics guy searching her. It's not enough."

"We had a team go over her, top to bottom. There's nothing there."

"Of course there is, otherwise Perez wouldn't have run. They just haven't found it yet."

"I can't waste precious resources, Agent Finn."

Finn gave up. He got up to go.

"One moment, Agent Finn. The IA agents want to speak to you, obviously. I've arranged an interview for tomorrow morning, nine A.M."

"An interview?"

"To establish the facts."

"You could've just e-mailed them my incident report."

"They said they want to hear it from you."

Finn walked toward the door.

"Oh, and one more thing," said Glenn. "Obviously, you're going to have to stay under the radar for a while."

Finn narrowed his eyes. " 'Under the radar'?"

"I'm pulling you off the water and seconding you to field operations. Just until this blows over."

Glenn, in his perfectly pressed uniform, behind his gleaming, empty desk with the framed photo of his prize on it, leaned back in his chair.

"I've got the highest intercept rate on this station, *sir*," said Finn.

"Cargo inspection is a worthwhile job. You'll do fine. And above all, don't talk to any media people. Any journalist tries to talk to you, you send them to me, you hear? Any questions?"

Finn pointed at the photo on the desk. "What bait did you use?"

It took Glenn a moment to understand. "Mackerel," he said.

Finn nodded. "That's a striped marlin," he said. "Protected species, right?"

"Not down in Mexico. I took that one off Alijos Rocks, in Mexican waters," said Glenn, his voice swelling with pride.

"Mexican waters," said Finn. "Right."

He left the room.

Finn walked out of the Long Beach Air and Marine Station, a single-story, cinder-block, flat-roofed building behind a stand of drooping gray gum trees that did nothing to disguise the architect's half-assed effort. Put some razor wire on the wall and you'd think it was a prison block like the ones down the road, he thought. Like every other CBP agent stationed on Terminal Island, Finn had to drive past the brand-spanking-new coast guard HQ, all glass and steel and irrigated lawns, on his way to work. And in Washington they wondered why the CBP had the lowest morale of any federal agency.

He walked through the lot to his dual-cab Tacoma, pressed the remote key without taking it out of his pocket, stepped up into the driver's seat, and pulled the door shut behind him.

He flipped down the visor and looked in the vanity mirror. His nostrils flared with each heavy breath. Angry red lines webbed from his pale blue irises. The crow's-feet at the corners of his eyes had deepened. He flipped up the mirror, unlocked the glove compartment, unclipped his holster, and put his service weapon in the box, next to the binoculars and Maglite he kept there for when he was doing boat-ramp surveillance.

Finn locked the glove compartment and sank back in the seat. He wanted a drink. Back in the old days, he would've gone out and had one. A year and a half ago, he'd almost lost his job and his marriage to drink. He thought about Mona, how close she'd come to walking away. He was thinking about the things she'd said that day, and about the promise he'd made to her, when knuckles rapped on his window, startling him. A heavy man of medium height with thinning black hair, an unshaven chin, and the kind of quick smile common to guys who never grew out of their high school wisecracking habits stood on the other side of the glass. Garrett Smith, a crime reporter with the *Los Angeles Times,* was wearing a tie, loosened over an unbuttoned and poorly ironed shirt, no jacket. Finn had known him for a few years now—Customs and Border Protection was Smith's beat. Finn rolled down the glass.

"You here to apologize?" he said.

"You see me holding flowers?" said Smith.

"What do you want, Smith?"

"Jesus, you're not being too friendly to your friendly beat reporter."

"I read your article."

Smith straightened his smile. "Hey, listen, I know the suit's bullshit, Finn. Edsall, Luna, Cheng? Come on. But I had to write it. It's my beat."

Finn frowned. "You quoted Edsall saying I was racist. He said I liked to shoot Mexicans."

Smith wagged a finger. "He implied it, he didn't say it. There's a difference."

Finn drummed his fingers on the steering wheel.

"What are you doing here, Smith? Apart from being an asshole?"

"I heard you stole breakfast from a shark."

Finn said nothing.

"You know there's been a bunch of sightings lately off Catalina?" said Smith.

Finn looked at him blankly.

"Come on, Finn. Shark attacks sell newspapers. Give me something."

Finn wasn't feeling generous.

"Can you give me something about the victim, at least?" said Smith. He had his pen and spiral pad out.

"Sure. The victim is definitely dead."

Smith tapped his notebook with his pen. "Any idea what kind of shark it was?" he said.

"A hungry one."

"All right, I get it. You're mad at me. Forget the shark. How do you respond to the allegation that you used disproportionate force when you put a bullet through the Mexican fisherman?" said Smith.

Finn flipped him the bird as he drove away.

CHAPTER THREE

Finn and Mona rented half a stucco-fronted duplex two blocks back
from Redondo Beach. They couldn't afford a view of the sea but
could afford to live close enough to smell it, which Finn figured was
good enough for the time being. Since there was no garage, he kept
two beach cruisers chained to a downspout out behind the house
to get them to the pier. The bikes smelled of the WD-40 he con-
tinually sprayed on their chains and sprockets to guard against the
salt. Mona complained that he put so much on, it stained her clothes,
and then the chains rusted anyway, but Finn was dogged about it.
On weekend mornings when he wasn't on shift and she wasn't working a pro bono case, they would make love, then ride the push-bikes
to the fish market and waterside restaurants.

The summer before, Mona had worn a wide-brimmed straw hat
she'd seen in a fancy boutique, which he'd bought for her even
though he'd privately thought it was way too expensive for a straw
hat. Once, Finn had glanced at Mona pedaling away alongside him,
her hair lifting off her shoulders and the brim of the straw hat
curling back, and he had realized he was happier than ever before.
That was why he was so diligent with the anticorrosion spray.

By the time Finn got home, Mona had left for work. He showered
and shaved, plugged his phone into the charger on the bedside table,
and got into bed.

He woke to find Mona sitting on the edge of the bed. Late-afternoon light gilded the edges of the palm fronds that scraped against the windowpane.

"You're home," he said.

Mona had her sable-colored hair back in a ponytail. She was wearing a tan suit skirt and a collarless white blouse tucked into it. The suit jacket, along with her black "good fake" handbag, lay on the end of the bed next to Finn's feet. She was wearing what she called her no-nonsense lawyer outfit. Mona was a voluptuous woman, even in her most somber clothes: her blouse stretched tautly over her breasts, her skirt curved around her rump. Her long brows arched over kind, almond-shaped eyes. She smiled and her cheeks dimpled.

"How was your day?" he said.

"It's good to be home."

She leaned down and kissed him, still smiling. He was wide awake now. He wrapped his arms around her and flipped her onto her back.

"I read the article in the *Times*," she said.

The smile fell off his face.

She stroked his cheek. "You okay?" she said.

"I was worried you might write a letter or something."

"Oh, I did. I wrote to the editor saying I was going to sue them for publishing insinuations and fabrications and for showing you in a false light. I said the suit was frivolous, opportunistic, and totally inappropriate. I said the man in the article is *not* the man I married. I know who you are."

Finn saw the laughter in her eyes. "You didn't send it, did you?"

She laughed. "No. But I wanted to. I was so *mad*."

The muscle at the base of Finn's neck twitched and unraveled.

"You know who I am, huh?" he said.

"Every inch of you. What about you? You know who I am?"

He kissed her neck, her cheek. "Sure," he said.

"Oh yeah? You sure? Tell me who I am."

He stroked his chin, made a show of collecting his thoughts.

"You were raised in Lincoln Heights. Your dad worked construction. Retired, moved out to Glendale, but can't stop working, so he's set himself up as a part-time carpenter out there. Your mom's a mom. You have one brother who got shortchanged, since you got the looks *and* the brains. You graduated from Lincoln High and were the first person in your family to go to college. You went to USC on a full scholarship and majored in politics with minors in French and Spanish. Then you went to Gould School of Law—"

"You sound like you're reading my CV."

"You're a woman who helps people who need help."

She rolled her eyes. "Could you make me any more boring," she said.

"Like everyone in your family, you like dogs."

She feigned a yawn. "Tell me something no one else knows."

"Okay. You're the finest piece of ass on the West Coast."

She opened her eyes wide in mock umbrage. "Let go of my hand so I can slap you. What about the East Coast?"

"You're the world's slowest cyclist."

"What's the rush?"

"You curl your toes when you come."

She giggled. "Better," she said.

She pushed him onto his back and straddled him.

"You just earned yourself a *cinq à sept,* monsieur."

"What's that?"

She started to unbutton her blouse. "It means you're busy for the rest of the afternoon, baby."

Later, Finn cooked rice and marinated two tuna steaks in soy while he fixed a salad and waited for the griddle to heat. Mona was in the shower. When he heard the water turn off, he put the steaks on, the soy spitting off the griddle. Finn wore sweatpants and a fresh T-shirt and was barefoot. He was drinking a club soda from the bottle. He fetched Mona's half-full bottle of white wine from the fridge door, then dimmed the lights in the eating area. He piled rice on two plates, put the tuna steaks on top of that, and carried them to the table.

Mona walked in, also barefoot, drying her hair and wearing her favorite jeans and blouse, the one with a flower print. When he poured her a glass of wine, the smell of the alcohol triggered a feeling he hadn't felt for a year and half. He quickly got himself another club soda.

They sat facing each other, grinning like teenagers.

"You've forgotten something," she said. She went to the sideboard and came back with a couple of candlesticks and a box of matches.

"We got it the other way around," said Finn, across the flickering candlelight.

"What do you mean?"

"Usually it's dinner first, then sex."

She smiled. "You're talking about dating rules, baby. The rules change when you get married."

"Different game, huh?"

"No. It's the same game, just for higher stakes. This is *good*," she said, forking the tuna into her mouth. "Tell me about your day."

"It ended well," he said with a wry grin. Then he told her the rest of it—about the phantom's reappearance and disappearance, about the floater, about his meeting with Glenn, about his being seconded to cargo inspection, and about the IA investigators.

"You've got that Zorro look on your face," he said, "the one you have when you're getting ready to fight injustice."

"It *is* injustice. I'm gonna sue them!"

"Who?"

"All of them! Glenn, the CBP, Homeland Security . . ."

"Homeland Security?" He laughed.

Mona couldn't walk by an injustice and not try to right it. It was her natural tendency, one of the things Finn loved about her. Back when they'd first become patrol partners, Diego had bantered to Finn about his "liberal lawyer" sister, making it clear that he was using the terms *liberal* and *lawyer* pejoratively. Diego didn't approve of his sister's vocation.

Finn, however, did. When Diego did finally introduce him to Mona, Finn had liked pretty much everything he saw. But Mona had taken one look at his CBP uniform and said, "I don't date my brother's friends."

If she'd meant to discourage him, it hadn't worked. Finn had found out that she was speaking at a forum called "No More Deaths: Toward a Safer Border" at the Self-help Graphics and Art Center, a hub of Latino activism. When she spotted him in the audience wearing civilian clothes and holding flowers, she smiled.

They were married six months later.

"I don't trust Glenn one bit," she said.

"I'm with you there."

"Someone must've leaked the story."

"Why would Glenn leak a story that makes the CBP look bad?"

"Because he knew the story was coming out anyway and he needed a fall guy. A rotten apple to throw away, make it look like it's just you instead of the whole system. I keep telling you, honey: it's not the apple that's rotten, it's the *barrel*."

"He opened fire. I don't think I did anything wrong."

She hesitated for a fraction of a second—long enough for Finn to notice.

He let it slide.

"That doesn't matter," she said. "They're going to try hard to make it look like you did. That way it's on you, and they stay on their promotion tracks. That's how rank works."

She sipped from her wineglass.

"We need a strategy in case they go after you. We can't focus on the fact that you fired in self-defense—even though you did—

because there's no evidence that Perez was even armed, let alone that he opened fire—"

"But if both Diego and I say he did . . ."

"It might not be enough. Why risk it? No, we need to show that Perez was the type of person who would fire on U.S. federal agents—that he was a gangster, basically. Of course, what would be best of all is if we could prove that he was engaged in criminal activity at the time of the shooting."

"He was a hundred miles north of the line without an entry permit."

Mona frowned. "That's not good enough, Nick. I mean a real crime."

He shrugged. "His gun went in the water. It's two and a half thousand feet deep out there. We're not getting it back. We're searching the boat, but so far we've found nothing."

"We need to find out everything we can about him. Find out who he really was and what he was really doing."

Finn scratched his chin. "I keep coming back to this one thing."

"What?"

Finn drained his club soda and said, "When we fished the body out this morning, there was a shark hanging around nearby."

"You think it was the one that took the poor guy's legs?"

"Probably."

"Oh my god." Mona put her hand to her mouth. "That's awful, but you're right, it's not relevant," she said a moment later. "It's got nothing to do with Perez. We need to find out what Perez was doing, whether he was smuggling narcotics or something else. We already know he was a bad guy, since he shot at you. Now we need the investigators to know that, too."

Finn didn't think the shark was irrelevant, but he let it go. "How do we do that?" he said.

"I'll start by asking my contacts to find out if he was involved

with any of the trafficking networks. Meanwhile, you need to contact the Mexicans and find out if he's on any of their cartel lists."

Finn nodded, said nothing, scratched his face.

"What?" said Mona.

"I was just thinking, we found the floater off Two Harbors, not
far from where we intercepted Perez."

"A week's gone by. I can't see how they're connected."

"I don't know. It just seems like a lot's happening in what used
to be a quiet patch of sea." He remembered Garcia talking about
the shark sightings off Catalina. "A quiet patch of sea," he murmured
again.

Mona reached across the table and put her hand over his.
"Honey . . . did you make the appointment?" she said.

After Finn had killed Perez, Mona had given him the name of a
counselor. Mona believed that counseling should be made mandatory for every CBP agent who shot someone, nationwide.

"Not yet," he said.

"You promised . . ."

"I know, and I will. I just haven't had the time."

Mona nodded slowly. She didn't look like she was buying his no-
time thing, but she didn't say anything about it. Then she said, "I
worry about you, honey. I don't want this to mess with your mind.
It's the machine that's broken—not you. I don't want you to get
ground up in the gears."

Finn gave her a lukewarm smile. He loved his wife, but he couldn't
understand that kind of talk. He'd served eight years in the military. Perez hadn't been his first firefight. Sure, he hadn't been sleeping right since he'd shot him; sure, he'd felt like a drink for the first
time in months; but he didn't see how talking to a stranger would
help. He hadn't needed to talk to anyone when his dad died; he'd
stopped drinking without having to go to those meetings she
was always on him about; he'd been through worse, guarding oil
terminals in southern Iraq, without having to blab about it. He

couldn't figure out how everyone talking about themselves all the time helped anything. His view was: just move on; everything passes eventually.

He took the plates into the kitchen. She followed him in, leaned against the counter, and watched him scrub plates at the sink for a while.

Then she said, her voice softer now, "Promise me, Nick."

He used a dishrag to dry his hands. "I promise," he said.

She smiled and kissed him. Her lips tasted of wine. He felt the tingle on the tip of his tongue.

"You know, I've been thinking," she said. "What if you quit?"

"Quit what? My job?"

"Yeah. Quit the CBP entirely."

"And do what?"

She smiled. "You said to me once, your dream was to have your own commercial fishing boat? We could move to Monterey, you could get your license . . . get your own boat eventually—"

"How would we live?"

She looked at him in mock surprise. "*Mi amor,* did you forget I am a lawyer?"

She must've seen Finn bristle because she laughed and said, "Look at you, all old-school! Don't like the idea of a woman keeping you, huh? Don't worry, honey, you'll have plenty of time to look after me later, when I'm pregnant. Then you can be my breadwinner. But first"—she put her wineglass down and pressed herself against him—"I need to be pregnant."

Finn grinned.

This felt better than talking.

CHAPTER FOUR

Finn parked his Tacoma in a bay at the CBP station. Mona pulled up next to him in her RAV4. Finn got out of his truck and into the passenger seat of hers. He was wearing his dress uniform. Mona was wearing her no-nonsense lawyer outfit, a barrette holding her hair back in a ponytail. Today she had taken her "cheap fake" handbag along with her briefcase.

"Remember, these people aren't your friends," she said. She had the vanity mirror down and was doing something around her eyes. "They're going to try their hardest to pull apart your story, so take it slow and think carefully before you say anything. If they ask any leading questions or try any tricks, let me do the talking. Got it?"

"Got it."

She leaned over for a kiss.

It was a beautiful fall day, cool and bright. Ruining it was Garrett Smith, loitering on the steps of the station. He thrust a micro-recorder into Finn's face.

"How do you feel ahead of today's hearing into the Perez shooting, Agent Finn?"

"What hearing?"

Garrett gave a lopsided smile. "Don't insult me, Finn. You're not the only one who can do his job."

Finn brushed his way past the reporter and entered through the swing doors.

"How did he know?" he said.

"Because this place leaks like a sieve," said Mona, "The system's—"

"Broken, I know."

Diego was waiting for them in the lobby.

"I got an ID from our floater's prints," he said. "Good news—he's got a state rap sheet. His name's Juan Miguel Espendoza, sixteen years old, and he's a U.S. citizen. His sheet gives an address in East L.A."

Diego smiled. "You look surprised," he said to Finn. "You were expecting him to be Mexican?"

"What's on his sheet?" said Mona.

"Always the lawyer, little sister," said Diego. "Auto theft and possession of controlled substances, same instance, busted by LAPD last June. He pleaded guilty, but he was fifteen at the time, so it was a juvenile case and he didn't do any time."

"Nothing since?" she said.

"Nope. But he's a gangbanger. Or was."

"How do you know?" she said.

"The rap sheet."

"Juvenile offenses. I'm surprised it wasn't sealed. Doesn't make him a gangbanger."

"Ever the optimist. People don't change, Mona," said Diego.

"Sure they do," said Finn.

Now it was Diego's turn to look surprised. "Agent Finn, has my sister turned you into a bleeding-heart liberal?"

"Diego, you're a moron," said Mona. She glanced at her watch.

Diego grinned. Then he lowered his voice and said to Finn, "We ought to go see the Irishman, see if he can give us anything on Perez."

Finn nodded. The Irishman was an informant who ran a bar in San Pedro called Bonito's. "Sure," he said. "Tomorrow night."

Diego nodded.

The door to the conference room opened and Glenn's secretary beckoned them in.

"Ready?" said Mona.

A rectangular wood-veneer table stood in the center of the meeting room. There was a microphone plugged into a recording device on it, three empty chairs down one long side, the chair at the head occupied by DMO Glenn—meticulously dressed, as usual. Two men unknown to Finn were sitting on the other long side. The blinds were down on both windows and the overhead fluorescent lights were on. The room was airless and too warm.

The two men, whom Finn assumed were the IA agents, wore white shirts and ties, their jackets hanging on the backs of their chairs. Both men were sweating. One was tall and thin and carried his weapon in a shoulder holster. The other was heavy, had a shaved head and no neck, and wore his gun on his belt, cowboy-style.

Finn assumed they were the ones who'd closed the windows and turned off the air-conditioning. He turned it back on at the thermostat by the door, then sat down in the center chair, Mona to his right and Diego to his left.

The heavy IA man frowned, got up, and turned the air-conditioning back off.

DMO Glenn made the introductions. No one shook hands. Glenn seemed to Finn by far the most anxious person in the room.

"You guys like to sweat, huh," said Finn, taking off his jacket. He knew that overheating a room was an interrogation technique designed to make the subject uncomfortable.

The one with the shoulder holster—the taller, thinner one whom Glenn had introduced as Agent Ruiz—tilted his head at Mona and said, "You brought your wife with you?"

"I'm here as Agent Finn's counsel," said Mona.

"And as Agent Jimenez's sister, right?" said Ruiz, smiling in a way that Finn didn't like.

"It's a family affair," said the thick-necked one, Agent Petchenko, who'd turned the air-conditioning back off.

"Why'd you bring a lawyer, Finn? This isn't an interrogation," said Ruiz, his voice fake friendly.

Mona leaned forward and spoke into the microphone.

"For the record, my name is Ximena Finn of Holguin Associates, and I am present as counsel to Nicholas Peter Finn, marine interdiction agent with the Custom and Border Protection's Office of Air and Marine, Long Beach Station. Agent Finn is here of his own volition, as is his patrol partner, Diego Jimenez, who was present at the time of the incident. Today's date is Thursday, October twenty-second. The time is nine fifteen A.M. Also present are the OAM's director of Marine Operations, Scott Glenn, and Agents Anton Ruiz and Andrew Petchenko, from the Office of Internal Affairs in Washington, D.C., both in their shirtsleeves," she said.

"Just seems mighty cozy to me, everyone being related," said Petchenko, glaring at Mona. He had a deep, sodden, drinker's voice, and delivered his consonants lazily.

"I think we should get started," said Mona.

Ruiz looked from Mona to Finn. "Why don't you start by telling us how you joined the CBP," he said.

Finn was about to speak when Mona butted in.

"That question is irrelevant to the purpose of today's hearing. Agent Finn is here to talk about the events that led to the death of Rafael Aparición Perez on the eighth of October. He will talk about that and only that. Let me repeat that this is an impartial hearing and *not* an interrogation. Agent Finn is *not* under arrest, has *not* been charged with any crime, and has *not* been read his Miranda rights. Agent Finn is here to help establish the truth of what happened during events that led to the death of Rafael Aparición Perez. Ask any more irrelevant questions, Agent Ruiz, and I will counsel my client to cease cooperating immediately on the grounds that you are prejudicing this hearing."

No one said anything for a moment. Both IA men looked unhappy.

"Fine," said Ruiz. "Agent Finn, could you please relate to us the events that led to you shooting dead Rafael Aparición Perez on the morning of the eighth of October, as you remember them."

Finn glanced at Mona, who nodded.

"Like I wrote in the report, I was on patrol with Agent Jimenez," said Finn, "Toward the end of our shift, at about six A.M., we come across this boat running with her lights out—"

"Is that illegal?" said Ruiz.

"At night, yes."

"At night . . . what about at six A.M.?" said Petchenko, looking up from a printout of the report Finn had written.

Finn straightened his back. "It's October," he said. "It's still dark at six A.M."

Petchenko shrugged.

"Go on," said Ruiz with a reassuring smile.

"We're about a mile northeast of Catalina Island. We approach the vessel and discover that she's a big sport fisher. Her lights are out and she's not fishing. We see no one aboard. We turn on our wailer and blue lights, and I signal her with the spotlight."

"You didn't try to contact her verbally?" said Ruiz.

"We didn't have time. She took off as soon as we switched on our lights."

"Why didn't you have time? Did you sneak up on her in the dark?" said Petchenko.

"We approached the boat stealthily."

"Why?"

"Because she was suspicious."

"Why?"

Finn wondered whether Petchenko was really this stupid or this was some kind of brilliant circular-reasoning strategy internal affairs agents used to catch people out.

"Because she had her lights out."

Petchenko looked stumped.

"Then what happened?" said Ruiz.

"Then we knew we had a twenty-two-thirty-seven. . . ."

Finn waited to see how well they knew their code. Neither agent said anything. He figured they didn't want to lose face by asking.

"That's Title Eighteen, Part One, Section 2237 of the Federal Code, namely, 'failure to obey an order from a federal law-enforcement officer to heave to,'" Finn said helpfully. "So we set out after him. We signal him again with the spotlight. He still doesn't stop. So I fire a warning shot across his bow."

"You opened fire?" said Ruiz.

"As I wrote in my report, I fired a flash-bang from our shotgun. I aimed it ten feet ahead of the fleeing vessel, so that there was no chance he couldn't see it."

"So he thought he was being shot at."

"Flash-bang shells have no projectile. They're harmless."

"But he doesn't know that, does he? All he knows is a boat sneaks up on him in the dark, then he sees a big flash and hears gunfire. Easy to panic in a situation like that, when you're being fired upon. Sorry—*think* you're being fired upon," said Ruiz.

Finn took a breath and wondered why these guys had such a hard-on for him. He glanced over at Mona, who had a stony look on her face.

"Okay. What happened next?" said Ruiz.

Finn knew the next bit was the tricky one. Firing a warning shot across a recalcitrant vessel's bow was standard procedure. It was perfectly legal, and they were trained to do it.

Setting a line to tangle around a vessel's propeller shaft, on the other hand, was Finn's own initiative.

"Normally, when a panga doesn't obey our order to heave to, we fire at its outboard and disable its means of propulsion. But this boat had an inboard engine, so we had to come up with another way to disable it. I used a rope."

"A rope. Is that standard procedure, Agent Finn?" said Ruiz.

"Is it even legal?" said Petchenko.

Before Finn said anything, Mona stepped in. This was her area. She gave Petchenko a rundown of Title 19 of the U.S. Code, especially Chapter Four and the Enforcement Provisions of the Tariff Act contained therein. Then she gave him a dose of Chapter Five, the Anti-Smuggling Act. Finally, for good measure, she ran through myriad sections of Title 46, Shipping.

Mona said a lot and said it fast and with great conviction. Finn wasn't sure that any of it cleared up whether his trick with the rope had been legal or not, but the investigators looked bamboozled. He listened to his wife draw to a close and tried not to smile.

There was a moment when no one said anything, the dust settling. Both investigators looked a little deflated.

"Okay. So you've managed to lawfully stop *La Catrina*," said Ruiz, gamely. "Walk us through what you did next."

"Agent Jimenez took the wheel while I fetched the M4 from the locker and fixed it to its mount on the starboard rail."

"Why you?" said Petchenko.

"I served eight years in the navy. I'm more comfortable with . . . with that kind of hardware," said Finn.

Petchenko wrote something down and showed it to Ruiz. Ruiz gave a little nod and said, "Go on."

"The suspect emerged from the cabin. There was something off about him. He didn't look like an angler. He was wearing the wrong clothes. A dark suit, a town suit. Not a spray jacket. Not something you'd go to sea in. We told him to put his hands up—"

"In what language?" interrupted Ruiz.

"I spoke to him in Spanish," said Diego.

"Because you don't speak Spanish, do you, Finn?" said Ruiz.

"That question is irrelevant," said Mona.

"I don't think so," said Ruiz. "I thought it was a requirement for all CBP agents to be bilingual."

"Today's hearing is about the Perez incident, not Agent Finn's linguistic abilities. Do you intend to follow this line much further, Agent Ruiz?" said Mona.

Finn felt a surge of gratitude for his wife.

"No, no. Please go on, Agent Finn," said Ruiz.

"The guy's not responding. He doesn't put his hands up. I've got a bead on him. He starts making his way up the ladder to the flybridge—the platform at the top of the boat. A moment later, I see him come out with a gun—"

"This is at dawn, right?" interrupted Ruiz.

"Correct."

"And he's in a position east of you?"

"That's right."

"So the sun's behind him, right? I mean, you were looking directly into the sun?"

Finn paused. He had to be careful here. "I could see them clearly."

"What about the smoke? On account of the engine being on fire? You sure you could see him right, through the smoke, holding a weapon?"

"I'm sure."

Ruiz didn't look convinced.

"Can you describe the weapon?"

"Some kind of assault rifle. It sounded like an AK-47—"

"It *sounded* like an AK-47?"

Finn nodded. "I heard enough of them in Iraq to recognize one anywhere."

"Even with the noise of the four engines on your boat? Even with the sound of your own weapon firing?"

Nice try, thought Finn.

"Outboards are loud, but guns are louder, especially when they're being fired *at* you, and anyway we were idling. As for my own weapon, it was silent at that moment, as you know from my report."

"I saw Perez open fire," said Diego.

Ruiz frowned. "We'll stick with Agent Finn's account for the moment, Agent Jimenez. So what happened next?" he said, turning back to Finn.

"I shot him."

"More precisely, Agent Finn."

"I aimed at the individual's torso and fired one three-round burst."

"You didn't think to evade his fire?"

"No, sir."

No one said anything for a moment.

"How many rounds did you say he fired at you?"

"I didn't say. He fired for maybe five seconds. He got off maybe twenty rounds."

"Twenty rounds? Yet there wasn't one bullet hole in your boat?" said Petchenko.

Finn shrugged. "Boats move. You ever tried firing from a moving platform at another moving platform? Especially with a gun as inaccurate as an AK?"

"Yet you managed to put a hole in Perez's chest in just that situation."

"The M4 is a far more accurate rifle. Plus, I was trained. I served eight years with the Maritime Expeditionary Security Force."

From the corner of his eye, Finn saw Glenn wince.

"What's that?" said Ruiz.

"Inshore boats. Mainly we did port security in the Gulf. Guarded oil terminals, that kind of thing."

"Inshore boats . . . is that like, swiftboats?" said Petchenko.

Finn frowned. Ever since John Kerry had been swiftboated, anytime he mentioned Coastal Warfare, everybody always thought swiftboats. The perversion of the word bugged the hell out of him.

"And you were a sniper?" said Ruiz.

"I did some marksman training," said Finn. Playing it down. He'd been the best shot in his unit and had spent most of his tours manning the M4 mounted on the bow of a thirty-four-foot Dauntless-class patrol boat.

"What happened then?" said Ruiz.

"The impact caused the deceased to fall backward. He went over the rail into the water. His weapon fell with him."

"You saw that?"

Finn nodded. "Yes."

"And then?"

"Then I went across and extinguished the fire in the engine bay."

"Where was Agent Jimenez while you were doing this?"

"He remained on our boat."

"So you were alone on the victim's boat?"

"Yes."

"And then?"

"We recovered the deceased from the water."

A moment passed.

"Have you seen the autopsy?" said Ruiz.

Finn hadn't.

"The M.E. didn't find any gunpowder residue on him," said Ruiz. "Not on his fingers, not on his clothes."

"He fell into the water. The water washed it off," said Finn.

"Maybe so. But we've got nothing showing that he shot at you. No residue on him and no bullet holes in your boat. We don't even have any evidence that he *had* a weapon, since you say it sunk to the bottom of the sea."

"You've got the sworn testimony of two CBP marine interdiction agents."

Ruiz sniffed. "Perez's family's lawyers say he was fishing."

"I heard," said Finn.

"So? Was he fishing?"

Mona leaned forward, but Finn spoke before she had a chance to interrupt.

"He wasn't fishing."

"You seem mighty sure about that," said Petchenko, squinting at him. He was either myopic or he'd watched too many Clint Eastwood films, thought Finn.

Finn felt his right eye twitching, the way it did whenever he got angry. He took a deep breath, steadied his heart, the way he'd learned in marksman training.

"I have several reasons to believe that the deceased was not fishing. First, he was on his own, which is unusual on a boat that size and which is especially unusual for fishing expeditions. Second, to fish, you need bait, and there was none on the boat. None of his rods were rigged. He was not wearing fishing gear. But more than that, it's *where* he was. You boys are from D.C., so you wouldn't know this, but if you want to catch game fish nowadays, you go south *to* Mexico, to Los Coronados, Alijos Rocks, somewhere like that. Isn't that right, sir?" he said, turning to Glenn.

"What's your point?" said Ruiz.

"My point is, no one comes *from* Mexico to go fishing a mile off of Catalina. People go the other way. Perez was fishing about as much as I was."

"So what do you think he was doing?"

Finn shrugged like it was obvious. "He ignored our signal to heave to. He used dangerous tactics to evade us. He had an assault weapon aboard his vessel and fired it at U.S. federal agents. He was a cartel man."

"Yet you found no drugs."

"We're still looking."

"It's been two weeks."

"It's a big boat."

"You say in your report he was coming from Catalina? Is that a drug hot spot?"

"Not that I know of. And I said he *appeared* to be coming from Catalina. I have no way of knowing where he had actually been."

Now it was Ruiz's turn to breathe loudly through his nose. He drummed his fingers on the table.

"You see our predicament, don't you, Agent Finn?"

"No, I don't."

"Perez is a foreign national. You're a U.S. federal agent. There's no evidence he was doing anything other than enjoying his motorboat. No residue, no weapon, no bullet holes, no drugs. All we have is you and your partner saying he pointed a metal object at you. Then you opened fire. That's right?"

"No, that's not right. It was a rifle. And *he* opened fire. I returned it. On top of that, he failed to obey our order to heave to."

"His lawyers say what you thought was an AK-47 was actually a fishing rod. They also say that you spooked him and that he couldn't speak English."

Finn couldn't suppress a laugh.

"You think this is funny?" said Ruiz.

"You think I can't tell the difference between an AK-47 and a fishing rod?"

"Maybe you weren't sure what it was; maybe you were nervous and let off a burst without really meaning to. Hell, anyone could understand that," said Ruiz, trying to bait Finn with a friendly-sounding compromise.

"Or maybe you couldn't see clearly on account of the sun being in your eyes," said Petchenko, squinting at him.

Finn held his gaze. "If that's the case, what motive would I have to kill an unarmed man?"

Petchenko shrugged. "What do I know? Maybe you got a thing against Mexicans."

"That's it. This meeting's over," said Mona. She stood up and pointed a pen at Glenn.

"Director Glenn, this hearing is a travesty and I will be contacting the commissioner's office immediately. Agent Finn came of his own volition in the hope of establishing the truth. Instead, he walked into a set-up, an interrogation in all but name. I will make it clear to the commissioner that you have failed in your duty to chair an impartial hearing. This is an outrage."

Ruiz got to his feet. "Oh, get real. This hearing was prejudiced the minute Agent Finn walked in with half his family," he said.

Everyone jumped to their feet and started shouting at one another.

Finn stayed seated, eyeballing Petchenko, his right eye twitching like a Morse code ticker.

CHAPTER FIVE

Finn walked Mona to her car. Petchenko's racist jibe had hit a nerve. He was still angry.

They were standing by the driver's-side door. Mona opened the door and threw her briefcase and handbag across to the passenger seat.

"I wish you hadn't heard that," murmured Finn.

"Are you kidding? I'm glad I was there. You're *lucky* I was there. That was a set-up. They're trying to build a case for prosecution."

Finn was puzzled. "Prosecution?"

"They're looking for a scapegoat. If they think they've got enough evidence against you—and believe me, they *want* to have enough evidence—then they'll contact a U.S. attorney and present the case for prosecution. The U.S. attorney then goes to a grand jury to get an indictment against you. Then they get a judge to sign a warrant, and next thing you know, you're in jail awaiting trial."

Finn's head was spinning. "Maybe you're right. I should just resign."

"You can't now. They'll use it against you. We have to clear your name first." She looked at him and smiled. "Relax. It so happens you married one of the best lawyers in the nation. I think I may have mentioned once or twice that I topped my class at law school. They probably still speak about me in awed tones."

Then, in a different tone, she said, "You know you're the first border agent I've represented? Usually I'm assisting migrants *against* the CBP. It's . . . interesting and feels weird at the same time. Like sleeping in someone else's bed."

Finn cocked an eyebrow. "So? Are we as bad as they say we are?"

She smiled but her eyes didn't. "Are borders necessary?" she said quietly.

"What?"

"It's the title of a paper I wrote in college. Seeing this . . ." she tapped the Customs and Border Protection patch on his shirtsleeve, "made me think of it."

Finn was quiet for a while. Finally he said, "What do you think would happen if we opened the borders?"

Now she had a twinkle in her eye. "We'd all move to Canada," she said.

He laughed. But he'd meant it as a serious question.

"Hey, why so serious? We'll get through this, okay? Trust me, I deal with assholes like them every day—you find them in every government department. If you're going to dig up dirt, you're going to bring up the worms. But we've got the truth on our side, Nick. And truth stands by itself. Jefferson said that."

He smiled. "You're quoting Jefferson to me now?"

"I'm trying to school you, baby."

His mood lifted.

She got into her RAV4.

"I'm going to put out the word, see if anyone has anything on Perez," she said through the window. "I'll call you the minute I hear anything. In the meantime, see if the *federales* have anything on him. And keep your head down. Don't say *anything* about the shooting to anyone without checking with me first, okay?"

He nodded.

"One more thing," she said through the car window.

He turned back toward her.

"I love you, baby," she said. "And I can't wait till Monterey."

Before getting into his truck, Finn noticed a card under his windshield wiper. He pulled it out. Garrett Smith from the *Times,* a note on the back of the card: "Let's talk."

Finn crushed the card in his fist and threw it onto the dash. With a sinking heart, he drove over to the cargo terminal and reported to the Office of Field Operations. He was about to do the most deadening thing he knew of: spend the day in front of a computer monitor. This particular monitor was in a cramped, airless cell built onto the bed of a special-purpose eighteen-wheeler. The truck was the much-trumpeted crowning glory of Homeland Security's technological push against fake Vuitton bags and Golden Triangle heroin. Everyone in the CBP knew it by its acronym, VACIS—for Vehicle and Cargo Inspection System—and it worked like this: the truck traveled slowly alongside a row of inbound containers lined up along the dock. A hydraulic arm attached to the top of the truck scanned a gamma-ray gun through the containers, feeding images into the computer and ruining Finn's life. He spent three hours staring at one X-ray image after another of container-loads of athletic shoes, iPods, automotive parts, flat-packed furniture, guitars, motorcycles, roof tiles, LED tubes, soft toys, and, above all, clothing. At lunchtime, he shut down the machine, pulled out his cell, and dialed a number in Mexico City.

"Policia Federal Ministerial, digame," said the voice that answered the phone.

"Vega? It's Finn."

"Finn. How's it going?"

"I need to track a name. You think you could run it through your database for me?"

There was a slight pause on the line. "You know we just elected a new president, right?"

"Congratulations."

"So things have changed. We're supposed to do everything through official channels now. You got a request for information from us, then you gotta send a form to the National Drug Intelligence Center, who's gotta liaise with—"

"I don't have time for official channels, Vega. I got twenty-four hours, tops."

"I don't know, Finn. Things are different. Everything's gotta be by the book."

"I won't say where it came from. And I'll owe you."

Another pause. Then: "*Cabron.* Give me the name."

He'd only just clicked off the call when his cell rang.

Mona.

"I found someone you should talk to," she said.

"Where?"

"The Self Help."

Finn stepped out of the VACIS control room, squinted in the bright sunshine, and stretched his back.

"I'm on my way."

He'd be damned if he was getting back in that airless coffin.

The Self Help was a two-story building that took up half a block on East Chavez. It had a curved portal painted sky blue, same as the corner blocks. The ground-floor wall was inlaid with shiny stones. The upper wall was earth-colored. A big sign, SELF HELP GRAPHICS AND ART written in fancy letters, hung beneath the second-story windows. A store in the mini-mall across the street advertised itself in two languages: "hardware" and "*ferreteria.*" On the wall enclosing the adjacent block, someone had painted a vast mural.

At the center of the mural was the Virgin swathed in pastel robes, her hands clasped in prayer. She gazed with gentle eyes upon a motley crowd of Mexican archetypes—mustachioed revolutionaries with bandoliers across their torsos, indigenous women in head scarves carrying infants, factory workers in blue overalls, peasants under giant sombreros, a couple dancing, musicians strumming guitars—all of them striding toward an oversize, monstrous Aztec sun god with a grotesque face, cruel eyes, a mouth wide open, and a big pink tongue spilling out over sharp teeth.

Finn parked at the curb and stared at the work through the windshield. An uncanny sensation came over him, and for a moment he felt as though he was being drawn to the same place as the striding Mexicans, being sucked into the same devouring mouth.

He shook off the feeling, entered the building, and followed the signs up the stairs and down a corridor to the Immigrant Legal Resource Center. The young woman at the reception counter had half her hair shaved, the other half long, a long-stemmed rose tattooed up her neck, and a metal bar through her eyebrow. She scowled at Finn as though he were smoldering sulfur.

Mona appeared from a door behind the counter and rolled her eyes.

"Jesus, Nick, you should've changed out of your uniform. You'll freak everybody out."

He followed her down the corridor.

"You think *I'm* the freak? Where do you find these kids, anyway? The circus?"

"She's a good kid. Just a bit aesthetically challenged."

She stopped outside a door.

"The lady you're about to meet is a legend in the community. Everyone calls her La Abuelita, 'Grandma.' She's an artist, been exhibiting at the Self Help since before you and I were born, lived here forever but prefers to speak Spanish. That's not important. The main thing is, she knows *everybody* who's anybody in L.A.'s immigrant community. They say that if La Abuelita doesn't know about it, it never happened."

"Does she know Perez?"

"Just listen to her story. You need to hear it from her."

Mona opened the door. Finn saw a very old woman sitting in front of a desk. She looked older than anyone he had ever met. A lightweight cotton dress with little flowers printed on it hung loosely from her ample frame. A gold crucifix rested on her bosom. Her shoulder-length gray hair framed a face with deep lines contoured around a large nose, thin lips, and bright eyes that looked far younger than the rest of her.

La Abuelita held a cigarette between two hard-worked, arthritic fingers, the knucklebones protruding like bubbles on giant bubble wrap. The cigarette surprised Finn—the last person he remembered smoking indoors in L.A. was his father, decades before, and he knew Mona hated it. He figured that La Abuelita's venerable age gave her impunity to antismoking pieties.

Mona said something in Spanish and the old lady fixed her unflinching gaze on Finn.

He smiled, said hello. She didn't say anything, just looked at him like she was reading his face. He sat in a chair facing her. Mona sat by her side.

"Nick, I'd like you to meet Señora Gavrilia," she said. "She's from Sinaloa State. She lives here now."

Finn knew better than to ask about her legal status.

"I'm going to ask Mrs. Gavrilia to repeat the story she told me," said Mona.

She said something in Spanish. La Abuelita started talking, her voice raspy, her cadence slow and deliberate. She spoke like a woman used to speaking without interruption. Mona interpreted.

"My husband's cousin, Felipe, lives in a small village in Sinaloa. He is a fisherman. He despairs for his son, also called Felipe, who is . . . *flojonazo*. . . ." Mona repeated the word in Spanish before continuing. "It means he won't work.

"My cousin tries to interest his son in the profession of fishing, but the boy doesn't like it. Then he tries to help him find other work, first with a fishmonger, then as an assistant to a marine mechanic. But the boy won't work. Finally, the father gets angry and kicks the young man out of the house."

"What was the name of the village?" asked Finn.

"Puerto Escondido," said Mona.

The old lady dropped her cigarette into a coffee cup that Mona had provided. The coffee cup had FOLGERS printed on it. A cloud of smoke hovered around La Abuelita.

"One day during holy week, my cousin is at the bullfight in Mazatlán. He looks down and sees Felipe, his son, sitting in the expensive seats in the shade, down by the *ruedo*.

"He is sitting with some men the father recognizes because they are infamous. They are Caballeros de Cristo."

Mona looked at Finn. The Knights of Christ were one of the biggest cartels in Mexico.

The old lady continued, with Mona interpreting. "He becomes scared. He doesn't want his son to be involved with men like these. After the bullfight, he seeks out his son outside the arena and begs his forgiveness. He asks him to come home.

"But the boy laughs at his father. He is wearing expensive clothes and has a thick gold chain around his neck. He humiliates his father in front of these men.

"My cousin's son goes home to his village. His heart is heavy.

"Then one day some people come to the village. *Enganchadores* offering money to villagers to go and work in the United States. Felipe sees that with them is his son. He sees that his son is working for the *enganchadores*. He sees his boy offering money to the young men he grew up with, who he went to school with and to Mass with, to go to America and work. He is offering large sums, which many young men don't resist. My cousin's son tries one more time to reason with his boy, but again he is rebuffed.

"Early one morning, Felipe is on his boat preparing his nets, getting ready to leave with the first light. He sees a boat arrive at the dock. An expensive boat. He hides beneath his nets, because no one has that kind of boat in that part of the country except cartel men. From his hiding place, he sees the villagers who were recruited by the *enganchadores* go aboard the boat, along with his son, Felipe. He counts five of them. The boat heads out to sea."

Here, the old woman paused, lit another cigarette, and gazed out the window at a big sign that read CHECKS CA$HED and then at the mural on the wall next to it. A minute passed. The room got smokier. Finn slumped in his chair. He felt tired and frustrated. He wanted to open a window. He wished she'd get to the point. The woman turned back to Mona and continued her story.

"Felipe never heard from his boy again. He went to the families whose sons had gone with the *enganchadores*. No one had heard from any of the boys who boarded that boat.

"Felipe wanted to know what had become of his son. Even if the boy was dead, it was better to know. He learned from the other families that the boys had told their parents the boat was taking them first to Los Angeles, where a truck would be waiting to take them to the orange groves. When Felipe learned that they were to come here, he called to see if I had heard anything.

"I asked everyone I knew if they had heard of five boys from Escondido arriving on a boat and going to the orange groves. But no one had heard anything, not in Los Angeles and not in the Central Valley.

"Then last week I saw on Univision the news bulletin about the *migra* shooting that man on the boat."

The woman looked intently at Finn now.

"I remembered that the name of the boat Felipe's son and those other boys went aboard was *La Catrina*.

"I called my cousin and told him I had seen this boat on television. He went on the computer and searched for the story. He looked at the photograph of the boat on the newspaper on the Internet. He telephoned me and told me the boat in the photograph was the same boat that he had seen at the dock. It was the boat that had taken away his son."

Finn was sitting up straight now.

"Those boys never touched the shore of America," said La Abuelita through Mona. "If they had, they would've contacted their families."

A moment passed. Finn looked out the window at the mural, at the Aztec god's inhaling mouth. *Five young men disappeared into the sea.* He thought about the floater, the stumps.

The old lady's story confirmed that Perez was a bad guy, but it wasn't evidence. Finn needed more. He turned to Mona.

"We need to find the cousin. I can ask Vega to send someone to Puerto Escondido, show him a photo of Perez. If he fingers Perez as a Caballero, we'll blow the bullshit lawsuit out of the water."

Mona spoke to the old lady.

The old lady shook her head.

"She says if you send someone from the capital, the cartel will certainly kill her cousin," said Mona.

In other circumstances, Finn thought, he could've played hardball. He could've brought up Mrs. Gavrilia's immigration status, put pressure on her to give up the cousin.

But he couldn't bring himself to do that. Maybe Diego had been right: maybe Mona *was* turning him into a bleeding-heart liberal.

He looked out at the mural again, deciding what to do.

"Le gusta?" said the old woman.

"She wants to know if you like it. The mural," said Mona.

"I was looking at it before I came in," said Finn.

"Mrs. Gavrilia painted it. It's called *The Fifth Sun.*"

"Why?" he said.

La Abuelita started speaking again.

"It's from a Nahua creation myth," translated Mona. "Before ours, there were four other cycles of creation and destruction. To make sure the fifth sun burned, the young god Nanahuatl threw himself bravely into the fires. In this picture, the Virgin is blessing the people who have thrown themselves into the fires so that the light should remain for those who come after."

Finn nodded.

People were always so afraid to be alone in the dark.

He turned to the old woman and said, "If your cousin wants me to find his son, he must talk to me directly. Otherwise, I can't help you."

The old woman gave a spluttering laugh. "I did not come here to ask for your help," she said in English, "I came to help *you*."

CHAPTER SIX

The next morning before sunrise, Finn slipped out of bed, taking care not to wake Mona. He stood by the bed for a moment and watched her sleep. The evening before, they had gone for dinner at a Korean crab place near the pier at Redondo. Mona had had a glass of wine and something inside Finn had seized up. He'd found himself resenting her without reason, and had pulled away a little. He'd woken in the middle of the night and lain in the dark next to her with his eyes open, listening to her breathe, wishing away the part of himself he'd kept from her.

Now he put on a pair of shorts, a T-shirt, and running shoes and headed out the door into the pale, predawn light and ran toward the sea.

When he got to the beach, he took off his shoes and socks and put them under one of the legs of a lifeguard tower. Then he hit the cold, hard sand down by the water. A bleakness had crept into his heart after he'd shot Perez, a dark mood that left him feeling restless and ill at ease all the time. It was a familiar feeling—he was a teenager the first time it had inhabited him, after his father's suicide—and for years he'd dosed himself against it with alcohol, until he'd found that he was allergic to alcohol, and that his way of drinking was incompatible with marriage and the kind of steadiness that marriage is supposed to beget.

He'd tried to ignore it, and to carry on as normally as possible, doing one thing and then the next, day after day, waiting for it to pass; but the pall had remained stubbornly in place—if anything, it had reached deeper into him after the Internal Affairs hearing— and the urge to dose himself against it was growing stronger, and this was the thing that frightened him, so much so that he was having trouble admitting to himself that it was even real.

This was also the thing he was keeping from Mona. He knew that if he told her about it, she'd say it was all the more reason to go talk to that counselor, and Finn knew that that counselor would want to talk about everything, especially all the things he'd made a habit of never talking about. His father's suicide, for instance. Finn never talked about that.

Ever.

He didn't talk all that much about what he called his "lost years," either, by which he meant the five years between the ages of sixteen, when his father had died and Finn had dropped out of high school, and twenty-one, when he had signed up for the navy.

Finn had always had trouble reading—in school, he'd felt like it came much harder to him than it did to other kids. It hadn't mattered so much in junior high, where the teachers had been kind. But in high school, with its overcrowded classes and overwhelmed teachers, and with no support at home, Finn had sunk to the bottom of the curve and settled there. On a skateboard or surfboard, he'd been peerless; in class, however, he'd felt ashamed, angry, and ultimately bored by his own incomprehension. Years later, when Customs and Border Protection had obliged him to sit through Spanish-language lessons during training, Finn had felt the same shame and anger at his lack of proficiency at learning new words and conjugation tables as he had at school, and by the end of it he came out with only a tenuous grasp of elementary Spanish—only just enough to qualify for the job. It was only during on-water training that he'd felt competent. Out on the water, he always let his patrol partners handle the conversations with the people they intercepted. Finn figured his job was to handle the boat.

He had thrived in the navy—its discipline had helped keep both the black mood and his drinking contained, and there'd been none of that Dr. Phil kind of talk. We don't give a damn as long as you get the job done, the navy had told him. Which had suited Finn fine. He'd discovered that he was very good at getting the job done.

From the navy's Maritime Expeditionary Security Force to becoming a marine interdiction agent had been one small step—Finn had followed other guys into it; and even though the CBP was nominally a civilian organization, so many agents were ex-military that the culture had a militaristic feel to it, especially in the Office of Air and Marine, where, with its high-powered boats and planes and helicopters, the testosterone levels were especially elevated. Finn saw a lot of similarities between what he had done in navy gunboats guarding Iraqi oil terminals and what he now did in CBP Interceptors patrolling the waters off Southern California. Mona was forever trying to remind him of the differences, forever telling him he wasn't in a war zone anymore, which was fine for her to say, but he was the one out on the water, and for him the similarities trumped the differences, no matter what she said.

The difference that had the greatest consequence for Finn was that his job in the CBP had let him drink in a manner he would've found impossible while serving in the navy. People smugglers and drug traffickers put to sea at night, so that's when marine interdiction agents went looking for them, and there was nothing unusual about Finn's sleeping through the day. For years, his schedule had let him hide his binge drinking.

Nor was he an alcoholic of the most hopeless variety. In some areas of his life, he retained complete control. He never let his drinking impact his work, for instance. Even after his worst benders, Finn abided by one rule: he never, ever stepped aboard a boat inebriated, or drank while at sea. His alcoholic father, of all people, had taught him that.

Finn fared well at sea. It was ashore where he struggled, and before he was married he'd lived a fitful life, observing an iron discipline aboard the Interceptor, then drinking to blackout between shifts.

Then he'd met Mona and fallen in love and they were married, and for the first few months he'd managed to keep his drinking in check.

In law school, Mona had been pursued by a series of calculating and ambitious men who had wooed her with the same aloof self-interest with which they practiced contract negotiation. She'd made a point of avoiding corporate lawyers ever since, which hadn't proved too difficult after she'd chosen to devote her career to immigrants' rights.

She'd met plenty of good men in the not-for-profit sector, and had even dated a few, only to discover that good men tended to leave her a tinge dissatisfied—90 percent satisfied, say, as though their good intentions prevented them from reaching that final 10 percent. She'd felt like she had an itch that was always just out of their reach.

There'd been nothing calculating about Finn's courtship. His pursuit had been frankly carnal, reckless even, and while he had shown genuine interest in her work and her ideas, he hadn't seen her work as worthier than his own; as far as he was concerned, she was doing her job and he was doing his. He was interested in her mind, but it was her body that he wanted first. Mona had been attracted to his directness, his blue eyes, and, if she was honest with herself—and this she found hard to reconcile, given her vocation—even his job. *That Interceptor you spend all night driving over the sea . . . how much horsepower did you say it had?* In bed, the corporate lawyers hadn't cared about her, while the social activists had done nothing but. Finn seemed both to care and not to care. There was nothing calculating about Finn.

They were married and they were happy, especially in bed, but then a year into it Finn had disappeared on a binge. When he'd slunk back through the front door, there'd been tears and apologies and promises, and then a couple of good months. Then he did it again. That time, Mona moved back to her parents' house, and for a while she'd even refused to take his calls and Finn had had to plead his case through Diego. Eventually, she'd caved—she dreaded that out-of-reach itch—but she'd been self-aware enough to realize she was caving, so she'd negotiated a contract with him, which amounted to: once more and I'm gone. So Finn had made her another promise and so far he'd stuck to it, even though he refused to go to those meetings she wanted him to attend. After a year and a half without a drink, she'd stopped mentioning the meetings.

Now, however, with the shooting, she wanted him to see a counselor. Post-traumatic stress, she'd said. Grief processing. Talk it out.

But talking wasn't Finn's way. His way was to keep going. Stay busy. When the darkness creeps in, crowd it out with relentless activity.

His plan now, down on the beach with the cold hard sand beneath his bare feet, was to sweat it out, no matter how much it hurt.

He ran steady for minute-long stretches, then sprinted as fast as he could for short bursts, using landmarks on the beach like lifeguard towers and storm-water outlets as finish lines.

His body warmed, his heart thumped, his legs burned. Sweat trickled down his forehead and streamed down his back. He dodged the surf swooshing up the shore. He ran past wet-suited surfers carrying their boards underarm down to the sea, other runners with earphone cords dangling from their ears, housewives walking their dogs even though dogs were forbidden, and svelte young women in leggings doing yoga with their backs to the water, facing the rising sun. He ran past a group of young people in fancy clothes sitting on the sand who had obviously been partying all night. He noticed the bottle in a brown paper bag they were passing around.

He ran interval sprints the length of Hermosa to the pier that divided it from Manhattan Beach, a distance of two miles. At the pier, he stopped and realized that his legs were trembling. He walked up to the dry stuff, lay down, and did crunches till his abdomen burned. Then he did some more.

When he was physically spent, he let his body flop onto the sand and lay there for a moment listening to the waves breaking around the pylons. The sun was up now, and a couple of big brown pelicans were sitting on the rail atop the pier above him. Finn gazed at the huge, placid birds. As a teenager, he'd spent hours surfing the pier, and he'd always liked watching the wildlife between sets. Not just the pelicans but the ospreys that circled above and the seals and dolphins that sometimes showed up.

He hauled himself up and looked out at the ocean. Out in the takeoff zone, five or six guys were sitting on their boards, waiting for the set, their seal-black wet suits glistening in the early light. Finn had run hard; his body hurt. Yet the pall still hung there.

He figured he'd just have to run harder on the way home.

Finn came through the front door breathing hard and drenched with sweat. Mona was sitting at the table, eating toast. She was smartly dressed but barefoot. Her shiny black leather heels were on the floor by her case, which sat with its telescopic handle extended by the front door. She looked up at him and smiled.

The organization that Mona worked for was championing, among other things, a bill that outlawed California employers from withholding overtime pay to workers who had irregular immigration status. Mona was flying to Sacramento to testify before the state assembly's labor committee, and to persuade it to send the bill to the floor. She was staying overnight.

It wasn't the first time that members of California's legislature had heard from Mona Jimenez, and, if she had her way, it wouldn't be the last. Mona had been only ten years old in 1994, when Californians had voted in a referendum to exclude undocumented migrants from the state's health care, education, and social security programs, and she had never forgotten the tears on her mother's face or the worried looks in her father's and uncles' eyes. She remembered how the atmosphere seemed to have changed that November day, how she had sat in the backseat of her father's truck driving through the streets of Lincoln Heights, in the city where she'd been born, and had felt as though when Anglos looked in their direction, their gazes had lingered a moment longer than usual.

Since Finn was confined to shore duty and no longer did night patrols, their schedules coincided, and he'd promised to drive her to the airport. At the drop-off zone at LAX, he set her case on the sidewalk and opened the passenger door for her.

She got out and took the handle of her case.

"Promise me you'll call the counselor today, Nick," she said.

"I promise."

She smiled. "Thank you," she said. Then: "Wish me luck?"

"Are you kidding? With that brain and those heels, they don't stand a chance. That bill's going through, I know it."

She grinned, kissed him, and swayed into the airport. Finn sat behind the wheel and kept his eyes on his wife's behind until an airport attendant waved him along.

Finn walked into the field operations station at Long Beach. The supervisor handed him a clipboard full of shipping-container manifests and took it upon himself to mention the shift Finn had skipped the afternoon before. Finn gave him a long look, and the supervisor didn't say anything more about it; shooting Perez had made Finn famous—or infamous, depending on your point of view—throughout the CBP.

He walked along the giant wharf to the truck with the mobile

VACIS system installed on its flatbed. It was sweltering inside the operator's cabin. He tried the air-con; nothing happened. He couldn't keep the door open on account of the radiation that the VACIS produced—the system wouldn't operate unless the cabin was sealed. He rang the supervisor.

"Air-con's not working. It must be ninety-five degrees in here," he said.

"Nothing we can do about it until tomorrow," said the supervisor.

Finn swore, loosened his collar, and looked at the pile of cargo manifests. His job was to read the manifest, then look for inconsistencies on the X-ray image of the container—false walls or ceilings, areas of high density, things that didn't match the manifest—that warranted opening the container. In other words, his job was to stare at the screen for hours.

He powered up the system. In an attempt to get comfortable, he took his keys, wallet, and phone from his pockets and put them on the desk next to the monitor. The corner of the card that Mona had given him, for the counselor, was sticking out of his wallet. Finn remembered the promise he'd made.

He felt irritated. He had a job to do, hadn't he? It was too hot to call from this damn coffin. And anyway, there was nothing to talk about. Perez had shot at him and he had shot back and now one of them was dead and it wasn't him.

What more was there to say?

By the end of his shift, Finn was mentally drained. He'd been sweating for six hours. His clothes clung damply to his body. His eyes were tired. He'd forgotten to bring a bottle of water and now he was thirsty. He finished looking at the last container on his list, powered down the machine, and opened the door.

It felt good to get some air. He climbed down the steps and walked off the dock. He'd arranged to meet Diego at Bonito's, a bar in San

Pedro, so that they could ask an informant about *La Catrina*. When he got to his truck, his phone rang.

It was DMO Glenn's secretary. "Hold the line for the DMO," she said.

The man's too important to dial his own calls? thought Finn.

"Agent Finn? I wanted to be the one to tell you that the Internal Affairs investigators have made their report. It's not good, I'm afraid. Not good for you, I mean. They're saying there's insufficient evidence showing that Perez opened fire or even had a weapon when you discharged your weapon and killed him."

Finn rubbed his eyes. The pall over his soul darkened.

"Agent Finn?" said Glenn.

"I'm here."

"Well, I'm sorry, Agent Finn, but there's really nothing I can do about it: they're recommending the case for prosecution to the U.S. attorney."

CHAPTER SEVEN

Bonito's was a dim, narrow bar in a single-story block stretching back from a glass front on a barren patch of Harbor Boulevard, just across the Vincent Thomas Bridge from Terminal Island. Its glass front was painted black to chest height, the band of darkened glass above that stenciled long ago with the bar's name, the lettering now flaking off. There was a little bell above the front door that jingled each time a patron walked through it.

Diarmud Cutts, an Irishman actually from Ireland and the bar's current owner, liked to tell that Bonito's had been the local drinking place for the Japanese fishermen and cannery workers who had once lived on the island, but Finn, who had grown up around Long Beach, knew better: the island's Japanese population had been interned after Pearl Harbor and had never returned, and anyway the Vincent Thomas Bridge, which connected the island to San Pedro, hadn't been built until twenty years after the war.

Cutts also liked to say that *Bonito* was Japanese for "tuna," and most everyone let him say it, even the Spanish speakers. If anyone dared challenge his knowledge of all things nautical, Cutts would tell them how many years he'd been in the merchant marine before settling in Long Beach, and of all the seas he'd crossed. The numbers varied according to his mood and degree of sobriety.

Among Bonito's regulars were the tugboat crews, longshoremen, shipbuilders, marine surveyors, port police, and cruise-ship maintenance workers from Long Beach and Terminal Island, as well as the crews of the commercial fishing boats that docked in the port of San Pedro. Collectively, they knew more than anyone else about the hidden worlds of the nation's busiest two ports, and what they didn't know they could learn discreetly at Bonito's. Cutts himself had the reputation of knowing everyone and everything. As a source on all matters relating to contraband, he was peerless.

Finn had been a good customer before his marriage. But for the last year and a half, he had avoided Bonito's and Cutts. The former was a dive, and the latter was patently a criminal and reminded him of his father and of the life that had killed him. Whenever goods that had plainly come out the back door of one of the port's bonded warehouses showed up in Bonito's, Finn had to turn a blind eye if he wanted to keep the line that trawled for bigger fish baited. Cutts didn't shy from making the most of his immunity: the bar's old, hardened, chestnut-and-maroon-blotched carpet had a rancid smell rising from it, but all three TVs mounted on the walls were brand-new, flat-screen Toshibas. Although Finn had been avoiding the place, tonight, the mood he was in, he felt in his element.

The bar itself extended down the left side and was the room's principal source of light. Diego sat slouched on a stool next to a bowl of nuts and a Dos Equis. He was wearing a black T-shirt over tan cargo pants, his leather jacket on the stool beside him.

Finn had changed out of his uniform and into spare clothes that he always kept in his truck. He had on an Everlast sweatshirt over Levi's, his feet cushioned in a pair of pigeon-gray New Balance low-tops. He was nursing a club soda.

It was a Friday night in the middle of football season. On the Toshibas, a panel of pundits was discussing Sunday's games. Finn and Diego were discussing Finn's situation. When Finn told his friend about Glenn's phone call, Diego wasn't surprised.

"The DMO never had your back," said Diego. "You know why they brought him in, an outsider? Because he's supposed to be media savvy. He was supposed to give the branch a makeover. Now three months into the job, he's got a runaway story about a trigger-happy agent? Please. He's throwing you to the wolves."

Finn said nothing.

"Of course when they call me up to testify," continued Diego, "I'll tell them what I saw, end of story. Perez went up that flybridge, came out with a gun, and fired. Then you fired back. Then he went into the water. I was *there; that's* what happened and that's what I'll tell them."

Diego drank from his bottle. Finn toyed with his Schweppes. Without looking, he saw the bourbon on the top shelf behind the bar.

"You sure it was a gun?" he said.

Mid-swig, Diego swiveled his neck in Finn's direction and said, "You're kidding, right?"

Finn ground his teeth. "There *was* a lot of smoke. And the light *was* bad."

Diego stared at Finn. Finn looked at the counter.

Diego said, "You feeling all right, Finn?"

"Fine."

"I mean, you need to talk about what happened . . . ?"

"That's what we're doing, isn't it? Aren't we talking about it right now?" said Finn, sounding sharper than he'd intended.

Diego put down his beer. "Sure. All right. Whatever you want." Then he added, "What did Mona say about it?"

"I haven't told her yet. She's in Sacramento at a committee hearing."

Diego hesitated, then said, "You know a lot of people hate her, right? Her doing what she does, working for that not-for-profit, all the trouble she's caused CBP? The lawsuits? You made it hard for yourself, marrying my sister."

Finn thought for a moment and said, "She's *your* sister. Doesn't it make it hard for you?"

Diego smiled. "Yeah, but you can't choose your sister. You get married, you've only got yourself to blame. Everybody knows that."

"This from a guy's been married twice," said Finn.

"Exactly. You should learn from my mistakes. Now I live with my dogs, life is simple. I've got no problems."

Finn smiled. *No problems. Right.*

"You're a real lady-killer, Diego. I can't understand why your wives left you."

Diego grinned. "The first one left because of the second one. There was an overlap."

Finn said nothing, waited for the punchline.

Diego paused, getting his timing right, then said, "And the second one, she liked me better when I was married to the first one."

It wasn't the first time he'd heard Diego deliver that line, but Finn gave him the laugh anyway.

"Mona's right," he said. "You *are* a moron."

Diego chuckled. "You marry a woman like my sister, there was always going to be trouble. I've been arguing with her my whole *life*. She is *righteous*."

Finn shook his head. "We never argue. Not like that," he said.

Diego's eyebrows popped up and he said, "Sure, okay. Whatever. What I'm trying to say is, you're a Customs and Border Protection agent and she's a . . . what do you call it?"

"An advocate?"

"Yeah. An advocate for illegals. So, you know, opposite sides. Look, I'm only saying this because you're my favorite brother-in-law."

"I'm your *only* brother-in-law."

"Don't pick nits. My point is, as far as the CBP is concerned, you're sleeping with the enemy. So Glenn is a career guy. A civilian, like me. He came over from ICE, right? Worked his whole life in Homeland Security in one branch or another, working his way up? Now he's got a directorship, he's up there in his office, he's got all these field guys under him, most of them ex-military, not giving him any respect; he's got to make his mark somehow, right, if he wants to make commissioner someday? So if one of his guys is accused of shooting dead an unarmed suspect, and it turns out the guy is the *husband* of the attorney who's brought more excessive-force lawsuits against the CBP than anyone outside Arizona, then—"

"You think he's going after *Mona*?" Finn interrupted.

"I think Glenn needed someone to hang out to dry. If you go down for shooting Perez, he can tell the media he got rid of the rotten apple in the station. At the same time, he can tell his higherups in Washington how he got rid of a thorn in the CBP's side, because if her own husband goes down for excessive force or even murder, Mona's got no credibility left, does she?"

Finn stared at him. He wondered if he had heard right. *"Murder?"* he said.

Diego was deadly serious. "That's what people are saying they'll charge you with, Finn. Remember those border-patrol guys in Texas, shot that dope smuggler in the ass? He claimed he was unarmed, they couldn't prove otherwise, they got put away for twelve years. And he *admitted* he was a dope smuggler."

"Didn't the president commute their sentences?"

"You're gonna bet your life on that?"

Finn remembered what Mona had said after he'd told her about shooting Perez: *"You're not in a war zone anymore."* And that other thing, too: *"The system's broken."*

This nightmare could ruin his life, Mona's, and even Diego's, he thought. He wished he could make the whole thing go away. He glanced up at the top shelf.

"It's a bummer. Anyway, whatever happens, you know you can count on me, right?" said Diego. "And on Mona, too, obviously. Actually, *especially* on Mona. She can be a pain in the ass, but she's the most determined person I know." As an afterthought, he added, "Like a dog with lockjaw. And I mean that as a compliment."

Finn straightened, patted his friend on the back. "Thank you," he said.

Diego nodded. He gave Finn a look, like he wanted to say something more. Whatever it was stayed unsaid.

"Mona got a lead on *La Catrina*," said Finn. He told Diego what he'd learned from Mrs. Gavrilia down at the Self Help.

"So let me get this straight," said Diego, "She's saying those boys went aboard *La Catrina,* then . . . what?"

"Exactly," said Finn. "No one knows."

They were both quiet for a moment.

Then Finn said, "We found Espendoza's body in the same patch of water as *La Catrina.*"

Diego looked doubtful. "Espendoza was from East L.A., not Mexico. And we found them almost two weeks apart. If he came off *La Catrina,* no way we would've found him after two weeks. Not with all those sharks around."

Finn nodded. He wanted it to be coincidence. But his gut told him differently.

"I called Espendoza's probation officer," said Diego. "She confirmed that he definitely'd been on the streets, messing up, trying hard to become a gangbanger. She said she would notify his mother. It's too bad. Kid was only sixteen."

"What about the father?"

"Far as I know, there isn't one."

He'd lost his father when he was Espendoza's age, and he'd gone off the rails, too, Finn thought. He glanced up at the TV. In a replay, the Cowboys' offense was setting up a shotgun formation. The pundits, with all the genius of hindsight, were explaining why it had been a bad idea.

Diego continued, "I told the probation officer we found him out in the channel and right away she says, 'I knew he shouldn't have gone on that boat. He couldn't swim.'"

Finn turned away from the game. "What boat?" he said.

"Part of the deal to stay out of juvenile was, the kid had to get a job. He wasn't in school, obviously. She said he'd found a gig on a commercial fishing boat out of San Pedro called the *Pacific Belle,* operates out of the commercial port just down the road here. So I called the port authority. They said the *Pacific Belle* came in Wednesday morning, six A.M."

"Six A.M. Right after we lost—"

"The phantom's signal. Right."

"You check if—"

"Anyone called in missing crew? I checked with the coast guard. No one did. So I dropped by the port on the way here and found the boat, but there was no one aboard. I asked around the rest of the fleet, but they're a tight-lipped bunch, those fishermen."

"Should be easy enough to figure out who owns her," said Finn. "Just call the DMV, get her registration." He nodded in Cutts's direction. "Meantime, we can ask the Irishman what he knows."

Cutts, behind the bar in a short-sleeved white shirt, was sliding glasses into racks. Finn, who hadn't seen him for a year and a half, was shocked by how much the man had aged. The Irishman seemed a decade older. He was moving slowly and avoided bending, as though favoring a wound in his gut. He hadn't shaved, and the ash-gray stubble on his pale face was doing nothing to cloak his pock-marks. Finn had never seen Cutts unshaved before. The man was usually meticulous about his appearance. He looked pale and gaunt, frail despite the coarsened tattoo, visible on his left forearm, of a Kalashnikov underscored with the words THE PRICE OF FREEDOM, and of some words scrolled in Irish under a Celtic knot with a ship in it on his right arm. Finn had once asked him what the words meant. "There's hope from the sea but none from land," Cutts had told him.

Diego signaled Cutts over and ordered another round.

Cutts put a Dos Equis in front of Diego. Then he used the soda gun to fill a glass with club soda. "And another soda for the lady," he said.

Finn let it go. "You ever heard of a smuggler called *La Catrina*? A sport fisher, going into Catalina, maybe?" he said.

Cutts wiped the counter. "Smuggling what?"

"We were hoping you'd tell us," said Diego.

"I never heard of *any* smuggling boat going to Catalina. What would be the point?"

Cutts winced, reached for his side.

He hasn't answered the question, Finn thought. "You feeling all right?" he said.

"I'm fine. Some trouble with my insides, is all."

"Nothing serious, I hope?" said Diego

Cutts flipped his bar rag over his shoulder and scowled. "For a while there I thought I was going to fulfill Mrs. Cutts's dearest wish and die. But then last week I had an operation, and the doctors put things right. I got out of the hospital this morning. The doctors told me I have a few more years in me yet."

"Never believe what doctors tell you, Cutts. You're going to die," said Finn.

"Here's to Mrs. Cutts," said Diego, raising his beer, "May all her prayers be answered."

"I didn't hear anything about your boat, lad," said Cutts, looking at Finn, "but while I was in the hospital I did see on the news how a marine interdiction agent shot a fisherman dead. Would that be the sport fisher you mean?"

"Don't believe everything you see on TV, Cutts," said Diego.

Cutts seemed keen to cut the talk. "*La Catrina*. I hear anything, I'll let you know. Always happy to help my friends in Customs and Border Protection."

He wandered down the bar to serve another customer. Finn watched him go.

"He looks sick, doesn't he?" said Diego.

Finn shrugged. "He's old. You get the feeling he knows more than he's telling?"

Diego nodded. "You think we ought to put the pressure on, ask to see the receipts for these TVs?"

Finn picked up his soda. It tasted of nothing. He put it down again.

"So what now?" said Diego.

"I put in a call to Vega down in Mexico, asked him to run Perez through their computer. Meantime, I still think the answer's on *La Catrina*. I'm going to take another look. Also, that fishing boat Espendoza was on? I think we need to talk to her captain. You think you can meet me down at San Pedro at first light tomorrow?"

Diego glanced at his watch. "In that case, I'm going home. Those guys start real early."

Finn nodded. He noticed that Diego hadn't finished his beer. He couldn't remember ever having left a drink unfinished.

"Yeah, me too," he said.

They both slipped off their stools. Cutts came over to clear up.

"I got an easy one for you this time, Cutts," said Diego.

"Go ahead."

"The *Pacific Belle*. That name mean anything to you?"

Cutts's eyes darted to the ceiling, then back to Diego. "What's that, lad, a boat?"

Diego gave Cutts a look of mock indignation. "No, it's a brand of bra. Of course it's a boat."

"A commercial fishing boat out of San Pedro, just down the road here," said Finn.

"Never heard of her," said Cutts.

"You mean no one from the *Pacific Belle* ever drinks here?" said Diego, disbelieving.

"If they did, I'd have heard of her, wouldn't I?"

Diego tsk-tsked. "It's hard to take you seriously, Cutts. What kind of informant are you, doesn't know anything?"

Cutts gave Diego a hard look. "I never heard of the *Pacific Belle* or of the other one. But doesn't mean I can't find out what you want to know. What are you lads working on?"

Finn knew that informants were a two-way street. It was best not to give them information you wanted to keep confidential. But before he could stop him, Diego leaned in and said, "We found a floater out in the channel might belong to her. A *cholo* from East L.A. named Espendoza. Thing is, she hasn't reported any missing crew."

Cutts's pale eyes stayed fixed on Diego for a moment. Then he set down a pad and pencil. "Give me your cell. I learn anything, I'll call."

Diego wrote down his number on a square of paper. Finn watched Cutts slip it into his shirt pocket, then walk away. He glanced up at the bourbon on the top shelf.

Finn and Diego left the bar. Each got into his truck, pulled out, and slipped into the traffic. Diego was in front. Finn kept his Tacoma below the speed limit, letting cars get between him and Diego's black Silverado. Then he got caught at a light, and Diego's truck went out of sight. Finn flicked on his indicator, went around the block, and parked in front of Bonito's again.

He took out his wallet, pulled out the card for the counselor. Ruth Grace, Ph.D., specializing in trauma and bereavement. There was a phone number, along with an e-mail and a street address. Finn got out his phone.

Then he flicked the card onto the floor, locked the phone next to his Heckler & Koch in the glove compartment, and got out of the truck.

He walked through the door back into the bar, feeling like a shook-up soda can, ready to pop.

CHAPTER EIGHT

Finn stood swaying on the sidewalk. He was trying to remember where he'd left his truck. It was late. He wasn't sure how late, but he knew it was late because the sky was dark. He looked up at the halos around the vapor streetlamps and decided that they made him happy. He had no right to be happy, yet that was how he was feeling. What he was going to do now, he decided, was get into his truck and drive home. There was something about that proposition that seemed not quite right, but whatever it was slipped from his mind like an oyster from its shell.

Staring at the vapor lights, he realized, was making him dizzy. He lowered his head, blinked a few times, and stumbled south along Harbor Boulevard, looking for his truck. He walked past Bonito's, past an empty block, past a cut-price dry cleaner's. By the time he got to the end of the block, he'd forgotten what he was looking for. He considered the gutter for a while. Then he turned around and stumbled back toward the bar, paying no mind to the two figures walking toward him. Finn stopped and stared at a truck with a dent in its front left panel. The dent looked familiar. After a minute, he realized he was looking at his truck. He stumbled toward it and felt around in his pocket for his keys.

"Hey, sailor," said a voice.

Finn looked up and a knuckle caught him square on the nose. He fell back and slammed against his truck, dropping his keys.

Another fist came in, this time into his kidney. The hit forced all the air out of him. He tried to take a swing, but he wasn't seeing straight and he didn't have anything to aim at. His eyes were all messed up and he couldn't see the faces of whoever was hitting him. But he could smell them—they smelled of fish—and he definitely felt the knuckle-bones crash into him the third time, slamming into his jaw now, a good left hook with plenty of hip-swivel in it. Finn's head hit the ground and decided to stay there awhile. His vision returned briefly, and he stared helplessly at two pairs of shoes. Finn noted, absurdly, that both his assailants were wearing sneakers. He saw something shiny on the ground between him and the shoes. His keys. A hand, not his own, picked them up. He tried to look up at the face that belonged to the hand. Before he could, he saw one of those shoes coming at his face.

Finn came to and through swollen eyes saw a stretch of dark sidewalk. He pushed himself up to his feet. That alone took everything he had. Every part of him ached. Especially his jaw, his nose, and his teeth, as well as his back, knees, elbows, ribs, kidneys, and eye sockets. He looked around. The sidewalk was deserted.

His truck was still there. He leaned against it and felt his face. There were lumps in all the wrong places and his hand got wet with blood. He groaned and patted himself down. His wallet was still there, which surprised him. He pulled it out and checked it. It contained no cash, but then it probably had been empty when he'd walked out of Bonito's. His credit cards and driver's license weren't missing.

He lurched over to Bonito's and tried the door, but it was locked. He move back toward the truck, looked down and saw his keys on the ground. Pain seared through his body when he bent down to pick them up. He got into his truck, closed the door, and leaned over to the passenger side. The glove compartment was open. He felt around inside.

He found his phone and checked the time: 2 A.M. He felt around some more.

"Goddammit," he said.

His Heckler & Koch was gone.

A noise woke him. He opened his eyes, took a moment to realize that he was at home, in bed. The palm was scraping against the windowpane again.

Finn couldn't remember driving home. He looked down and saw that he'd fallen asleep on the bed fully clothed. Mona's bottle of white wine lay on its side on the floor. Next to it lay another bottle, of bourbon. Also some cans of beer.

Finn didn't remember drinking any of it. He'd have to clean it up before Mona got back. White wine, beer, and bourbon. It didn't strike him as a wholesome combination.

His stomach agreed: he stumbled to the bathroom and threw up in the toilet. Then he went to the sink and splashed water on his face. When he looked up, he saw, reflected in the mirror, Mona standing in the bathroom doorway.

"I had to take a cab from the airport," she said. "You weren't answering your phone."

Finn suddenly remembered that he had promised to pick her up at LAX. He wanted to disappear. He turned to face her.

"I'm sorry," he said.

Her eyes were wide. "What happened to your face?" she said.

"These two guys . . ."

"Which two guys? Who? What happened?"

He shook his aching head. He didn't know.

She turned and ran from the bedroom, down the stairs. Finn went after her. She'd left her suitcase, the handle extended, by the front door. He knew it was because she'd just returned from Sacramento, but it looked like she was all packed, ready to go, like she'd been planning to leave all along, the way Finn's mother had left, all those years ago, her case ready by the door, his mother on the couch with her hands on her lap, waiting for his father to come home from the pub to tell him she was leaving.

Mona had the door open and her hand on the suitcase handle when he caught up with her.

"Mona, please, wait . . ." Feeling pathetic and terrified at once, he stood in front of the door, blocking her exit.

She was crying. "Please, just let me go." She avoided meeting his gaze.

He put his arm out, blocked her way. "Mona, I'm sorry."

Now she did meet his gaze. "Sorry is easy. You were sorry last time, too. Remember?"

"It won't happen again, I swear."

"Just like last time. This is déjà vu."

Finn was getting angry. Didn't she realize how much pressure he was under? Then he remembered, he hadn't told her about the indictment hanging over him. Once she heard that, he figured, she'd go easy on him. She'd give him a get-out-of-jail-free card. Of course she would, once she knew what kind of pressure he was under. Any woman would, unless she had a stone in place of a heart.

But when he told her, the flare-up in her eyes didn't subside.

"So, what? You expect me to stick around and help you? Is that it?" Mona was speaking really fast, spitting her words. "You want me to say, 'Poor Nick, he's in trouble, he's stressed, so it's okay if he leaves me stranded at the airport? It's okay if he gets wasted, blacks out, comes back with broken teeth not knowing who broke them'? You're not sorry for what you did, Nick. You're just feeling sorry for *yourself.*"

Finn held his ground. "We're a family, Mona. This time, I promise—"

"Don't make promises again. It's insulting. You think I want have a baby with you *now*? So she can see you drunk, with two black eyes? Get out of my way."

Finn felt the fight go out of him. He wanted the ground to open up beneath his feet. He stepped aside. Mona rushed out the door, got into her car, and was gone.

He searched through the kitchen drawers until he found the Advil. He washed down four with water that he drank directly from the faucet. Then he put the coffee on, sat down at the table, and waited.

He listened to the fridge hum. He listened to the percolator hiss. Every now and then a car passed outside, but none of them stopped outside the house. None was the sound of Mona coming back.

I've fucked it all up. Just like my father, he thought.

Finn dug out his cell from his pocket. There were eight missed calls from Mona. He called her cell. It rang twice, then went to voice mail. She'd rejected his call.

"Sorry," he said. He wanted to say more, but the words didn't come. He clicked off.

Last time it had happened, she'd gone to her parents' house. He considered calling them, or even going over there. Then he remembered the state he was in, the bruises and scrapes on his face, the alcohol soaked into his shirt.

He poured himself some coffee and sat back down at the table. None of this would have happened if he hadn't shot Perez, he thought. He needed to clean himself up, get back on the wagon, set things straight. Maybe he'd try one of those meetings she was always talking about. Yeah, that's what he would do. He would clean up, then he would call her and say he was ready to go to a meeting.

Before that, though, what he needed to do was figure out who had beaten him up and stolen his Heckler & Koch. He needed to get it back. It was his service weapon, and it would be the nail in the coffin of his career if he had to go down to the station and report it stolen.

He also needed to sort out the Perez thing. He wondered how Diego had done with the fishing boat down in San Pedro. He pulled out his cell and called Diego, but it went straight to voice mail, which meant his phone was off.

That's okay, he thought. He'd have a shower, change his clothes, then go down to the dock himself and ask around.

On the way, he'd look into Bonito's first, see if anyone had seen anything out on the sidewalk the preceding night that might help find the bozos who had taken his gun.

Maybe he'd have a little pick-me-up while he was there. Just to help keep his head straight while he ironed out his problems.

CHAPTER NINE

San Pedro's commercial fishing fleet docked along a quay about a mile down the road from Bonito's, in a narrow bay off the deepwater channel that led to the main container terminals of the Port of Los Angeles. The bay itself had received cargo ships once, but now it was too small for the leviathans that carried the modern world's trade, and so had been largely abandoned except by the fishing fleet, which itself was dwindling. The last local cannery had closed in the nineties, a year or two before Finn's father had been caught smuggling narcotics aboard his fishing boat.

Finn turned onto the road that ran along the concrete quay. Trawlers and seiners lined the side. Nets lay in great piles on the concrete, tarpaulins pulled over some of them. Finn drove slowly, examining each boat. He had a buzz going from his pit stop at Bonito's on the way in. Cutts hadn't been able to help him work out who had mugged him the night before, but the pick-me-up Finn had enjoyed while there had worked. He was looking forward to finding the *Pacific Belle*. Before he could figure which one she was, he noticed a commotion at the end of the wharf: blue lights, police cars, a chopper bearing down. He drove down to take a look. A port-police officer flagged him to stop. Finn rolled down his window.

"This area's off-limits. You'll have to turn around, sir."

The Office of Air and Marine and the port police often cooperated on port operations. Finn recognized the officer.

"Wilkins? It's me, Finn."

"Finn, Jesus. What happened to your face? I didn't recognize you."

"What's going on?" said Finn. He was closer to the water's edge now and saw a barge crane raising something heavy out of the water. The port police dive-team boat was alongside the crane barge, her blue lights on and her white-striped red flag out, indicating that she had divers down. The barge didn't have its own means of locomotion, so there was a tug alongside it, smoke rising from her funnel. The chopper hovered over them all, her down-blast whipping the water.

"We've got a submerged vehicle."

"What happened, somebody kill himself?" said Finn.

"More like homicide," said the port-police officer. "Divers already pulled out the body, looks like he's got bullets in him. Jesus, you really do look like crap, Finn. Is that alcohol on your breath?"

Finn leaned away from the window. He kept his eyes on the crane. Finally, the vehicle emerged. Finn gripped the steering wheel so tightly that his knuckles turned white.

The crane lifted a black Silverado from the water. Finn immediately recognized the two decals of dog silhouettes that Diego had stuck on either side of the Chevy emblem on the tailgate.

Finn parked as close as the port police let him and hurried along the outside of the crime-scene tape to the very edge of the wharf. Diego's Silverado was dangling from four chains fitted from the crane; water streamed from its undercarriage. The crane swiveled till the truck was over the quay.

It was the end of a beautiful afternoon. The sun conspired with the onshore breeze to stipple the water beyond the barge with a million flecks of gold. Finn leaned over the edge of the quay and threw up till his gut was hollow.

He wiped his face on the back of his sleeve, turned his back on the scene, and walked back toward his truck. Officer Wilkins was talking to a man in a suit standing on the other side of the tape, the two of them looking in Finn's direction. The man ducked under the tape and approached Finn.

"Mike Benitez, LAPD," he said. Finn knew that the port police didn't have its own homicide squad, so they must've called in the LAPD.

Benitez's trim, squared posture and buzzed hair marked him as ex-military. Despite the glare, he wasn't wearing sunglasses, and Finn saw him look at him carefully through clear, steadfast eyes.

"Officer Wilkins says you knew the victim?"

"We work together. Customs and Border Protection, marine interdiction agents. He's also my brother-in-law. And my friend," said Finn.

Not yet ready for the past tense.

Benitez explained that they'd found Diego's wallet, so they knew who he was.

Then he cleared his throat and said, "Did he live with anyone, have any family?"

"He lives alone, with two dogs. He has two ex-wives. No kids. His parents live in Glendale."

"Okay. I'll call Animal Control about the dogs," said Benitez. He wrote something down on his notepad. Then he said, matter-of-factly, "You're the guy I read about in the paper who shot that fellow off of Catalina couple of weeks back, right?"

Finn was surprised. "Yeah, that's me. Except the paper said I shot the wrong guy."

"They got that wrong, huh?"

"He was the right guy."

Benitez nodded. "I never believe everything I read in the paper. Was Agent Jimenez with you when it happened?"

Finn nodded. "We work as a team."

"When was the last time you saw him?"

"Last night. We met for a drink after work, place called Bonito's, up by the bridge. He left at maybe ten thirty, eleven, around
then."

"He say where he was going?"

Finn nodded. "Home. He had an early start. We were supposed
to meet here this morning. We wanted to talk to the captain of a
fishing boat here called the *Pacific Belle*."

" 'Supposed to'?"

"I didn't show."

Benitez made a note, then asked, "What were you investigating?"

"We found a body out in the channel Wednesday morning. Diego
ID'd him from his sheet. His probation officer said he worked on
the *Pacific Belle*."

Benitez wrote some more, then asked, "What happened to him?"

"Shark got his legs, but we don't know if he was dead already or
not. We're waiting for the medical examiner's report."

A blank look came over the cop's face. "Jesus. I hate sharks," he
said.

"Yeah," said Finn.

Benitez turned, looked out at the water. "There a lot of them out
there?"

"It's the ocean," said Finn.

"Sorry. Dumb question," said Benitez.

Finn let his shoulders drop. He realized he'd been abrupt, that
most people knew little about the ocean.

"You get leopard sharks and great whites sometimes hunting seals
in the kelp forests on the ocean side of Catalina. You don't see them
so much in the channel but of course they're there."

Benitez wrote something down. Finn couldn't help but be impressed, the cop noting unusual details, however unrelated.

"Is that usual for you guys to investigate bodies?"

Finn shrugged. "It's not a regular part of the job. We do it sometimes."

"How long have you known Agent Jimenez?" Benitez said.

Finn thought about when he'd met Diego, at the National Marine Training Center in Saint Augustine, Florida. "Five years," he said. "We joined Air and Marine at the same time. He introduced me to my wife."

The cop nodded and stayed silent while he looked through his notes. Then he looked over Finn's face. "What happened to you?" he asked.

"Two guys mugged me."

Benitez cocked an eyebrow. "You file a police report?"

Finn shook his head.

"Where did it happen?"

"Outside Bonito's."

"Last night?"

Finn nodded.

"So you stayed at the bar after Agent Jimenez went home? Were you with anyone?"

Finn scratched the side of his face. "Yeah, I stayed. No, I drank alone."

"What did the two guys look like?"

Finn looked at the ground. "Don't worry about them," he said. "Worry about finding Diego's killer."

"That's what I *am* worrying about, Agent Finn. I think we'd better send someone to take a look at this *Pacific Belle*," he said. Then he asked, "You know much about fishing?"

"My father was a fisherman."

"Where? Down here?" Benitez indicated the row of fishing boats tied up alongside the quay.

Finn nodded.

Benitez seemed to be waiting for more, but Finn didn't give it to him. Finally the detective said, "Well, like I said, I'll go see this fishing boat and ask around, but we're investigating Agent Jimenez's death, so we can't do much about your floater unless we can connect them. What was his name, by the way?"

"Espendoza."

Benitez noted the name, took Finn's contact details, and handed him his card. Then he flipped his notepad shut and, in a different tone, said, "I'm sorry for your loss."

Finn nodded, said nothing.

"I know what it is to lose one of your own," Benitez continued. "You want to get out there and deal with it yourself. My advice? Stay out of it, Agent Finn. I don't believe everything I read in the papers, but I still read them. Go home, look after your wife. Let us do our job."

Benitez held out his hand and Finn took it.

"Don't call Animal Control," said Finn. "I'll pick up the dogs, take them to his parents. They know me."

Benitez nodded. "I'll let the team at Jimenez's house know you're coming."

Finn got back into his vehicle and watched Diego's Silverado get lowered onto a flatbed truck. He got out his phone. For the first time in his life, he dreaded calling Mona.

CHAPTER TEN

Later that night, Finn pulled onto the Glendale street where Diego's parents lived, a wide, tree-lined, gray-green strip of the California Dream within a short drive of a golf course, a mall, and a mega-church. He cruised past their single-story house, saw Mona's RAV4 parked in front of its double-wide garage; the curtains were drawn, and there was no cop car out in front of the well-kept lawn, the hedges neatly trimmed. He kept going, shook his head at his own cowardice, and turned around and parked on the street, not in the driveway. From the storage compartment in the door he pulled the half pint of Jim Beam he'd picked up along the way. Just a small swig of navy courage, he'd figured.

By the time he'd managed to do that, the bottle was half empty. He popped some mints into his mouth and got out of the Tacoma.

Diego's dogs knew the house, of course. They were Rhodesian ridgebacks, big rambunctious dogs named Ronald and Nancy. He opened the door and the dogs jumped out, no leashes, and ran across the lawn and up the front steps to the porch, barking. The front door opened before Finn got to it. Diego's mother, Maria, small and stout, stood in the entranceway. His father, Carlos, only slightly taller, stood behind her. Finn stamped up the walkway, wishing he'd had more to drink.

Maria Jimenez wore beige slacks and a loose linen blouse. Her reddened eyes had a vacant look that seemed to him the saddest thing in the world, until he saw her husband, Carlos. The man had tears streaking down his cheeks, no shame about it, just letting them roll quietly, wiping them away with the back of his hand. The only thing that bothered Finn more than a woman crying was a man crying.

Inside, he found Mona sitting on the brown leather couch in the living room, rubbing the dogs' heads. She looked ten years older. He stared at her, realized he was staring, and averted his gaze by awkwardly looking around the room at the clean beige carpet, the sideboard loaded with picture frames, the wood-and-glass coffee table.

Finn remembered what Diego had said on the boat, joking about whose death would upset Mona most. *If you could see her now,* he thought. *If you could see all three of them . . .*

Maria sat on the couch with Mona, Carlos across the table in a big, old armchair worn in the seat. No one told Finn where to sit, so he sat in the other armchair.

"Mona says you were the last person to see him," Carlos said eventually.

Apart from his killer, thought Finn. He leaned forward, rested his arms on his knees. "Last night, we met in a bar after work."

"What did you talk about?" said Maria.

Finn told them about the floater. He told them a little bit about Perez, too. "We went to see an informant," he said. "But he didn't tell us anything."

There was an awkward silence.

Then Carlos said something in Spanish to his wife and Mona sharply rebuked him. Finn couldn't speak the language, but he understood the tone. He knew they were talking about him.

"DMO Glenn called to offer his condolences," Carlos said finally, his voice low, gruff. "I ask him about the funeral. I say to him, 'You're gonna give my boy a proper ceremony, right?' But he doesn't give me a straight answer. I ask him straight, 'Is there a problem?' and he says to me that Diego wasn't in the line of duty when he was shot. And then he says something about an investigation, how maybe Diego perjured himself, trying to protect you."

Finn's gut knotted up.

"What does that mean?" said Carlos, looking at Finn for an answer.

Finn didn't have an answer. Even the dogs seemed to be looking at him reproachfully.

"You're the one who shot the guy on the boat, right?" said Carlos.

More sharp words in Spanish from Mona.

"No. I have a right to know," said Carlos. "You shot the guy, Finn. *You* are the one who's under investigation, *not* my son." His eyes drifted over to the framed portraits on the sideboard. "He died for his country. They should honor him. They should give him a proper funeral, in the big cemetery by the sea."

"There'll be a proper funeral," said Finn, real quiet.

Out on the porch, Finn offered Diego's parents his condolences, then walked down the front steps. Mona walked with him. When they were out of hearing of the porch, they stopped and stood together on the brick pathway that bisected the Jimenezes' lawn, the city's innumerable lights producing in the sky a glow great enough to dim all the stars.

"How are you doing?" he said.

There was a moment of silence.

"There's a big hole, you know?"

Finn looked toward his truck. He knew.

"Did Diego ever tell you about the time we found a million bucks?" he said.

Mona said no.

"This was before you and me met," said Finn. "We find this go-fast way out in the channel. Just drifting out there, on its own. We board, there's no one aboard, blood all over the Naugahyde, bullet holes in the glass, and a gym bag packed with wads of cash in the forward locker. I'm talking about bricks of money here, thick as books, hundreds of them. We figured it had to be at least a million. The boat is sinking, too. So we haven't radioed it in yet, right, and the boat's so sleek and low it's hardly on the radar, and we know the drone's way out east. The only people in the whole wide world who know about the million bucks are me and Diego and presumably whoever did the shooting, except they forgot to take it. So anyway, the whole way back to shore, Diego's joking about what he's going to spend it on. How he's going to build himself his own playboy mansion, get himself a robe like Hugh Hefner, and build a special garden just for his dogs. We get back to the station, we hand in the bag, he says, 'Hugh Hefner, man, what kind of man spends all day in his pajamas?' "

Mona laughed softly. It was a sound Finn relished.

They were quiet for a while.

Then she said, "I want to be part of it."

"Part of what?" he said.

"Of what you said to my parents. Of looking for who killed my brother."

"Mona . . ."

"Listen to me. He was my kid brother, and I need to find who killed him. Do you understand?"

"And I *will* find whoever—"

"No. *I* need to be part of it. I'm not asking, Nick."

"We're talking about a murderer here. Maybe more than one person. Killers."

"Exactly."

Finn ran his tongue along his teeth. "So we're what, a team? Like *Law & Order*?" he said. Immediately, he regretted his sardonic tone.

Mona crossed her arms and shook her head. "I can smell it, you know. The mints do nothing. The mints are useless. We can all smell it."

She looked at him with hate or hurt—he wasn't sure in the dim light.

"You were drunk when he was killed, weren't you?" said Mona.

Finn said nothing.

"You were supposed to be with him."

He stayed quiet.

"You're the one who's ex-military. You're supposed to be the tough guy. He looked up to you, you know? He was in awe of you, God knows why."

She put her hand over her mouth and looked back up at her parents, who were still standing on the stoop, watching them.

"He didn't know his way around guns like you. He was gentle. You were supposed to look after him. He was . . ." She started to sob. "He was my *kid brother*."

He tried to put his arm around her, but she shrugged it off.

"Just meet me at the Self Help at nine A.M. so we can start working on leads. You can still be sober at nine in the morning, can't you, Nick?"

She walked back up the path to her parents. They went inside and closed the door.

Later that night, Finn drank himself to sleep. In his sleep, he had an erotic dream. In his dream, he was lost in Mona's long tresses. Then he heard a man laughing. He looked up and saw Diego watching.

"I told you she'd miss me more than you," said Diego in the dream. Finn turned back to Mona, but when he did, she was gone. In her place was a void. He started falling.

He woke in a cold sweat. He didn't go back to sleep. He went downstairs, turned on the TV, and waited for dawn. Then he took a shower, not bothering with the hot water.

CHAPTER ELEVEN

Early that morning, Finn drove back to the fishermen's dock where Diego's truck had been lifted out of the water. He pulled up next to a couple of refrigerated trucks, killed the engine, and rubbed his eyes with his knuckles. His eyes ached, and the bruises and scrapes on his face throbbed and smarted, just to remind him that they were there.

He looked through the windshield at the row of commercial fishing boats parked alongside the dock. He saw a longliner with a big coil drum on its stern deck, and green nets heaped over the gunwales or on the decks of the seiners, which made up most of the fleet, and the trawlers with their gantries. He noticed the rust streaks around the welds and bolts on most of the boats. The usual seagulls flocked around the pylons and clung to the rigging and rails, and the usual stench of fish and of an industry in terminal decline hung over the whole place. A handful of men with cigarettes hanging from their mouths were loading plastic boxes laden with fish and ice into refrigerated trucks. Everything about the place reminded him of his father.

He got out of the truck and walked down the dock, past the fishermen unloading their catches. If they noticed him at all, it was with suspicion. Finn knew that they were a dying breed, and from the pall that hung over the port it was clear that they knew it, too, despite the hopelessly optimistic names they had given their boats:

Free Spirit. Daisy. Sea Fox. China Doll. High Hope. And then *Pacific Belle.*

She was a seiner, her bridge set forward and high, but she didn't look comfortable with her rig—with her mast and boom and all the gear crammed onto her stern deck—and Finn figured she'd been a bait boat once, converted for seining. Finn gave her about forty feet, which made her tiny compared to the boats next to her. Her red hull looked rustier than her neighbors'. No one was unloading her catch. There was no one on her deck, but he glimpsed movement in the wheelhouse. He stepped aboard, walked across the deck, past the foot of the mast, and up the steps to the bridge's thick steel door, and knocked. A woman opened it.

She wore a tight-fitting, pale-green T-shirt, body-hugging blue jeans, and worn sneakers, the laces loosely tied. She was about five-and-a-half-feet tall, which was smaller than he was, but he was standing a step below her so she looked taller, and she had a determined, ferocious look about her. Her green eyes were speckled with gold. Unbrushed, dirty-blond hair spilled down past her high cheekbones and the soft-looking skin of her neck, which had that even, permanent-looking tan of someone who spends a great deal of time outdoors. She had the looks of a beauty-pageant queen and the straight-spine bearing of a professional athlete.

Finn hadn't expected to meet a woman, let alone an attractive one. He was even more thrown when he noticed the child.

A skinny, very pale girl of around eight or nine stood staring at him behind the woman's leg. She had the same color hair as the woman, the same intelligent green eyes and small, round-tipped nose, the same small, pouty mouth.

"Can I help you?" said the woman.

Finn took off his sunglasses. It seemed more friendly.

"Good morning, ma'am. I'm with Customs and Border Protection," he said, glad that he was wearing his uniform. "I'm looking for the captain of this vessel."

Her eyes twitched. "You're looking at her."

Finn hoped his surprise didn't show.

"What's this about?" she asked.

He glanced at the child and said, "Can we speak privately?"

She raised one corner of her mouth and considered him. Finn became acutely aware of how repulsive his face must've seemed to her. She turned to the child and said, "Lucy, Mommy needs to talk to this man outside. Why don't you go practice your knots for a few minutes?"

The kid shook her head and stared at Finn.

"Now, Lucy."

The kid shook her head again and just kept staring, her expression saying that she was amazed, *amazed,* that someone like him should exist. Feeling self-conscious, he rubbed his hand over his face and watched her mother walk to the chart table, from which she picked up a picture book and a length of rope.

"Look at all these knots you can learn, sweetie," he heard her say, pointing at the book. The kid wasn't interested; all she wanted to do was stare at the bruiser in the doorway.

"Mind if I come in, ma'am?" said Finn.

The woman gave a noncommittal shrug.

Finn put on a smile and bent at the knees so that he was at the kid's eye level.

"It's Lucy, right? My name's Finn. I work on boats, too. I make knots all the time, tie all kinds of things, not just my shoelaces. You know how to tie a bowline, Lucy?"

The kid moved back behind her mother's legs and shook her head some more.

"It's easy. I'll show you. Can I borrow your rope?"

Lucy hesitated, then peeled away from her mother's leg, walked over, and handed Finn the rope. He held up the rope in front of her and made a loop.

"What you have here, see, is a rabbit hole"—he showed the kid the loop—"and a rabbit who lives in it." He wiggled the end of the rope. "You want the rabbit to come out of the hole and look at you, like this." He pushed the rope end through the loop and wiggled it. "The rabbit runs out of his hole, around the tree"—he looped the end around the rope—"then runs back down his hole." He passed the rope back through the loop, tightened it, and showed the girl the noose. She was looking at the knot now, not at Finn.

"That's a bowline," said Finn. He untied the knot, showed her again, patiently, and then again.

Finally he handed the girl the rope. She approached him, her eyes on the rope now, not his face.

"Now you try. Remember, you want the rabbit to come out of its hole towards you."

He stood up and smiled at her. She smiled back.

Finn and the woman stepped outside and stood on the landing, under the power block hanging from the end of the raised davit. She left the door open and kept glancing back at her daughter, who was fiddling with the rope as she sat at the table.

"You have kids?" she said.

He shook his head. The woman lit a cigarette.

"You should," she said.

"Mrs. . . . ?"

"Blake. Linda Blake."

"Mrs. Blake, were you on your boat about this time yesterday?"

"No. Why?"

"Was anyone?"

"You want to tell me what this is about?"

"I just need to ascertain whether another CBP agent, same uniform as me, came aboard your boat about this time yesterday. A marine interdiction agent named Diego Jimenez."

Linda Blake barred her right arm across her chest, supported her left one on top of it, and blew a plume of smoke in his direction.

"Who?" she said.

He looked at her and told himself to forget that she was beautiful. She was sucking too hard on her cigarette, getting an uneven burn.

"Agent Jimenez?" he said. "Came up here yesterday at first light to see you?"

"Maybe he did, but I wasn't here till the afternoon, so I didn't speak to any Agent Jimenez yesterday morning."

"Can you tell me where you were?"

"At home."

"You were at home all morning?"

"No. I took Lucy to her doctor's appointment about nine. I met my sister, Rhonda. We did some shopping. I didn't get down to the boat until after three. That's when I saw all the commotion at the end of the dock. You mind telling me what's going on?"

"Do you live alone, Mrs. Blake?"

She screwed up her eyes. "That's none of your business."

"Mrs. Blake . . ."

"And as far as I can tell, you've got no business at all here on my boat."

"An agent's been killed, Mrs. Blake."

She held his gaze. "Is that what all that was yesterday?"

He gave a curt nod. She dragged some more on her cigarette. She was down to the butt.

"I'm sorry to hear that. I still don't get what you're doing here on my boat. You're not a cop."

"You got a lot of experience with cops, Mrs. Blake?"

"My husband was a master-at-arms. You know what that means?"

"Sure. I did eight years in the navy."

"Which boat?"

"Maritime Expeditionary Security Force."

"David—he was my husband—we were both on the *Roosevelt*. It's where we met."

"Well, it's nice to meet a fellow squid, Mrs. Blake."

"Linda. My husband's dead. Being called by his name freaks me out. Makes me think he might reappear, you know? But he won't." She ran her hand through her hair. "So, you going to answer my question?"

"Agent Jimenez was my patrol partner and my brother-in-law."

"I get it. It's personal."

"Yeah, it's personal."

"And you think he came here."

Finn realized that she was asking all the questions. He took back the initiative.

"When was the last time you saw Miguel Espendoza?" he said.

He caught the tremor at the corners of her eyes.

"Is *he* involved? I haven't seen him in over a year."

"But he used to work for you?"

"He did one trip. And like I said, that was over a year ago."

"Know if he worked any other boats after you?"

"I doubt it. If he'd crewed on any of the other boats in the fleet, I'd have heard."

"Why just the one trip?"

"He realized it wasn't the life for him. Too much hard work. Did *he* kill your brother-in-law?"

Finn rubbed his chin. "He's not a suspect."

She looked surprised. "So why are you looking for him?"

He fixed his gaze on her and said, "We're not. We found him floating out in the channel."

If she was rattled, she was hiding it well.

"You mean he was murdered, too?" she said.

"I didn't say that."

"You didn't say anything." She lit another cigarette.

The little girl came out of the wheelhouse. "Look!" she said. She held up the rope. She'd tied a bowline, almost.

Finn smiled, squatted down beside her. "That is sweet. You're a sailor now, Lucy," he said, saluting her.

She beamed. Then she said, "What happened to your face?"

"I bumped into the floor."

She laughed. "Here," she said, handing him the rope, "It's a present."

Finn smiled and thanked her. He put the rope in his pocket.

Linda took the little girl by the hand. "All right, Lucy, it's time for your medicine. Say good-bye to the funny-looking man."

She turned to Finn and said, "We live with my sister, Rhonda. She takes care of Lucy when I'm at sea. Speak to her if you want to check my alibi."

Finn handed her his card. "You think of anything else regarding Espendoza, anything at all, you give me a call."

" 'Nick Finn,' " she read. "What do people usually call you? Nick or Finn?"

"Nick's fine," he said, surprising himself. Everyone called him Finn except Mona.

"I prefer Finn. Suits you better." She put the card in her jeans pocket. "You look like a dangerous guy, Mr. lone-wolf, expeditionary-force, no-warrant marine interdiction agent, with your beat-up face and all, but I bet you're not. I bet you're quite nice to look at when you're not so ugly."

The little girl giggled. Linda laughed outright, opening her mouth and revealing sharp little canines. Finn obliged them with a smile and headed toward the stern.

At the gangway, he turned and said, "One last thing, Linda. This time of year, you're fishing for what?

"Mackerel."

"Any luck?"

"With what?"

He pointed to the nets. "With the catch."

She pulled her child closer and said, "The fish are all gone, Finn. We're *all* out of luck."

CHAPTER TWELVE

At the Self Help, Mona met Finn in the reception area and led him to the small room where they'd interviewed La Abuelita. It smelled of stale cigarette smoke. Mona took a seat behind the desk, with the window behind her. She looked thinner and older, with bags under her eyes, her clothes loose rather than form-fitting. Her eyes seemed to have dimmed, the shine gone out of them. She hadn't bothered with makeup. Mona, it quickly became clear, was there to work and nothing else. She had greeted him curtly. She avoided all physical contact.

Finn told her about his visit to San Pedro that morning.

"The *Pacific Belle* links Espendoza and Diego," she said.

Finn nodded. "There's a link with Perez, too: we found Espendoza's body in the same patch of sea where we intercepted *La Catrina*."

Mona picked up the handset and asked for a whiteboard. A moment later, the door opened and the kid with the face jewelry rolled one in. She gave Finn her usual glower.

When the door closed behind her, Mona got up and stood in front of the whiteboard with a marker. On the left side, she wrote Diego's name. In the middle, she wrote Espendoza's. On the right, Perez's.

Then she turned to Finn and said, "Perez, Espendoza, Diego. Let's get down everything we know that links them."

"Diego was found in the San Pedro fishing port, where the

Pacific Belle docks," said Finn. "Diego and I found Espendoza out in the channel, off of Two Harbors. Espendoza's probation officer said he had a job on the *Pacific Belle*."

Mona wrote "Pacific Belle" on the board, drew a line linking it to Espendoza and another to Diego. She wrote "San Pedro" under Diego's name. She stepped back and looked at her work for a moment.

Then she said, "All three of them were at one time or another in that same patch of sea where you found Espendoza: Diego on patrol, Perez on *La Catrina*."

She drew more lines linking the three men, forming a triangle on the whiteboard. In the middle of it, she wrote "Two Harbors" with a red marker.

"Looks like the Devil's Triangle," she murmured.

Finn thought of all the shark sightings that had been reported in that area. "Here's another possible link," he said. "The port authority told Diego that the *Pacific Belle* returned to port the same morning we found Espendoza's body. So it's possible, in theory at least, that she was out there in the channel, in the Devil's Triangle, that morning."

Mona drew a line linking the *Belle* to Two Harbors and put a question mark next to it. "So you think Espendoza might've come off the *Pacific Belle*?" she said.

Finn shook his head. "Espendoza was floating; bodies sink and don't surface until they gas up, which can take days. If he'd come off the boat that morning, he would've sunk first. He'd been in the water awhile."

Just then his phone rang. The screen showed a Mexico City area code. Finn answered. It was Vega, his contact at the Mexican Federal Police, whom he'd asked to run a check on Perez before Diego's murder. Finn had forgotten all about it.

"You sitting down?" said Vega.

Finn said he was.

"Perez was a cop."

"What?"

"He was with the Policía Municipal Preventiva up in Rosario, in Sinaloa."

Finn was glad he was sitting down. He said, "I thought he was—"

"A gangster, yeah, I know. But listen, he was a *local* cop in Rosario, and the Caballeros own Rosario. That means they own the judges, the mayor, and the cops, too."

"So you're saying Perez was dirty?"

"He was alive, wasn't he? I mean, before you shot him? If you're a cop in Caballeros territory and you're not dead, that means only one thing: you're working for them."

"Sinaloa. That's miles from Tijuana."

"At least a thousand."

"What was he doing off Catalina? Why does he own gas stations in Tijuana?"

"I can't answer that. All I can tell you is, you shot a dirty cop from Rosario."

"I need proof Perez was dirty."

Vega laughed. "You're joking, right?"

Finn thanked him, hung up. On the whiteboard, Mona wrote "Caballero" under Perez's name.

Finn thought, *What if the Caballeros killed Diego in retaliation for Perez? What if they killed the wrong* migra *agent?*

From the black look she was giving him, he guessed Mona was thinking the same thing. He felt a hollowness in his gut. He regretted holding back from taking a drink that morning. He thought about the bottle of Jim Beam waiting for him in his truck, the seal unbroken. He breathed hard through his nose, tried to set his thinking straight, focus on the task at hand. He looked at the board, at all the lines and arrows connecting each name to the others. A crooked cop from a small town in Sinaloa; a teenager from East L.A.; a marine interdiction agent.

Mona had referred to the patch of sea outside Two Harbors as the "Devil's Triangle." It seemed appropriate. He remembered pulling Espendoza's body from the water, the bloodied stumps in place of legs, the great dark shape gliding beneath him. He got up and took a pen from Mona and circled the "Pacific Belle" on the board.

"It keeps coming back to the boat, doesn't it," he said.

Mona nodded. "You met the skipper. You trust her?" she said.

"She seemed cagey," he said. "Like she was scared of something and didn't want me to know it."

"Maybe she's doing something she's not supposed to be doing."

"She's supposed to be fishing, so that's easy enough to find out," said Finn. He still had his phone in his hand. He dialed a contact at the California Department of Fish and Wildlife.

"Can you e-mail me the most recent catch log for a seiner out of San Pedro, the *Pacific Belle*?" he said. He also asked for a copy of her commercial fishing license. He gave his personal e-mail address and hung up. Mona was back in her seat.

"I'll contact the DMV and chase down the *Pacific Belle*'s registration," she said. "See where that leads."

Finn told Mona he was going to take another look at *La Catrina*. Perez had been ready to kill federal agents to protect her, he said. He was convinced the answer was still hidden aboard her somewhere. They arranged to phone each other at the end of the day, or as soon as either one discovered important information.

When he left, they parted with the same stiff manner with which they'd met. A stranger watching would've been surprised to learn that they were married.

CHAPTER THIRTEEN

Finn drove to the CBP station. Along the way, he picked up a pint of Jim Beam and a large bottle of Coke. He poured out half the soda on the road and replaced it with bourbon. By the time he got to the boat he had a nice buzz going.

La Catrina was still cradled in the hoist parked at the top of the boat ramp. It was Sunday and there were no forensics guys around. Finn had her to himself.

He started on the outside. He walked slowly around the entire hull, tapping it every few inches, listening for hollows that shouldn't have been there. He scrutinized the fiberglass, running his fingers over it, looking for sections that might've been cut, then patched over and resprayed. When he got to the stern, he saw that the line with which he'd stopped her was still tightly wound around her propeller shaft. He tapped the rope with his knuckle—it was synthetic rope, which was why it had melted and then fused around the shaft. He couldn't help smiling at his own handiwork: the rope felt as hard as concrete.

After tapping his way around the entire hull, Finn stepped back to get a broader perspective of it. But looking at the boat close-up or farther back, he couldn't see any signs of tampering.

He climbed up the rolling ladder, stepped onto her deck, and began searching. He started in her engine bay, which was hardly bigger than a crawlspace and still smelled of burning plastic and oil. The fire extinguisher with which he'd tried to put out the fire was still there, leaning uselessly in a corner. He checked every nook and cranny.

He climbed back out of the engine bay and methodically went over *La Catrina*'s stern deck, making sure to feel along the lining of all her storage compartments for false bottoms. He checked the refrigerator, the bait box, the drinks holders, the rod holders, and the storage compartment under the bench seat.

He went through the tinted-glass door into the cabin. Inside, he was pleased to see how thorough the forensics guys had been before they'd been pulled off the job. They'd dismantled pretty much everything that could be dismantled. They'd pulled the flat-screen TV out of the wall to check the cavity behind it. They'd knifed through the throw cushions and the tan leather banquettes to check for contraband hidden within. They'd unscrewed the air-conditioning vents. They'd even pulled out the recessed light fixtures in the ceiling and left them dangling on their wires. They'd taken everything out of every drawer and cupboard in the galley, then taken the drawers off their rails and dumped it all into one corner. They'd opened all the canned food and all the food cartons, searched through their contents, and then thrown it all into a lidded plastic bin. Finn was hit by the smell when he lifted the lid, all the food beginning to go bad. Still, he poked through it all.

He went through all the charts and pilot books and paperwork in the drawers of the chart table next to the control console. He went into the bedroom and the bathroom and found the mattress slashed and the vanity unit dismantled. He found a flashlight, located the bilge hatch, then lay down on the floor, lowered his head through the hatch, and shone the flashlight around the bilge.

He went back out to the stern deck and climbed the external ladder to the flybridge. There was a second console up there, so the boat could be driven from up high as well as from the cabin. There was also a second icebox, in which, Finn assumed, Perez had kept his weapon. If he was going to find traces of gunshot residue anywhere, it would be up here. Yet when the forensics team had run all their fancy tests, they'd come up negative.

Of course, it didn't take a genius to see why, thought Finn. The flybridge was completely exposed to the elements on all sides. Because of his trick with the rope, *La Catrina* had been unable to travel under her own steam, and in the six hours it had taken to arrange for a boat to come out and tow her back to Long Beach, a Santa Ana had blown down off the mountains, and *La Catrina* had been towed straight into the eye of a wind gusting upward of forty miles per hour. It would've blasted away whatever residue there might have been on the exposed surfaces of the flybridge.

Finn thought about all this, and then thought how flimsy that would sound in court. *Ladies and gentlemen of the jury, I assure you, the wind blew away the evidence . . .*

He climbed off the boat empty-handed, walked back to his truck, and grabbed the bourbon-laced Coke from the storage compartment in the door.

When the liquor's glow had blunted the edges of his anger, he drove home.

He spoke with Mona on the phone that night. He was sitting at the kitchen table in their Redondo home with his laptop open in front of him, a drink with ice cubes in it next to that. He was bare-chested. She asked him whether he'd found anything on La Catrine and he said no, but he wasn't done looking.

She told him that she'd gotten the *Pacific Belle*'s registration details from the DMV, and he was impressed by her powers of persuasion. He'd never gotten any document that quickly from the DMV.

"Linda Blake owns forty-nine percent," said Mona over the phone. "The rest is owned by a corporation called Muir Holdings. I did a company search to try to find out who that is, but whoever's behind Muir Holdings doesn't want to be identified. The company's held by a trust, and there's no way of finding out who the beneficiaries are. It means 'sea,' by the way."

"What does?"

"'Muir.' It's the Irish word for 'sea.' I googled it."

Finn never did have a head for languages.

"Did you speak to La Abuelita?" he said.

"She's never heard of the *Pacific Belle*."

When they'd said everything they had to say about the case, the conversation ran out of fuel and sputtered to a halt. Finn wanted to keep Mona on the line. He said he hoped she was planning on taking time off work. She was, she said. He asked how her parents were doing. He closed his eyes while she told him. Then he asked about the dogs.

"They lie on the floor whimpering, staring at the front door," she said.

Finn couldn't count the number of times Diego had told him that Rhodesian ridgebacks had been bred to hunt lions. "Strongest breed in the world, kick any dog's ass, including pit bulls," he used to say, prompting Finn to nod politely and try to keep a straight face. He'd known Ronald and Nancy since they were puppies, and he'd never met a softer, more spoiled pair of canines. They might've looked tough, but Finn pictured them bolting behind their favorite couch the moment a lion so much as glanced in their direction. For Diego, they'd been family.

"What are you doing, Nick?" said Mona.

"I just want to talk, Mona. That's all."

"Are you drinking right now?"

He picked up his glass. The ice cubes in it clinked. "Yes," he said.

The line clicked off.

He put down the phone. It was very, very quiet in the room. One of these days, he thought, he would have to do something about his drinking.

One of these days.

CHAPTER FOURTEEN

Finn spent the rest of night lying on the couch, the TV flickering in the background with the sound down low, the bottle of bourbon he was working his way through his only defense against the black dreams. He slept in fits and starts only, afraid to sleep too deeply or too long lest the dreams return.

He got to the dock at first light, the sky streaked with gold and purple. Linda Blake was standing on the quay by her boat, talking to a refrigerator-size man wearing a grizzly beard, yellow bibs, and Xtratuf knee boots. Finn saw her see him and say something to the man, who turned and ambled past Finn, eyeballing him.

Linda was wearing the same sneakers and jeans as yesterday, plus a green fleece. An elastic band held her hair away from her face, and he caught the green-and-gold shimmer in her eyes. She didn't look pleased to see him.

"I'm busy," she said.

"This won't take a minute."

"Like I said, I'm busy."

"You said yesterday that you'd been out on a weeklong trip."

She stuffed her hands into her pockets. "That's right."

"How many crew?"

"However many I can afford. Two, this time."

"Same crew, usually?"

"Whoever I can get."

"You gonna tell me their names?"

"You gonna get a warrant?"

Finn tried a different tack: "Where'd you go?"

"Out past the banks."

Finn nodded. "You were fishing mackerel, huh?"

"Mostly."

Finn ran his tongue along the inside of his teeth. "Yesterday when I asked you how it went, you said the fish are all gone. But you must've caught something, right? A week at sea, you have to come back with something?"

She stiffened. "What's this got to do with anything?"

"Why didn't you go farther out? A week, that's hardly worth the effort, seems to me. Why didn't you head out farther west?"

"You seen the size of my boat? I'm lucky if I make it past Cabo. I can't compete with those big boats go out all the way to Japan. I don't have a helicopter for spotting schools. And anyway, no one wants radioactive fish. You got a point?"

"I called Fish and Wildlife," he said. "I saw your catch log."

She gave him a hard look.

"You haven't caught anything this season. Fish and Wildlife says you're not even close to your quota. So I figure three things could be happening here. Either you're the unluckiest fishing boat in the Pacific, or you're not declaring your catch, or you're not fishing at all." He held her gaze. The green-and-gold shimmer had sharpened. "You don't declare your catch, you could lose your license," he said.

"My generator gave out. I had to throw out the catch. I wasn't going to declare a catch I couldn't sell."

The lie was so blatant, Finn could only admire her for telling it with a straight face.

"My dad worked a seiner back when I was growing up in the nineties," he said. "Small boat, like yours. He used to go after the tuna every spring. Then the tuna stopped coming inshore, and only the big boats could go out far enough to get them. The industry collapsed. All those men out of work, boats getting repossessed. You wouldn't be the first fishing boat to turn to trafficking. What did you do? Stop at some quiet fishing village in Baja, take on a few packages?"

She pulled her hands out of her pockets and lit a cigarette, the flame guttering in time with the tremor she was trying to hide. She took a deep drag and then, with the cigarette clasped between her index and middle fingers, waved toward the fishing fleet. "You see all these boats here?" she said. "All these guys, they go out there, risk their lives to catch fish. This is the most dangerous business in the world. There are lots of accidents. Men die all the time."

An image of his father's fake leg came to Finn's mind. "If you've got a point, I missed it," he said.

"What I'm telling you, Finn, is that this is a dangerous business, and we look after our own. We don't talk to outsiders. Especially not those who come around here disrespecting us, making allegations."

She was talking tough, but her tone didn't match her words. She sounded scared.

"Who's your co-owner?"

She blinked. "What?"

"Muir Holdings? Who is that? Who are you protecting?"

She dragged on her cigarette, fixed her eyes on his. "Go home to your wife, Finn. You have no idea what you're dealing with."

"What happened to Espendoza?"

"I haven't seen him—"

"Bullshit. I think you know exactly what happened to him. In fact, I think he came off this boat."

She started up the gangway. He hustled behind her, the metal clanging under his feet.

"How did you know I'm married?"

She turned and glanced at his left hand. Finn didn't wear a ring.

"Get off my boat," she said.

"Not before you tell me what happened to Diego."

Someone stepped onto the gangway behind him. He turned and saw the man in yellow bibs. He had two companions behind him, both the size of NFL nose tackles.

"Is there a problem here?" said the refrigerator.

Finn turned back to Linda. "I *know* Diego spoke to you, Linda. I don't give a damn what you do with your boat. All I want is whoever killed Diego."

"This guy bothering you, Captain?" said the man in bibs.

"Yes," she said.

Finn turned to the man. "This is official business. I'm a marine interdiction agent with Customs and Border Protection. There's no trouble here."

From their dead-eyed looks, Finn got the impression that the trio did not give much weight to the federal government or its agents.

"Captain says get off her boat," said the man.

"We're just having a conversation."

"Conversation's over."

Finn looked at the three men and wondered if he was about to get the crap kicked out of him again.

They looked like they were wondering the same thing.

He threw up his hands. "Okay, okay, I'm going," he said, glancing back.

Linda Blake had disappeared into the wheelhouse. She had more flint to her than he had thought. She wasn't going to give up Diego's killer without some arm-twisting, and he couldn't twist her arm with her sitting safely in the pocket. She had quite the offensive line around her, and, truth be told, Finn was relieved to get off the gangway before it collapsed under their combined weight.

He'd been waiting in his truck for two hours by the time Linda came off the *Belle* and appeared in the parking lot. He shrank down in his seat and watched her get into a white Tahoe. She pulled out of the lot and turned left. Finn gave her ten seconds, then pulled out behind her.

The sun was up now and the air was getting warmer. The roads were filled with people on their way to work. He followed the Tahoe down West Twenty-second, pulling up a couple of cars behind her at each of the lights. She turned left on South Gaffey, then right onto Twenty-fifth. A couple of miles down the road, Twenty-fifth Street turned into Palos Verdes Drive. Linda stuck to the speed limit. The farther they went into Palos Verdes, the more the neighborhood improved, with eucalypti standing guard over mowed front lawns, trimmed hedges veiling wide, pricey-looking houses with double-front garages, the street spotless, not a pothole in sight. The white Tahoe turned off on a local road. Finn knew what kind of money fishermen took home, and this wasn't the kind of neighborhood in which they lived.

Linda pulled into the driveway of a single-story, modern-looking, cement-and-wood house. Finn drifted past her. Through his tinted windows, he saw the front door of the house open and Lucy appear next to a woman who looked enough like Linda for Finn to figure she was the sister.

He got to the end of the street, turned around, and pulled up in the shade of some trees. He checked his watch. It was 9:45 A.M. Too early for a drink.

He had one anyway.

That Linda had led him to her sister's house disappointed him. He'd hoped, unreasonably, that she would lead him straight to Diego's killer. But all she'd done was go home. He searched around for a piece of paper on which to write down the address. All he could find was the counselor's card that he'd thrown on the floor.

He was about to leave when he saw Linda, Lucy, and the sister reappear from the house. The sister had on a nurse's uniform. She held open the Tahoe's back door while Lucy climbed in, then closed the door and got in the front passenger side, next to Linda at the wheel. For the hell of it, Finn pulled out from the shade and followed them. Linda navigated her way through the back streets of Palos Verdes, Hermosa Beach, and Manhattan Beach. She turned right onto Rosecrans, and Finn almost overshot the ramp when she veered onto the 405 northbound. He had to cut off a Suburban, whose driver honked exuberantly. He kept his eyes fixed on the Tahoe: if Linda had made him, she hadn't reacted.

Half an hour later, she took the Santa Monica exit and drove west to a large hospital. The white Tahoe went through a boom gate into the parking lot and headed down a row of parking spaces. Finn followed, took the next row, and pulled into an empty space. He watched Linda and her sister get out of the car and open the back door for Lucy, who was playing with a length of rope. The three of them walked into the hospital.

Linda had talked about taking her daughter to a doctor's appointment, but he'd imagined an office visit, not a hospital. His heart went out to her. He thought the kid must be sicker than he'd realized. Maybe his gut had been wrong about Linda. Maybe she had acted the way she had because she was stressed about her sick daughter.

CHAPTER FIFTEEN

Forty minutes later, Finn got out of his truck and walked up the set of stone steps, through the tinted-glass door, and into the air-conditioned, tube-lit foyer of the L.A. County Coroner's office.

He walked to a counter next to a set of double-swing doors marked CORONER STAFF ONLY and asked the receptionist, a light-skinned black woman with the elongated eyelashes and straightened hair of a pop star, to page Eugene Geisinger, the medical examiner. While he waited, he wandered over to the gift shop. The sign over the door read SKELETONS IN THE CLOSET, the font arranged out of little bones. In the shopwindow he saw beach towels, T-shirts, tote bags, and baseball caps printed with body outlines, skeletons, and L.A. County Coroner emblems. The boxer shorts were branded UNDERTAKERS.

A man in a blue lab coat came through the double-swing doors. He was a slim six feet and had slicked-back black hair. Intelligent, dark eyes peered out from beneath dense eyebrows.

"Jesus, what happened to your fucking face?" said the medical examiner, his hand extended.

Finn shook his hand and shrugged off the question. "What does it say about this city, has a morgue with a gift shop?" he said, nodding toward the shopwindow.

"This right here is a license to print money," said Geisinger. "People come down, make a positive ID of a husband or boyfriend, then head home with a fucking souvenir. Now, what *you* need is one of these beach towels with the body-outline print, on account of all the floaters you bring in."

Finn chuckled joylessly. "I heard you got Diego here," he said.

Geisinger didn't answer right away, so Finn waited out the silence by looking back at the display case. In the glass, he saw the reflection of Geisinger's jaw muscles twitching. Geisinger's face was ravaged looking, though from what, Finn didn't know. As far as he knew, the M.E. didn't smoke or drink, or at least didn't drink the way Finn did. For all his cussing, Geisinger was a classy guy. He listened to classical music while he worked.

"It broke my heart when I saw him," Geisinger said after a minute. "He was a good man. It's a fucked-up thing. Please give my deepest condolences to Mona."

Finn nodded. Then he said, "What about my floater?"

Geisinger brightened. "Oh man, your floater—he's a big celebrity around here. There are med students coming down from Keck just to take a look at that piece of shark snack, morbid fuckers. His legs, what's left of them, look like hamburgers. Put me off my lunch, which is saying something. But that's not the important thing. Someone who knew what he was doing cut an incision about seven inches right here"—Geisinger tapped his side, just below his ribs—"removed one of his fucking kidneys, then sewed him up. Only, they were less careful when they sewed him up. The sutures got infected. There's traces of puss."

Finn stared at their reflection in the glass. "Why would anyone do that?" he said.

Geisinger shrugged. "It's fucked up. You heard about the kid over in China, sold his for an iPad?"

"Jesus."

Geisinger sighed. "We also found water in his lungs."

"Back up a second. You're saying that they killed him first, then took the kidney? They stole it?"

"I doubt it. Why stitch up a fucking dead man? No, I think he had the operation, then died, but I can't say whether he died from post-op complications or from something else. We found traces of propofol in his blood."

Finn's incomprehension must have been evident, because Geisinger added, "That's a serious anesthetic used in surgery. It's only available in hospitals. Anesthesiologists call it 'milk of amnesia.'"

"Is that what killed him? Propofol?"

Geisinger shook his head. "It can kill you in high doses—Michael Jackson was pumped full of it—but your guy lost so much blood, there's no way of knowing if he had a lethal dose or not. All I can say for sure is that he was definitely dead when the fucking shark got his legs."

Finn scratched his bruised face. "So what's your best guess?" he said.

Geisinger shook his head emphatically. "Oh no, I'm not playing that game. Could've been the propofol, could've been all the fucking alcohol we found in his gut. Or maybe he just drowned. You guys brought us a real winner this time. I'm putting the cause of death as undetermined." Geisinger paused. "Though, of course, most guys in his line of work don't die naturally."

Finn thought for a moment. "What do you mean, 'his line of work'?"

Geisinger pointed at the side of his own neck. "You see the crucifix he had tattooed here?"

Finn shook his head.

"Caballeros de Cristo—the Knights of Christ—down in Sinaloa. You know the ones: shoot you to pieces, then give you a Christian burial?"

Finn couldn't believe it. If Espendoza was a Caballero, then it linked him with Perez. "But he was just a kid. Plus, he was from East L.A. An American citizen. The Caballeros are a Mexican outfit."

Geisinger shrugged. "Maybe they're franchising. Maybe it's NAFTA. Maybe they don't recognize the border. Hey, I'm just the medical examiner, what the fuck do I know? What I'm telling you is anyone who gets that tattoo on his neck and isn't a fucking Caballero and they find out, they're going to separate his neck from his head, right? So either Espendoza was a Knight of Christ or else he was so stupid he died of it."

Finn absorbed this, then asked, "Do you know when he died, or how long he'd been in the water?"

"You pulled him out Wednesday morning, the twenty-first. I would say he'd been in the water four or five days by then, maybe even longer. He had a lot of gas in him, more than most of them, probably because of the wound. As for whether he was already dead when he went in . . ." Here, Geisinger shrugged.

Finn calculated. Four or five days meant that he would've gone in Friday or Saturday of the week before last. He made a mental note to see if he could find out where the *Pacific Belle* had been on the sixteenth or seventeenth.

Then, in a concerned tone, Geisinger said, "There's been talk about you, Finn."

"What kind of talk?"

"Ugly fucking stuff. This morning, these two guys from CBP Internal Affairs came in. They said they were investigating Perez. But their attitude was all wrong."

"Wrong how?" asked Finn.

"They asked to see Diego's autopsy, not just Perez's. They made remarks about how Diego was wearing his sidearm but hadn't taken it out of his holster. They talked about how it was likely he knew and trusted his killer. Wanted me to say so, too. They wanted to know if the slug was from a Heckler & Koch P2000, the ones you guys are issued with. Then they started speculating on whether you'd had a beef with him. Right there in the cold room, in front of my team. In front of the fucking body, for Chrissakes."

Finn stared at his reflection in the gift-shop window. "What'd you tell them?"

"I said I was just the fucking medical examiner and they should go ask the ballistics guys. Fucking amateurs. They won't get anything from them anyway. I pulled out a slug, it was a total mess. It was lodged in his heart. He was shot in the fucking back, so the bullet bounced off his spine and got all messed up. Doesn't look like anything. They'll never identify the weapon, not unless they find a casing."

Benitez hadn't mentioned finding any casings at the San Pedro dock.

"You find anything that could tell you where he was shot? I mean geographically?" Finn asked.

Geisinger shook his head. "All I found in his stomach was beer and nuts. I thought the cops had the crime scene down at the fishermen's dock in San Pedro?"

"They do," said Finn. "I'm just . . . I'm just looking to see if they missed something."

"The water washed away most anything that might've been helpful on the outside," said Geisinger. "I'm guessing that's why the fucker who killed him put him in there. He must've hit the water reasonably hard, too. The impact knocked everything off him. He ruptured his spleen against the steering wheel, though he was already dead by then. There was tattooing around the entrance wound in his head, telling me they shot him at close range, but not enough to tell me with what, or where."

Finn rubbed his chin, then said, "I need to see him, Eugene. And the floater, too."

Geisinger gave him a long look. "Okay, let's go," he said, but not in a way that indicated he thought it was a good idea.

Finn followed the medical examiner through the swinging doors and down a pale green corridor to the cold room. He zipped up his jacket.

In the anteroom, Finn put on a lightweight gown over his clothes and slipped on a pair of latex gloves. Then Geisinger offered him some VapoRub. Finn scooped some out and rubbed it below his nostrils, clearing them instantly. The M.E., he noticed, didn't bother with either the gown or the VapoRub. Like a fishmonger, he'd gotten used to the smell of his trade.

Inside the examination room, orchestral music was playing from a couple of wall-mounted speakers. Espendoza was laid out uncovered on a metal autopsy table. Sea bugs had gotten into him, accelerating autolysis; Finn could tell by the blue color of Espendoza's face. He averted his eyes from the stumps and stared at that face. Despite its dead-man color, it seemed more natural to him now, or at least how Finn imagined Espendoza might've looked when he was alive. His youth was apparent now; he looked barely old enough to have a driver's license, just the faintest hint of hair on his lip. Finn had hoped that seeing Espendoza's body would help him work out what had happened to him, would reveal some connection that he had been blind to. He kept staring, waiting for it to come to him. He took in the gaudy tattoo of the Virgin on Espendoza's chest; he looked at the small cross in blue ink on his neck that Geisinger had mentioned.

Nothing.

He turned his attention to the other table. A body lay under the cover.

"That him?" he said.

Geisinger nodded. Finn walked over and stood next to it.

Geisinger just looked at Finn. After a minute, he said, "You sure?"

Finn nodded.

Geisinger rolled back the sheet. Diego's face was without color, or at least without one Finn could describe. His eyes were closed. A ragged, red-black wound the size of a dime marked the place where the round had entered on the right side of Diego's forehead. Finn breathed slowly and deliberately. He stood as still as possible and listened carefully, as though he were expecting Diego to say something, tell him who had killed him, where to find that person, what to do. But he didn't hear anything but the hum of the refrigerators.

He felt a hand on his elbow.

"Time to go, Finn," said Geisinger.

Finn nodded. They left the cold room and headed down the corridor.

"I thought I had something here," said Finn.

"Bodies play tricks on people," the medical examiner said. "Sometimes it's better just to let them be."

Finn thought that was funny, coming from him.

He walked out of the building and unzipped his jacket. He liked Geisinger, but he was glad to be outside. He stood at the top of the steps for a moment, letting the rays warm his skin, hoping they would seep the chill out of him. But the image of Diego's colorless face, the ragged wound ripped in his forehead, was burned into his mind's eye. The urge for a drink came on strong.

"Fuck," he said.

The receptionist was standing next to a potted plant on the other side of the steps, smoking a cigarette, one arm across her waist, her hand supporting her elbow. She glanced in Finn's direction.

"You grieving, hon?" she said.

He nodded.

"Uh-huh. Who'd you lose?" she said.

Everybody, thought Finn. "A friend."

She nodded matter-of-factly. "What happened, he get shot?"

"Three times."

"Yeah, that'll do it. You some kind of cop?" she said, looking at his uniform.

"Customs and Border Protection," he said.

"Uh-huh. I heard of that. You want my advice?"

He shrugged. "Sure," he said.

"Right now you need to be with the people you love and who love you. You're not bringing your friend back, standing there with all those bad ideas I can see in your eyes. Let the Lord be the judge. You got a wife or girlfriend?"

"A wife," he said, his voice cracking a little.

She crushed her cigarette into the side of the pot.

"Go spend time with her. That's the best place you can be right now," she said before heading back inside. Finn dialed Mona's cell. The call went straight to voice mail. He left a message, telling her what he'd learned from the coroner. He asked her to check with La Abuelita whether the Caballeros had moved north.

After hanging up, Finn stood there for a moment, listening to the cars passing on the nearby Golden State Freeway, the sound like waves breaking on a shore.

CHAPTER SIXTEEN

Finn slept for a couple of hours, then arrived back at the dock just as the sun was setting. He pulled up near the water, far enough from the *Pacific Belle* not to draw attention to himself. He got out the pair of binoculars he kept in the Tacoma for when he was doing surveillance on boat ramps, and trained them on the seiner. As he had expected, there was nobody aboard. He put away the binoculars, sat back, and waited for the sun to set. The smell and sight of the fishing boats was so familiar to him. Finn took a swig of Jim Beam and thought about his father.

When Finn was ten years old, his father had lost his right leg below the knee and four fingers on his right hand to a drum-winch cable on a purse seiner. After the accident, he couldn't fish anymore, and he had taken up drinking full-time, mostly at Bonito's. This was in the old days, before Cutts had taken over. Then he had started a second career piloting boatloads of Mexican pot up the coast. He'd known the waters, and he'd known how the coast guard and CBP patrolled them. He'd been a good smuggler, but he'd been a drunk, which meant he'd gotten careless, which meant he'd gotten caught.

"Takes a fierce storm, son," he'd said to Finn in the car driving back from the penitentiary when he came out on parole after a four-year stint, "for a man to realize the world don't care if he lives or dies."

After his parents split, Nick lived with his mother, but he had a key to his father's fleabag apartment in Harbor City and stayed there sometimes. One day not long after his sixteenth birthday, he'd walked in to find his father with a black-red hole under his chin, and bits of his skull splattered over the top of the tan leather recliner. His fake leg lay on the ground next to the recliner. To this day, what remained most vivid in Finn's memory was the gun in his father's good hand and the finger of honey-colored liquid in the bottle of Maker's Mark on the floor beside the recliner. He remembered wanting to drink it and to go where his father had gone.

He took a swig of his memory medicine. These were images he'd spent a lifetime trying to forget. He knew he had to keep going, keep doing what he had to do, keep moving toward the faint light ahead, no matter what. He told himself, *Forget about the past.* What he had to do now was find Diego's killer, get sober, and get Mona back. He looked at the bottle in his hand. Somehow, the first objective seemed more attainable than the second. He thought about what Diego had said out on patrol that morning, how he'd been shook up by the dead-eyed way Finn had killed Perez. And Mona, always telling him how he wasn't in a war zone, always wanting him to go talk to someone, like he needed to be guided back into the fold of the human race.

He took another swig. The truth was, he *hadn't* felt anything when he'd killed Perez except the rush of adrenaline. The feelings had come later, when he was back onshore. He'd started having unnerving dreams.

While he thought about all this, the last of the day faded from the sky. Finn looked out through the windshield at the almost full moon over the water in the bay, and at all the lights of the container terminal beyond.

He tried to imagine Diego's last moments on this earth. Had he been looking at this same moonlight reflection on the water? What thoughts had been his last? Had he pictured Ronald and Nancy bolting across the park?

Finn grabbed his Maglite from the glove compartment and a

blue CBP shell jacket from the backseat, the words CBP FEDERAL AGENT printed in large gold letters on the back. Then he stepped out of the cab and went to the back of the truck. He unlocked the steel toolbox in the load tray and pulled out his personal weapon, a Glock 17. From a separate drawer he pulled out a clip, which he slid into his weapon. A cool breeze was blowing in from the sea. Finn zipped up the shell jacket, stuffed the Glock into the deep pocket, and walked down the quay to the boat.

No one was around. Feeling more sober than he deserved to, Finn walked up the gangway and onto the steel deck of the *Pacific Belle*. His father had first shown him his way around a fishing boat, so he knew that the small skiff tied fast to the starboard rail was used to draw the net around schooling fish. He walked under the boom with the power block at the end of it, used to hoist the net. The boom was leaning at a thirty-degree angle off the mast and was only slightly shorter than it was. There was the cable drum, and there, the cover to the fish hold. There was everything Finn expected to see on a fishing boat, except for one crucial thing: there was no net. He glanced at the dock, where fishermen sometimes laid out their nets to repair, but there was nothing next to the *Belle*.

Finn climbed up to the wheelhouse and found the door locked. The door to the below-deck cabin, however, wasn't. Finn shone his flashlight over a diner-style table and bench seats, the vinyl covering of which was patched with gaffer tape in a color that didn't match. There was an ashtray on the table with butts in it. He opened a cupboard and found canned and boxed food. In the galley area there were a couple of burners mounted on gimbals, a fire blanket above them, and a fire extinguisher clipped into the corner. Finn opened a locker and found a box full of thick rubber gloves, the kind fishermen use to handle catch, as well as rubber aprons and neoprene-lined rubber boots. Someone had shoved an old rod and reel into a corner of the locker.

He went through to the next cabin forward, which was close

and airless and hardly bigger than the dual cab of his truck. Four uncomfortable-looking bunks were crammed into it, each with a stained, thin mattress and a dirty-looking pillow without a case. There were only two small portholes and both were clamped shut. Finn started to feel nauseous—a little bourbon-flavored vomit found its way back up into his mouth; he quickly made his way out into the fresh air.

Back on deck, Finn thought he heard something from the direction of the quay. He had switched off his flashlight when he came up from below, so it took a moment for his eyes to adjust to the darkness. When they had, he scanned the quay. He saw a creature, either a small cat or a large rat, scuttle between two bollards. He turned his attention to the fish hold. The hinges squeaked when he raised the cover. He peered in, but of course without turning on the flashlight he couldn't see a thing.

Finn gingerly made his way down the steel ladder, pulling the hatch shut behind him. It was pitch-black inside. The hold smelled of fish and of something else, too. Something a bit like spoiled milk. His feet landed on something soft, like a mattress. He switched on his flashlight. Its narrow white beam revealed refrigeration pipes snaking around the hold's fiberglass lining. He looked down and saw that he was standing on a neat pile of fishing net. He bent down and touched it. It was completely dry—it had been out of the water for so long that dry rot had set in. Which accounted for the sour smell, thought Finn.

Something else on the other side of the hold caught his attention: a large roll of thick neoprene—thicker than any wet suit he'd seen. Unrolled, there must've been hundreds of feet of the stuff. He got onto his knees and shone the flashlight's beam down the middle of the rolled-up material. The surface wasn't smooth. He reached in and touched what felt like kitchen tiles. He flipped over the end of the roll and found that it was covered in black, diamond-shaped tiles about the size of his palm and fitted closely together, like the scales of a crocodile's skin. He tried to pry one off, but the tile was fixed firmly in place. He had no idea what it was or what it was used for. It looked vaguely military. He took a photo of it with his phone.

He started feeling ill again. There was no reconciling a belly full of liquor with a fish hold. He climbed back up the ladder, pushed the cover open, and clambered gratefully back into the fresh air.

He was walking down the gangway back to the quay when he noticed the three police cars. As one, they switched on their head-lights and blue lights, blinding him. He shielded his eyes and cursed. Someone yelled at him to put his hands in the air. Officer Wilkins appeared with a set of handcuffs. He looked almost apologetic.

Finn was about to say, *How did you know I was here?* when he saw Linda Blake, her arms crossed, standing in the pulsating pool of blue-and-red light on the dock, glaring at him.

CHAPTER SEVENTEEN

It was close to nine thirty in the morning by the time Finn got home from the port police lockup.

Mona's RAV4 was parked outside. He walked into the condo, his head aching, and heard her moving around upstairs, in the bedroom. The living room was a mess. There were empty bottles and dirty plates on the coffee table and empty cans on the floor. His clothes were strewn across the furniture. The TV was still on. He'd been living like he had before he was married. In the kitchen, he saw that Mona had put the coffee on. He searched the back of the cupboard for a clean mug, filled it with coffee, drank it straight down, then took a refill upstairs.

She had all her luggage out. She'd taken all her clothes from the closet and laid them on the bed. Two cases were already packed. A third lay open on the floor, half full. She wasn't packing for a return trip—she was clearing out. The irrational hope Finn had entertained while driving home now evaporated.

"You look terrible," she said.

"Thanks," he said.

"You stink, too. Are you sober at least?"

Finn let that one through to the catcher. He noticed Mona's straw hat on the bed.

"Isn't that some kind of bad luck, putting a hat on the bed?" he said.

"I've had more than my share of bad luck this week. Can it really get worse?"

Finn privately thought so. In his view, it could always get worse.

Mona looked at her watch. "Where've you been?"

"The captain of the *Pacific Belle* called the cops on me last night. I've been lying on a bench in a cell down in San Pedro."

Mona stopped packing. "You find anything?" she asked.

"Her nets haven't been in the water in a long time. And this." He showed her a photo he'd taken on his phone of the neoprene roll with the tiles.

"What is it?" said Mona, screwing up her face.

"I have no idea." He sipped his coffee. "Did you speak to Mrs. Gavrilia?"

Mona nodded. "She said there was no way the Caballeros de Cristo have established themselves north of the border. She said when the Caballeros take over a town, they really take it over. I mean, they're fanatical, they're about total control—that's their thing. They move in and get rid of all opposition until they control everyone, from the mayor to the guy grilling tortillas by the side of the road. Anyone who doesn't like it . . . too bad for them. They can't operate like that in L.A. It would be a war zone."

"So how come Espendoza had that crucifix tattooed on his neck?"

"She said he probably went down to Mexico and joined the Caballeros there. They cultivate a kind of mystical aura around themselves, like a cult. You should see the songs they put on You-Tube about how great they are. She said kids in the neighborhoods hero-worship them, talk about how they're restoring pride. She said young men were heading south and signing up. It's no different, I guess, from those kids who grow up in Boston and Atlanta and then go fight for jihad in Syria."

None of that made any kind of sense to Finn. In his view, the Caballeros were narcotics traffickers and murderers. Where was the pride in that?

"I figured if he'd gone to Mexico, he'd have needed a passport," continued Mona, "so I checked with the Department of State. They say they never issued him with one. As far as they're concerned, Miguel Espendoza never once left the United States during his short life."

"Plenty of people cross the line without passports," said Finn. He thought of the bunks in the airless cabin in the bow of the *Pacific Belle*. "He could've gone by boat."

Mona nodded. "That's what I figured."

Then she said, "You know, if Internal Affairs sees you like this, it's one more thing they'll use against you. You know that, right? They'll say you've got an alcohol problem. They'll ask whether you'd been drinking when you shot Perez."

"The answer is 'no.'"

"Doesn't matter what the answer is. In court, it's the question that does the damage. Like those articles in the paper. They hurt you whether they're true or not."

He turned to face her. "I've given up alcohol," he said.

She laughed out loud. "I can smell it on you from here, Nick." She was standing on the other side of the bed.

"That's from last night. I haven't had a drink today."

"It's nine thirty in the morning."

"I've quit. I'm serious this time."

She shook her head sadly, stuffed the rest of her clothes without folding them into the case, and zipped it up. Then she picked up her straw hat.

"I can't have this conversation again, Finn. I have to go. I'm going to church with my parents."

That surprised Finn. Mona hadn't been in a church since their wedding day.

"I'm going to light a candle for Diego," she said.

"Mona, I mean it," he said. "This time, that's it. I don't want to lose you."

She fixed her eyes on his, making it a question. He tried to look at her as though he meant what he was saying—tried to give her a gaze that said *Believe me.* He didn't know what she saw when she looked at his beat-up, liquor-ravaged face. Much later, he would admit to himself that all he had been thinking about at that moment was how much he wanted to open the fresh bottle of Jim Beam that he'd picked up as soon as the port police had released him from lockup, which he had been careful to leave in his truck when he'd seen Mona's RAV4 parked outside the condo.

At least when she left, he had the decency to carry her bags to her car. And to wait until she was out of sight before retrieving the bottle from his truck.

CHAPTER EIGHTEEN

He spent the morning drinking and the afternoon sleeping. Now it was night and he was in the *Pacific Belle*'s galley. Rain started drumming down on the deck above—he had to listen closely to hear footsteps through it. The moment he did, he stepped to the side of the door, out of sight. The door swung open. Linda came in, set a bag of groceries on the counter, and switched on the light. Water streamed off her green slicker. She wheeled around when Finn said her name, then stepped back when she saw the gun in his hand.

"Sit down," he said, gesturing to the table.

She sat. He sat opposite her, still pointing the Glock at her.

"You're going to tell me who killed Diego," he said.

She looked at him fearfully. "I swear, Jesus, I don't know. Please . . . I have a daughter . . ."

She put her elbows on the table and started to sob. With his free hand, Finn reached into his pocket, pulled out the bottle of Jim Beam, and put it on the table between them. Then he took his finger off the Glock's trigger and put the pistol on the table next to the bottle.

Linda Blake stopped crying and gave him a quizzical look. Then she snatched up the gun and with both hands pointed it at Finn's heart. A long moment passed. The veins in her neck pulsed. He waited for her to pull the trigger. Instead, she weighed the weapon in her hands, feeling its lightness. The skin around her eyes slackened. "It's not loaded," she said.

Finn held her gaze. "You got any shot glasses aboard this rust bucket?"

It turned out that all she had were chipped and coffee-stained mugs. She sat tall and still, watching him while he poured bourbon into them. "Jesus, look at you," she said. "I've never seen anyone beat up that bad not in the hospital." She lit a cigarette with a Zippo, then put the lighter and the pack on the table. "Does it hurt when you drink?"

He raised his mug and threw back the shot it contained. "I don't feel a thing," he said.

She gave him a half smile and drank the bourbon from her mug. Finn poured them each another shot.

"On the bright side, at least things can only get better from here," he said.

"Don't kid yourself."

"You're a pessimist."

"I run a commercial fishing boat. You spend enough time off-shore, you learn things can always get worse."

"Is that how Diego got killed? Because things went wrong?"

The smile evaporated from her face. "I don't . . ."

He grabbed her wrist across the table. "I saw the dry rot in your nets down in the hold—they haven't been in the water for months. You've got no crew. Espendoza was no fisherman. You haven't filed any catch reports. You're covering for someone. Who killed Diego?"

"I don't know," she said, her voice rising. She writhed away from him, trying to free her wrist. He tightened his grip and gave her a hard look through the snakelike slit of his swollen right eye. He had no idea how menacing he looked with his face like a bruised apple, but he hoped it was plenty.

"You do and you're lying. Whatever you're into doesn't mean a damn thing to me, but there are plenty of people who'd be happy to make it their business: the cops, the CBP, the coast guard, Fisheries—everyone's about to get real interested in the *Pacific Belle*."

He leaned forward and, in a softer tone, said, "I know you're scared, Linda. You feel like you're caught between him and me. You're scared of him and you're scared of me. But he's not your friend—*I* am. I can help you. We can help each other."

She tried to yank her wrist away from him again but he only tightened his grip.

"You're hurting me!" she said.

"I'm your friend! Talk to me!" His voice was hard and unfriendly.

With her free hand, Linda Blake scooped up Finn's Glock and jammed it against his chest and pulled the trigger repeatedly: *click-click-click-click-click*. He knew it wasn't loaded, but his heart still jolted into overdrive. His face was so close to hers that he could distinguish the lashes above her green eyes, which gleamed like mossy stones in a shallow stream. She stopped pulling the trigger. Her lips began to tremble and Finn thought she was about to cry again. He released her wrist. She slumped back into her seat, but she didn't cry. She stuck out her lower lip and blew away an escaped lock of hair. Then she laughed.

"Bang bang, you're dead," she said, almost whispering, still pointing his gun at him. "You didn't think I would really shoot you, did you?"

His heart only now started to slow down. He slugged a shot of bourbon to collect himself.

"We both knew it wasn't loaded," he said. "You're not the type to shoot anybody."

"I was four years in the navy."

"Aboard an aircraft carrier. I bet you haven't fired a weapon since basic training. I bet you've never killed anyone in your life."

She tilted her head quizzically. He noticed the down at the bottom of her earlobe, the freckles on her nose.

"But *you* have, haven't you?" she said.

He couldn't help but think of Perez.

She must've seen the thought drift across his face like the shadow of a cloud over a patch of sea, because she said, "Did you like it?"

"What?"

"Killing that unarmed man in cold blood, the one I read about in the *Times*. Did you like it?"

"Now *you're* making me nervous."

"I bet it was a rush," she said.

Slowly, he raised his hand until it covered hers and took the gun away from her. He put it on the bench next to him, out of her reach. Loaded or not, she made him nervous.

"Even if you pull the trigger for the right reasons, it messes up your life. Does that answer your question?" he said.

Her face slackened, and the tears he'd been expecting began welling in her green eyes. He leaned forward, put his hand against her cheek. "It's okay, Linda. Whatever it is, no matter how bad, I can help. But you have to tell me: who killed Diego?"

"If I tell you—" A sob shuddered out of her. Tears streamed down her cheeks and onto Finn's fingers. She rested the weight of her head in his palm.

Her skin felt soft. "It'll be all right," he said.

She pulled away from him, wrapped her arms around herself, and started sobbing. "You don't understand, Finn. He said if I said anything, he'd kill Lucy."

CHAPTER NINETEEN

"Who did?" said Finn.

Linda composed herself, wiped her cheeks with the back of her hand, and drew a cigarette from her pack. Finn picked up the Zippo from the table and lit it for her. She took hold of his hand, held it up in front of her eyes, and stared at the flame.

"It was my husband's Zippo."

Finn flicked the top shut and turned it over. The metal lighter had a picture of an aircraft carrier etched into it, with USS ROOSEVELT engraved below. Linda pried the lighter from Finn's hand.

"After David died, all the other captains expected me to just sell the boat," she said. "But the inshore tuna ban had just come into effect and everyone had to go way out to fish, so no one wanted a small boat. People said to me, unless you've got a big boat, a factory boat that can be out for months, you're not gonna make it. Anyway, I couldn't sell her. No one wanted the *Belle*."

"How'd he die?" he said.

She took a drag on her cigarette. "There was a storm. He was swept off." She paused. The rain had dwindled to a pitter-patter on the deck above. "So I started working the *Belle* myself. I switched to mackerel. I had Lucy to take care of, I needed to make a living, keep us both afloat, right? At first I didn't catch enough. I couldn't even break even. So I went to the bank and took out a loan against the boat. I figured my luck would turn eventually and I'd start catching fish. Things couldn't get any worse, I figured. I was wrong."

She knocked the ash off the end of her cigarette and stared at the Zippo. "Lucy got sick," she continued. "Really sick. She needed specialist treatment, and it was expensive. I went to the VHA, but they wouldn't cover her. Medicaid said we didn't qualify. So I maxed out my credit to buy her private coverage. Then, when I tried to claim the costs, they wouldn't pay. They said it was a preexisting condition that I had failed to declare. Like I knew. I was going to sue, but then the credit crunch hit and anyway I'd used all my money on the premiums. Everything collapsed. I defaulted on the boat payments and the bank refused to negotiate. They were going to take the *Belle* and the *Belle*'s all I have, Finn. Her, and Lucy. I was desperate. That's when Little John—one of the other captains, you met him this morning—Little John told me about this Irish guy, owns a bar up the road, has some kind of maritime background, I never found out what, exactly. What John said was, this guy knows boats and likes to invest in fishing operations when no one else will."

Finn felt his temperature rise. His good eye started twitching. "Diarmud Cutts," he said.

She looked alarmed. "You . . . you know him?"

Finn nodded. "What happened next?"

"I went to see Cutts. He said, yeah, he could loan me some money, buy out the bank's share in the boat, get me off the hook, let me get back to fishing and looking after Lucy. All he asked for in return was a share in the *Belle*."

Everything started falling into place in Finn's mind. He remembered Mona saying Muir meant sea in Irish. He remembered the tattoo on Cutts's right arm: HOPE FROM THE SEA BUT NONE FROM LAND. Linda added another butt to the already overflowing ashtray.

"Then things got even worse," she said.

"How?"

"About a month after he paid off the bank, Cutts came to see me and said he wanted me to stop at this fishing village in Mexico, pick something up. That's all he said. I didn't need to know what it was, he said. Just pick up a small package and bring it back to me. You getting the picture?"

Finn was getting the picture. "Where's the village, exactly?"

"About forty miles south of Mazatlán."

Sinaloa, thought Finn. *Caballeros de Cristo country.* It kept coming back to them.

"What's the village called?"

"Puerto Escondido."

Where La Abuelita had said the young men had gone aboard *La Catrina* and disappeared.

"I told him I didn't want to get involved with anything like that," Mona continued. "I told him I had my daughter to think about. I said I needed to focus on fishing, making it pay for her treatment." She drew another cigarette from the pack but didn't light it. "That's when he handed me the envelope. I can still feel its thickness in my fingers. It was more money than I could make in six months at sea." She paused. Her lower lip was trembling again. "The kind of money that changes your life, Finn." She lit the cigarette and for a moment stared into some private space within her.

"The first time, all it was was a package about the size of a brick, wrapped in black plastic, easy to hide. I never saw what was in it, but of course I took a guess." She gave him a piercing look.

"Then it started happening more and more regularly. The shipments got bigger. Pretty soon, I wasn't even bothering to put the net out. On top of that, Lucy wasn't getting better, despite the treatment. The doctors said they wanted to try a different kind of treatment . . . an even more expensive kind. The pressure was getting to me, but the money helped. If you had kids, you'd understand. You wouldn't look at me like that."

Finn realized he was clenching his jaw. He'd been thinking of his father—how he had turned mule after his accident. How easy it must have seemed to him with a boat and an open sea, no one on the horizon. To Linda, too. Finn forced a smile. He watched her press her hand hard into her side, trying to stop it from trembling.

"Tell me about Diego," he said.

She contemplated him for a moment. "What difference does it make now if you know?" she said quietly, as though to herself. She took another drag before she continued.

"Last Friday, Cutts phones me. Right away, I notice his tone is different. Before, he used to speak to me like we were partners, even though we weren't, really. I mean, I didn't think I could refuse him, you know? Once I'd done that first run? Anyway, I was scared of him, but he'd never threatened me and he always spoke to me in a friendly way—asked about Lucy, how she was doing. That all changed last Friday. He called late. I was at my sister's. Lucy was asleep in bed. He told me to go to the boat. I said I couldn't, I couldn't leave Lucy, but then he said what he would do to Lucy if I didn't go. It was . . . shocking. I went numb.

"I went into autopilot. I just did what I was told. I left Lucy with my sister and I went to the boat. The dock was deserted. I came aboard and I waited."

She tapped the ash from her cigarette and glanced at Finn. "Then your friend showed up," she said. "Diego."

"What time?" he said.

"Really late. Around two in the morning."

"How could he have known that you would be there at that time of night?"

She shrugged. "No idea. But when he arrived, he acted like he wasn't surprised to see me. He asked me about Espendoza. He seemed to think that I was going to tell him something."

He was set up, thought Finn. "Keep going."

"All Cutts had said was, keep him there, don't let him leave. So I

did. We talked. I told him whatever he wanted to hear. He wanted
to hear about Espendoza, so I told him how the kid had crewed for
me. Then he said how you'd found him out in the water, and what
had happened to his legs. . . ."

She composed herself and took another drag on her cigarette.

"The whole time we were talking, I had my phone in my pocket,
waiting for Cutts to call, tell me what to do. I was going crazy. I
wanted to run away, go back to my sister's and grab Lucy and disappear. But I couldn't leave. She couldn't stop the treatment she was
getting at the hospital and I . . . I needed the money to pay for it."

"So Espendoza *was* on the *Belle*," said Finn, his throat dry.

She smiled weakly at him. "Yes. He dealt with the . . . with Cutts's
connection in Mexico. I told Cutts it would make everyone in the
fleet suspicious, me having this kid aboard who was obviously no
fisherman, but Cutts insisted. 'Make him blend in,' he said." She
laughed bitterly.

"Espendoza didn't blend in. He didn't do shit. He was just a stupid, arrogant kid with a gun, playing gangster. His job was to be
Cutts's eyes, wave his goddamn gun around, make sure I didn't
lose my nerve and go to the coast guard or anything like that. He
was dumb, he was lazy, he couldn't handle his liquor, and he had a
gun. I had to sleep with the door locked."

Yet he's the one who ended up dead in the channel, thought Finn.
"Then what happened?"

"Like I said, Cutts had told me to keep him there. So I . . . I kept
him there. It wasn't hard. He was sitting right where you are now.
We were drinking from these mugs. It was late. I didn't know what
would happen next. I was terrified, but I was on autopilot, just doing what I'd been told to do. He went outside to piss over the side.
I heard three shots. . . . Oh, Finn, it was horrible."

He tried to swallow, but he didn't have any spit left in his mouth.
"Who killed him?"

"I didn't see the actual . . . I was inside, I didn't see it happen. But then Cutts and this other man I didn't know came in. The man had a gun in his hand."

"The other guy—what was his name?"

"No one told me, and I was too frightened to ask. He had dark skin, and he was wearing a suit. He had a foreign accent, Arabic it sounded like. I had no idea they were going to kill him, Finn. You believe me, don't you?"

He smiled unconvincingly. "What happened next?"

"We went out on deck. The two of them carried the body off the boat. They told me to go back inside the cabin. I heard a car revving on the quay. I heard a splash. Then Cutts and the man came back. Cutts told me to scrub the blood off of the deck. While I was doing that, he told me what he would do to Lucy if I talked to anyone about what I'd seen that night. I said I hadn't seen anything, but he still told me. The things he said . . . I could barely stand to listen, Finn. It was bloodcurdling. He's a monster. He said if anyone asked, I was at my sister's, with Lucy. He said that that was my story. He said to make sure to get the details straight with Rhonda—that's my sister—in case any cops came around to ask her questions. Afterwards, I raced home, I held Lucy in my arms and didn't let go. I almost took off. I thought about it, believe me. I wanted to get in the car and drive somewhere far away, out of state. But where could I go? I had to stay near the hospital for Lucy. And I needed the money to pay for it."

She put her face in her hands and started sobbing again. Finn waited, trying to keep a lid on the rage seething inside him.

Linda stopped crying and took a breath before continuing.

"When you came around the next day, when I saw how kind you were with Lucy, I felt like I could trust you. I wanted to tell you everything. I almost did . . . but I couldn't. I knew I was in too deep, and I thought if I told you, you would arrest me, and then who would take care of my Lucy?"

She paused, looked at him with wet green eyes, and said, "You're not going to arrest me, are you, Finn?"

He didn't answer her question. "Do you know where Cutts is now?"

"He called me this afternoon and told me to get the boat ready to leave at dawn tomorrow. 'To resume operations,' he said. That's what the groceries are for. I told him it was too dangerous, the police were probably watching the boat. He told me there was nothing to worry about. He said the police had a suspect in their sights and that they were about to arrest him."

Finn sneered. "What suspect?"

She looked straight at him. "You."

Finn laughed. "Cutts thinks he can set *me* up for Diego's murder?"

"He said he has evidence."

Finn's feeling of incredulity started ceding ground to one of dread. He cast his mind back to that night in Bonito's when Diego had asked Cutts, "You ever heard of a boat called the *Pacific Belle*?" Then Diego had told Cutts about the floater, even telling him his name. "A *cholo* from East L.A. named Espendoza." Finn remembered him then saying to Diego, "Give me your cell. I hear of anything, I'll call."

Then, later that night, someone had mugged Finn and taken only his gun; they'd left him his wallet and his phone and his truck. His dread unfettered now, Finn realized that the killer had used *his* gun to kill Diego. And now all Cutts had to do was plant the pistol somewhere where Benitez would find it, and that would be that: the cops would have their evidence. If they needed a motive, all they had to do was ask Ruiz and Petchenko; they'd say that Finn had murdered Diego to cover up what had really happened on *La Catrina*.

He looked at the frightened woman sitting opposite him. She was right: Cutts *was* a monster. To protect his narcotics-smuggling operation, he had murdered Diego and set up Finn for it. But

Linda . . . Linda, with her beautiful green eyes, had played the honey trap. She'd been the lure that had fooled Diego. Finn's head said she was a victim, but his heart saw it differently.

"What happened to Espendoza?"

"I swear I don't know—"

"Bullshit. All this traces back to the floater. Diego didn't know you were running narcotics on the *Pacific Belle*. He didn't know any of that. All we had was Espendoza's body and his probation officer linking him to the *Pacific Belle*. Something spooked Cutts and it goes back to Espendoza. What happened to him?"

"I don't know—"

Finn slammed his fist on the table. "Don't lie to me, Linda!" He was shouting.

She started sobbing again. "I swear on my life, Finn, I don't know, I don't know, I don't know." She dropped her head in her hands.

Finn looked at her without pity. "To Diego," he said, and he emptied what was left of the bourbon into his mug.

She stared at him in horror, not touching her drink. He downed the bourbon, picked up the Glock, slid the clip back into it, and got to his feet.

"Where are you going?" she said.

"To Bonito's."

"Finn, no!" She jumped up and blocked his way.

"Listen to me, Linda. You're right, I could arrest you. You're in deep, maybe even as accessory to murder. What happens to you next depends on whether you knew Cutts was going to kill Diego, or whether you chose not to know. Either way, that's up to the law to decide. You're also looking at aiding and abetting, accessory after the fact, failure to report a crime, obstruction of justice, trafficking in controlled substances, and who knows what else. But here's the thing: if everything you told me tonight is the truth—if Cutts threatened your daughter's life—there's not a jury in the state that's going to put you away for it. Especially because now you're going to go home, pick up Lucy, go to the LAPD, and ask for Detective Mike Benitez. And you're going to tell him everything you just told me. You can trust him. He'll protect you and Lucy. You were frightened like any mother would be. People will understand. But you still did the wrong thing."

"But you promised you'd protect me!"

He shook his head. "No. I promised I'd make sure Cutts doesn't touch a hair on Lucy's head. And I will."

"He'll kill Lucy, Finn! You have no idea who you're dealing with!" She grabbed hold of him. "Please don't, Finn, please . . ."

He threw her off with more force than he'd intended to. She fell onto the bench and started sobbing again.

"Do as I say and everything will be all right," he said.

She looked up at him with utter desperation, her face wet with tears, her hair disheveled.

A voice inside Finn, a very faint voice struggling to be heard, told him that the right thing to do was to stay put for a moment, to give her a bit more time, to talk her through her terror, reassure her.

But he didn't feel like doing the right thing.

The best he could do was to say, "You got plenty of problems, Linda. I know it. But I promise you this: Diarmud Cutts is no longer one of them."

"Finn, wait!"

He walked out without turning back.

CHAPTER TWENTY

Finn stormed through the door of Bonito's, his hair and jacket wet from the rain, and his Glock double gripped in front of him. The first thing he saw was Cutts standing behind the bar with a shotgun, aimed squarely at him. There was no one else in the bar. The door swung shut behind Finn, its little bell tinkling, the door stifling the sound of the rain still falling outside.

"Drop it, Cutts."

Cutts kept the shotgun leveled at Finn. "A bit presumptuous of you, lad, don't you think?"

Finn took a tentative step forward.

"That's it, keep coming," said Cutts. "You ever seen what a shotgun will do to a man at close range?"

Finn halted. If he pulled the trigger, would there be time for Cutts to pull his? In the bar's yellow light, the white-haired Irishman, wearing his usual white, short-sleeve shirt, looked old and sick. Surely his reflexes were diminished, thought Finn.

On the other hand, Finn had been drinking for days. He didn't feel all that steady-handed.

"I'm giving you a choice, Cutts. Either give yourself up, or else we shoot it out here. Up to you."

Cutts contemplated Finn for a moment. Then he said, "Where I come from, negotiations always take place over a drink."

"I'm not here to negotiate," said Finn.

A smile flicked its tail at the corner of Cutts's mouth. "Of course you are. Think it through, boy. You're a murder suspect. I've got customers who'll swear on the Holy Bible I never left the bar that night. What have you got?"

"Linda Blake."

Cutts chortled. "Just a momentary lapse by the lady, Finn. Who can blame the poor woman, with all the stress she's been under? Or maybe it was those blue eyes of yours which persuaded her. Either way, she's since seen the error of her ways. She'll swear on her daughter's life that she was at her sister's all night the night of your partner's demise. Just like she is tonight."

Finn tried to make sense of what he was hearing. No more than fifteen minutes had elapsed since he'd walked off the deck of the *Pacific Belle*. What was Cutts talking about? Then he noticed the cordless phone sitting on the zinc-topped bar. He cursed himself. In that short interval, Linda had lost her nerve.

"You really think you're quicker than me, Cutts?"

"All the bluster of youth," said Cutts. "No man can know the hour of his own death, lad, but I'll lay my money down that this isn't mine. I'll even tell you why: if you were as sure of yourself as you would have me believe, you would've pulled that trigger by now."

Finn's Jim Beam buzz was wearing off. He felt a tremble in his forearms. His mind felt muddled, unfocused.

"And you forget," continued Cutts, "of the two of us, I'm the one with nothing to lose."

A voice inside Finn's head said, *Pull the trigger. To hell with the world. Just pull the damn trigger.*

Then he thought, *What if Mona spends the rest of her life believing I killed her baby brother?*

If there was an afterlife, thought Finn, would he be able to endure it knowing that Mona was hurting because of him? The Irishman was right: he had something precious to lose. If he died without bringing Diego's killer to justice, he'd be leaving Mona to a life without consolation. Finn didn't believe in closure—he had never shut the door on what his father had done, and knew he never would—but he did believe that justice was at least some kind of remedy. He wanted to give that to Mona. What he did with himself after that didn't matter.

He had to get out of Bonito's alive, grab Linda, and take her someplace safe, like he should've done in the first place. After that, he would come back for Cutts.

He started edging backward toward the door, keeping his gun on the old man behind the bar. But before he got to the exit, he heard the little bell tinkle and felt a gust of cool outside air and then cold metal against the base of his neck. A male voice behind him said, with a foreign accent, "Slowly put your gun on the floor."

Behind the bar, Cutts smiled.

Turned out, Cutts had been serious about the drink. Finn was sitting on a stool, a shot glass filled with amber liquid in front of him on the bar. Cutts was looking much happier. He'd put away his shotgun. The man with the accent was sitting a couple of stools away. He hadn't said another word since sneaking up behind Finn. In his hand, still pointed at Finn, was Finn's Glock. On the bar next to him, and out of Finn's reach, was Finn's service weapon. Like the guy was starting a collection of Finn's guns.

The man wore a dark suit over a dark shirt, no tie, his open collar revealing a gold chain. He had on a pair of suede slip-ons, the kind with the little tassels that Finn thought looked tacky. He looked like he was in his fifties, clean-shaven, with well-groomed black hair and intelligent dark eyes. He had light skin. Linda had said he sounded Arabic, but Finn had spent many months in the Persian Gulf and the guy didn't seem Arabic to him. Not that it made a difference to Finn one way or the other.

He eyeballed the man and said quietly, "I'm going to kill you for what you did to Diego."

The guy smirked.

"Come, come, forget about all that," said Cutts. "Take a drink, lad. Then we can talk."

Finn slowly turned his attention to the shot glass Cutts had placed in front of him. For the first time in his career as an alcoholic, he felt almost repelled by the sight of alcohol.

Almost.

Finn had screwed up big-time and was feeling it. He'd charged in like a bull, head down, straight at the billowing red skirts. The old man had outplayed him. *What difference would a drink make now?* he rationalized. He picked up the glass, threw back its empty promise, and slammed it down on the bar. The heat started in his gut, then rose through his chest and up to his head.

Cutts grinned.

"So then, Finn, now that you've wet your gullet with my whiskey, listen close to my offer: how about you come work for me?"

It took a moment for Finn's brain to register what Cutts was saying. When it did, he laughed and said, "You're not serious."

Cutts was straight-faced. "I have the supplier and the boat," he said. "With your knowledge of the waters and, more importantly, of how the government patrols them, you could get the product through easier than most. Think about it, Finn. There's no one better qualified to be a smuggler than you."

Cutts refilled Finn's glass.

"And if I don't?"

Cutts glanced toward the tassel-shoed man. Then he said, "I have no further use for you."

Finn scowled. "It doesn't sound like I'm in much of a negotiating position, am I?"

Cutts slapped the bar cheerfully. "There, I knew you'd be

reasonable. Here, another one to celebrate." Cutts poured Finn another drink.

Finn realized that he was drinking alone. The old man smiled apologetically.

"I must abstain on account of my insides, Finn. Doctor's orders. And Serpil here never drinks. But please: you go ahead." Then he added, "Of course, given the situation, I'm going to need some form of insurance against you. A guarantee, like. Something to make certain you won't run to the cops the moment you've left the dock."

"I go to the police, you turn in my gun and set me up for Diego's murder. Is that the insurance you had in mind?" said Finn, barely hiding his scorn. He was thinking about how his father had turned to smuggling and thrown away his life. Finn had no intention of going down the same path. He was just playing along with the old man's screwy fantasy, buying time.

Cutts looked at Finn coldly. "Check your phone," he said.

"What?"

"Take out your cell phone and go to your messages from Diego," he said, enunciating each word, as though speaking to someone slow on the uptake.

Finn looked at his phone. There was a sent message to Diego that he didn't recall sending. It was time-stamped 1:33 A.M. on October 24—the night Diego was killed. It read: "Can't talk. Got lead on floater. Can you meet me at the San Pedro fish dock?" Diego had answered: "When." From Finn's phone: "Now." From Diego: "On my way." Finn felt a rush of nausea.

"Diego's phone disappeared when it went into the water with him, which was a foolish oversight on our part," said Cutts. "But surely the police will have acquired his phone record by now. I expect they'll start looking for you as soon as they read those messages don't you?"

Cutts poured Finn another shot. "Here, have another. You look like you need it. Now, if I were in your shoes, I'd be glad to be

going on a little boat trip right about now. And, of course, I would
do everything in my power to avoid running into any of my old
colleagues in the CBP. That's what I would do, Finn, were I in your
fucking shoes." Cutts's tone slipping as he spoke, from falsely reassuring to hostile.

Finn downed the shot, slowly this time. It was worse than he'd
thought. But Cutts was still making a mistake.

"Okay. I get it," said Finn. "Collect the product or else take the
fall for Diego's murder. I get it. I'll do what you want."

Cutts held Finn's gaze. "I don't think you're taking this seriously."

Then he turned to the man he'd called Serpil. "You think he's
taking this seriously?"

Serpil shook his head.

"Neither do I," said Cutts. He seemed genuinely angry, his face
flushed, his eyes flared. He moved down the bar, picked up Finn's
P2000, and pointed it at Finn. "Let's go," he said.

When Finn asked where, Cutts told him to shut the fuck up.

They went to the San Pedro fishing dock. They went in Cutts's
Jaguar, Cutts driving, Finn in the front seat, Serpil in the back with
Finn's Glock 17 pointed at Finn's head. Cutts parked the car near
the deserted section of the quay where Diego's truck had gone into
the water. The rain had finally let up. Two glistening bollards caught
in the Jaguar's headlights threw long shadows across the concrete
toward the water. Cutts killed the ignition, and everything went
dark.

"Get out," said Cutts.

Finn got out. A few stars appeared in a gap in the clouds. Cutts
had said, "No man can know the hour of his own death." An image of his father, dead in his tan recliner, appeared in Finn's mind.
He tried to remember whether his father had been wearing a watch.
He wondered if his father had known his last hour.

Finn didn't wear a watch.

"What time is it?" he said to Cutts.

"Never you mind the fucking time," said Cutts. "Walk."

Cutts and Serpil shoved him down toward the water. When they got to the edge of the quay, Cutts told Finn to turn around. Serpil pressed the pistol to Finn's forehead. Cutts stood a little way back, holding his P2000 by his side.

"Your friend Diego thought I was fucking around," said Cutts. "He didn't take me seriously. What about you, Finn? Do you think I'm fucking around?" The old man was breathing heavily through his nose.

"No," said Finn.

Cutts made a show of cupping his ear with his hand. "What's that? I didn't hear you. You'll have to speak up, Finn. I'm an old man. My hearing isn't what it used to be."

"I said, no, I don't think you're fucking around."

Cutts nodded and said, "People ought to take it seriously when they have a gun pointed at their fucking heads. People ought to take that very seriously, Finn. Am I right about that?"

"Yes."

"Because I don't feel you were taking it seriously in the bar, Finn. I got the feeling you weren't taking it seriously at all. I got the feeling you were just humoring me, like. I thought, *This gobshite thinks he can outsmart me? He thinks he can go aboard the boat,* my fucking boat, *and take it to the authorities?* Is that what you were thinking, Finn?"

Finn didn't say anything.

"You know what will happen if you go to the authorities, Finn?"

"No."

"No, you don't know? Well, I can help you with that. I know someone who knows. She'll tell you. We'll go see her, and she'll tell you what will happen if you go to the authorities. Turn around and walk."

Finn turned and walked. He heard Cutts's labored breathing behind him.

They reached the *Pacific Belle*.

"Stop," said Cutts.

Finn stopped. Serpil went aboard ahead of them. Cutts didn't tell Finn to move, so he stayed put. He and Cutts on the dock, Cutts with the P2000, Finn with the bad feeling, wondering if this was his hour. He looked down the dock, vainly hoping that Benitez had posted someone to stake out the *Pacific Belle*.

There was no one there.

He heard a whistle from the deck of the *Pacific Belle*.

"Okay. Let's go," said Cutts.

Finn walked onto the *Belle*'s deck and into the cabin he had left not so long ago.

He found Linda kneeling on the floor with her hands clasped behind her neck. Serpil had Finn's Glock pointed at the side of her head. She was biting so hard on her lower lip, Finn thought she would draw blood. Tears streaked her cheeks. She was shaking uncontrollably. Her cheeks were hollowed. Her eyes darted from him to Cutts to Serpil and back again.

"Please," she said to Cutts, pleading. "Please, for Lucy's sake. For my daughter. I did what you asked me to do. You said you'd let me go. Please, let me go to my daughter."

"Shut the fuck up," Cutts said to Linda. Then, to Finn, he said, "You too. On your knees, you fucking piece of shite."

Finn knelt, put his hands on his head. He blamed himself for not staying with Linda, going with her to pick up her daughter, putting them both in a motel somewhere, giving her a chance to breathe, feel safe. He should've slowed it down. The truth was, he'd been angry at her for lying to him and angry at her for her part in Diego's murder. He'd blamed her for the mess he was in. He realized now that Cutts had been terrorizing her for months. She'd been *conditioned*.

Finn looked up at Cutts. "Let her go," he said, as calmly as he could manage. "I don't need her to work the boat. Look at her, the state she's in. She's no use to me. If anything, she's a liability. Let her go, and I'll do the run alone."

Cutts shook his head in disbelief. "You're still not taking me seriously, Finn. Look at you, the state of you, you're giving *me* terms? She's going with you. Because why? Because she's my insurance, that's why. You understand? I have her daughter. I have your little girl, Linda."

Finn glanced over at Linda. She looked like an animal heading into the slaughterhouse and knowing it. She tried to get up, but Serpil shoved her back down.

"No!" she shouted.

"You don't believe me? You don't fucking believe me? Get your phone, call your sister."

Sobbing, Linda pulled her phone from her pocket and dialed.

"Rhonda?" she said. "Let me speak to her. Let me . . ." She didn't finish her sentence. She listened to whoever was speaking on the phone. Then the phone slipped from her hand and Linda collapsed on the floor. Serpil picked it up and put it in his pocket.

Cutts turned his attention back to Finn. "You see how it is, Finn. You go to the authorities and the girl dies. You want to know how? Badly, Finn. She dies badly. I met Serpil here in Kosovo. I've seen him do things to people there that no man should ever see. Are you taking me seriously now, you cocksucking gobshite?"

Finn looked at Linda lying on the floor. She opened her mouth and released a terrible, suffocated moan. Serpil yanked her violently by her wrist back to her knees.

"You win, Cutts, I'll do it. Whatever you want. Just let her go," said Finn, raising his voice.

"You're not telling me a fucking thing," said Cutts, shouting now. "I'm telling *you*, Finn. I'm telling *you*. You go to the authorities, the child dies. You hear me? If you get intercepted, even by accident, the child dies. Are you taking me seriously now?"

Linda was wailing. Cutts was shouting, spittle collecting at the corners of his mouth. Finn's heart was racing. Only Serpil appeared calm. He seemed almost to be enjoying the chaos. Like it was all for show, for his entertainment. And when Cutts cracked Finn in the head with the side of Finn's P2000, Serpil laughed out loud. Finn felt blood trickle down his jaw.

"How do I know you won't just kill the girl anyway?" said Finn.

The question appeared to exasperate Cutts. He pointed the Heckler & Koch P2000 at Finn's forehead and said, "Fuck this shite. I've run out of patience, Finn. I've made my offer: you bring me the shipment, the kid lives. You can't ask for fairer than that. You *don't*, then you die now. Then I fetch the kid, and I kill her in front of her mother's eyes. Then I kill the mother. Then I go find your wife and I tell her, 'I'm the one that killed your brother and husband. Now I'm here for you.'"

Cutts caught his breath, looked at his watch, and said, "I'll give you five seconds to decide."

Finn glanced at Linda. Her eyes contained the question.

"Five . . ." said Cutts.

But there was no real question, of course. He thought of Mona, of their vanished future together. Tears welled in his eyes.

"Four . . ."

He thought of his father in his tan recliner. Finn had to tried to lift himself up, tried to become a better man than his father had been.

"Three . . ."

But he'd failed. He made a simple vow to himself. First, he would get Linda's daughter back. Then he would kill Cutts and Serpil.

"Two . . ."

Then he would follow his father's way out. Men like the Finns had been making deals with the devil forever.

"One . . ."

This was his.

He nodded at Cutts.

The Irishman raised the gun so that it pointed at the ceiling.

"About fucking time. You leave now," he said. Then he looked at Linda and said, "Our friends are expecting you. You can explain to Finn how it works on the way down. We'll meet you at Two Harbors at midnight on the sixth. I'll wait till half past the hour. If you don't show by then, or if we get word that you've contacted anyone—anyone at all—we'll do to your daughter what we did to Espendoza."

CHAPTER TWENTY-ONE

Finn wasn't a religious man in the conventional sense, but at sea he felt part of a natural order that vanished the moment he set foot ashore.

Thus, on the morning of their second day at sea, as he stood on the *Pacific Belle*'s stern and kept his eye on where his fishing line disappeared into the water, his CBP jacket zipped up against the chill, and the eastern horizon the color of rust, it seemed to him that this private disk of ocean, this moveable and sequestered world, was his reward for the resolution he'd made when he left the San Pedro dock. Aboard the *Pacific Belle,* he had come to realize that all he needed to restore clarity and grace to his life was firmness of purpose. He felt as though he had stolen away from the common world, as though he and Linda were the only beings in the universe God didn't have his eyes on. The sea was having its tonic effect. The cuts and bruises on his face were beginning to heal, and he felt like he'd been given these days at sea—days of blamelessness— on the condition that once they reached their journey's end and were sucked back into the undertow, he delivered on the promise he'd made to himself on his knees that night in the cabin below.

It helped Finn's condition, of course, that he hadn't taken a drink since Bonito's. He hadn't deviated from his father's counsel never to drink at sea.

Linda was still asleep in a cot below. He had told her that he would wake her at sunrise so that she could replace him on watch, but she had spent the night crying her eyes out over her daughter. Finn was happy that she was sleeping at last and didn't want to wake her. He wasn't tired and he was glad for the respite from her hurt. He had been navigating the *Belle* for eight hours on his own, but she was equipped with autopilot so there was very little for him to do in terms of actual navigation. Mostly, his watch consisted of keeping one eye on the gauges and another on the radar, for they had agreed that they would keep all other boats beneath the horizon.

Remarkably, they had managed to travel some 350 miles from San Pedro without passing within sighting distance of another boat. They were northwest of Cedros Island. Another 40 hours' sail would bring them level with Cabo San Lucas, at which point they would turn east toward the Sinaloa coast. For the time being, however, they were in rich fishing grounds, and Finn figured that fishing would keep his mind occupied. He fetched the old rod and reel he'd found in the storage locker below, along with a plastic box containing a motley collection of lures, rusty hooks, floats, and weights.

He spent the morning jigging off the stern. In the first hour, he caught so many jack mackerel so quickly that he figured the *Belle* must've been traveling above a school of them. Futilely, he wished he could call Mona, tell her that he was on a commercial fishing boat, just like they'd talked about.

Reeling in yet another fish, Finn started to feel more ambitious. If the mackerel were schooling so close to the surface, chances were that they were being corralled by something bigger. So when he pulled the fish out of the water and saw that it had swallowed the lure entirely, he cast it back out at once and gave it enough slack to dive.

The line reeled for a minute before slackening. The mackerel was slowing. Finn cautiously started bringing it back in. It resisted, but not much and he had no trouble until something hit it hard, and the line started running out again, much faster this time, catching Finn by surprise and bending the rod close to the breaking point. He thumbed on the reel lock and still the line ran out, smoke rising from the brake. He clicked off the lock and moved all around the deck, the line screaming off the reel, Finn working the rod to prevent whatever had taken his bait fish from passing beneath the hull.

The sun was high by the time he'd worked it to the surface. His forearms and back ached from the strain and his mouth was as dry as sandpaper. He was exhausted, but he still had the weight on the line. He was winning the battle. Then, where his line scythed through the water, he saw a flash of silver and yellow. His heart pounded. He made tiny adjustments to the drag, giving the line enough slack in case the fish still had enough fight left in him to dive but not so much that he could undo all Finn's hard work. Finn raised and reeled, raised and reeled until he'd maneuvered the fish alongside the boat.

Just then Linda appeared. Finn handed her the rod. "Don't let him throw the hook," he said breathlessly, pointing to the fish.

He grabbed the gaff and leaned over the rail, leaning right down, looking to get a clean shot, sweat dripping from the tip of his nose. A cloud passed overhead and darkened the water beneath him in a way that reminded him of the shadow he'd seen pass beneath Espendoza's body. He told himself he was imagining things. Suddenly, the *Belle* lurched awkwardly and he nearly tumbled in. With his spare hand, Finn took hold of the rail, leaned out, and contemplated his catch in the blue water directly below—a beautiful yellowfin, at least three and a half feet long. He had no idea what the fishing line he was using was rated for, but he was sure it was for less than whatever this fish weighed. He could tell that the fish was out of fight by the way it lingered at the side of the boat, like a boxer slow out of his corner in the late rounds. He held his gaff suspended over the water, his arm tense, waiting for his chance. Then he struck hard and fast at the fish's shoulder and gaffed it under the gills. The yellowfin was heavy; it took everything he had left to haul it up. He had it halfway up the side when he saw the water beneath him bulge and then the dark shadow turned into a shark barreling at him, its rows of triangular teeth thrust forward, its eyes rolled back, its underside a clean and perfect white. It launched itself from the water and locked its jaws around the fish on his gaff and tore it away with such force that the gaff went flying from Finn's hand. The shark fell back into the water with a heavy splash and backed away, violently shaking its catch, fading into the deep.

Finn found himself sitting on his ass on the deck. He realized he must've fallen back and that his legs must've given way, but he had no recollection of either event. His vision seemed sharper and time slower. He saw Linda leaning over him, her green eyes burning bright; he saw her lips moving, but instead of her voice, he heard a tinkling sound, like marbles being thrown against a mirror.

Finn lay on the cot, trying to sleep. Every time he shut his eyes, he saw the shark charging up at him, breaking clear of the sea, and swallowing up the big yellowfin, its maw just inches from Finn's arm. He figured the yellowfin must've been hunting the jack mackerel, and the commotion must've drawn the sharks. Prey being preyed upon by predators, themselves just prey to even bigger predators. The kind of convergence commonplace in nature. Finn had just been in the wrong place at the wrong time. Just like Diego had been that night on the *Belle*.

When he knew for sure he wasn't going to sleep, he peeled himself off the cot and went above, expecting to find the refreshing breeze that usually picked up in the afternoon in these latitudes. Instead, it was hot and sticky, and the sea had an unpleasant, oily sheen to it. The world seemed especially still and soundless, with nothing moving except the *Belle,* and nothing speaking except her diesel. He looked up at the pale sky, noted the high-altitude streamers, and remembered the redness he had seen on the eastern horizon that morning. His shirt clung to his skin. When he took it off, the sun felt harsh on his back.

It was near the end of Linda's watch. He joined her in the pilothouse, drank straight from a plastic gallon container of water, and checked the navigation screen. They were about five hundred miles north of Cabo, traveling. Then he checked the electronic weather chart. It was hurricane season. The heat, the streamers, and the red sky pointed to something. On the chart, he saw a low-pressure cell southeast of their position that he didn't like the look of.

"Your face is healing," said Linda. "I can see who you are now."

He looked up from the screen and smiled. "Whenever I was sick as a kid, my dad used to take me out on the water. 'The sea is the best medicine,' he used to say. He said salt water cured everything."

Linda drank from her mug. "It won't cure Lucy," she said.

When Finn asked Linda what was wrong with her daughter, he saw a sort of practiced emotional blankness creep over her face, like a room being emptied of its furniture. He leaned forward and put his hand on hers, not sure where he was going with it.

She smiled a joyless smile. After a moment, she pulled her hand away. "It's all right," she said. "My sister's a nurse. She takes good care of my baby when I'm at sea."

They sat in silence for a while. Eventually, Linda said, "We'll make landfall on Sunday. The Caballeros will meet us at the dock with the merchandise. Then we turn right around and head home."

After she said that, she gave up her seat at the helm and left the pilothouse.

Finn was sweating profusely, though he was doing no more than sitting on the stool behind the wheel, the ship on autopilot. There was no ventilation in the wheelhouse whatsoever, and it was clear to Finn that the *Belle* had been built for Alaska, not Mexico. He had turned around to see if any of the rear windows opened when through them he saw Linda standing naked on the stern deck. He watched her spread a towel on the sun-cooked fish-hold cover and lay herself down on it, arms stretched out as though she were on some millionaire's teak-decked yacht.

He gazed at her for a long time, at her tanned face and neck and how it contrasted with the white skin of her breasts, her stomach and thighs. He stared at the dirty blond hair between her legs until he realized that he had become aroused. He turned away lest Linda glance in his direction and catch the hungry look in his eyes.

Feeling guilty, Finn tried to think of his wife.

But his mind teemed with predators and prey.

CHAPTER TWENTY-TWO

At Cabo they turned east and headed across the mouth of the Gulf of California toward the Sinaloa coast. They made landfall early in the afternoon of November 1.

By then, the change Finn had felt coming the preceding day had arrived: the wind had picked up out of the southeast and brought with it low, heavy clouds that blocked out the sun and turned the sea the color of concrete. Finn knew a storm was coming. He felt the tingle in his legs as he stood on the foredeck, leaning on the rail, watching the small fishing village of Puerto Escondido come into view.

The village consisted of a huddle of flat-roofed buildings lining the pebble beach of a small bay. Rebars rose in awkward, forlorn clusters from their roofs, tokens of evaded taxes or of second floors to come in more prosperous times. An unpaved road led away from the village, past a lagoon and up a small, scrubby, treeless hill, over the rise of which Finn could just make out a cross atop a church spire.

Twenty or so small, open fishing boats had been hauled up onto the pebble beach. Their names were painted in big letters on their bows. A handful of bigger commercial boats—to Finn, they looked like shrimpers—were tied to the dock. From the electronic chart, Finn knew they were on a remote, lonely stretch of coast in Sinaloa

State, forty miles south of Mazatlán, near the mouth of a large lagoon fed by a river. The *Belle* passed through a plume of murky water on its way into the port, telling Finn that it had recently rained upriver, the mud now draining into the sea.

They entered the shallows, the *Belle* pushing aside water and sending a steady outflow of little waves to wash up on the pebble beach. The vegetation beyond the pebbles was mostly dun-colored scrub save a few clusters of spare-looking palm trees. The pier was in a sorry state: one of its pylons had rotted and fallen away, and the planking around the gap sagged. The *Belle* was the smallest boat in San Pedro, but she looked like a giant compared to the other boats lined up at the Escondido dock. A pod of pelicans had claimed the pylon tops, one per pylon. The usual gulls loitered. The stench of rot rose from the seaweed washed up along the high-tide line.

Finn was surprised by how quiet it was. There was none of the usual business of a port, even a small one. He saw no fishermen mending nets, no kids hand-spooling off the end of the dock, no harbormaster to push paperwork on them. In fact, he saw no one at all. The place was deserted, a ghost town. The only sign of human presence was a black Suburban with tinted windows and an out-of-place polished gleam lying in wait at the start of the dock.

Linda brought the *Belle* up alongside the dock, threw her into Reverse, and stalled her so that she would drift in. Finn was impressed. Getting a boat this size with no side thrusters to a dock this small was a tricky thing. Linda handled it perfectly.

He jumped ashore with a mooring line in hand and looped it expertly around a rusty bollard. Linda came out of the pilothouse, took the slack out of the line, and tied it off to a cleat on the foredeck. They repeated the operation with the stern line. They put a springer on.

Finn looked down the deserted pier. He pointed his chin at the truck. "I'm guessing that's for us," he said.

Linda nodded. They walked down the dock toward the Suburban. They got closer, and Finn noticed that the motor was running. He glimpsed an unshaven face and a mop of disheveled hair reflected in the tinted windows and realized it was himself. The car's rear passenger window descended. A man with black hair and wearing a black shirt, the collar open, looked out at them.

He said something in Spanish to Linda. She astonished Finn by replying in Spanish. She sounded agitated, her voice quavering a little, as though the man was giving her bad news. The man said something else, something that to Finn's monoglot ears sounded final, then rolled up the window. The Suburban lumbered away. The man had never once looked at Finn.

"We have to wait a day," said Linda.

"Why?"

"Because it's the Day of the Dead. He says nothing happens today."

Finn shook his head. "You're not serious," he said.

Linda rubbed the back of her neck. "He says they don't do business on holy days."

"They're fucking drug dealers."

"We have to wait."

Finn clenched his jaw. "So, what? We just sit here?" He had a bad feeling. He didn't like being back on land. He wanted to be out on the water. "I don't like it here. Let's go anchor out in the bay."

She smiled. "I got a better idea. There's a party in town."

He laughed humorlessly. "You're kidding, right?"

"What difference does it make?" she said. "I could do with the distraction. We'll be safe, too. The cartel owns Escondido."

Safe. Finn remembered La Abuelita's words.

Puerto Escondido was the town where the five boys had boarded *La Catrina.* Never to be heard from again.

They walked ten minutes along the dirt road, past the lagoon and over the hill, until they got to the main part of the town.

Finn's first impression from the boat had been of a dying,

isolated, desolate place, and the main drag did nothing to improve his opinion. He found himself in a sullen, cinder-block, dust-covered town not pretty enough for tourists, with no obvious industry other than fishing, and even that looked like its best days were behind it. He followed Linda through the church square and into what he guessed was the town's only hotel. A few local men loitered in the shade of the roof's wide overhangs and stared expressionlessly at Finn and Linda.

A vase of marigolds stood on the glass counter in the lobby, next to two statues of skeletons, one wearing an elegant green dress, the other in red, both with elaborate hairdos and carrying bouquets. He picked up the green one and examined it curiously.

"They're called Catrinas," said Linda. "They're festival decorations. They're meant to remind you that death comes for everyone."

He turned over the doll in his hands. "She looks happy enough," he said.

The room, which Linda said the concierge had told her was the best one available, was clean and simple. Finn noticed that it had only one bed, a low queen with a wooden headboard. The walls were whitewashed, the concrete floor painted ocher. There was a closet, a chest of drawers, and a mirror next to the bathroom door. Finn opened the sliding doors to the balcony.

The balcony was on the corner of the hotel, overlooking an alley. The square was visible to the right. At the far side, he saw the church, the spire of which he'd spotted from the port. On the other side of the alley was a two-story building with an internal courtyard. Kids were playing in the courtyard.

"What's that, a school?" he said.

"An orphanage," said Linda, looking away. "I'm going to take a shower."

She went back inside. Finn stood on the balcony and watched

the kids in the orphanage for a while, then turned his attention to the square. He saw workmen on ladders, hanging decorations on lines strung between lampposts. A stage and risers had been erected opposite the church. Off in the distance, he saw the bank of clouds he'd seen from the boat. It was moving in.

He went back inside and lay down on the bed, shifting around on the thin mattress till he got comfortable, then closed his eyes and let his body slacken. He saw again the shark launching itself from the water and stealing his fish. He saw Linda's naked body. He heard a noise and opened his eyes. Linda was standing in the doorway, her hair wet, a towel around her torso. She was crying.

"Are you okay?" said Finn.

She didn't answer.

She lay down next to him on the bed, put her head on his chest. Her wet hair smelled like a tangerine being peeled. She didn't move.

"I miss her so much," she said, whispering.

Finn put his arm around her, rested his hand on her bare shoulder. He lay like that, listening to the thrum of the ceiling fan and watching the shadows grow longer across the wall until his mind slowed and he fell asleep.

By nine o'clock, Finn, shaved and showered and wearing the crisp guayabera Linda had ordered up to the room for him, stood at a stall in the main square and bought two beers with American dollars that Linda had produced. He handed one to Linda, who was wearing a green dress with a lace neckline she'd conjured out of nowhere. It reminded Finn of the one he'd seen on the Catrina in the lobby.

He looked up at the black, starless sky. The clouds had moved in, darkened, and grown fuller, and there was a purple tinge on their sagging bellies. He expected them to burst at any moment. Though he had showered and was in a clean shirt, he was sweating profusely and didn't feel well. A kind of vertigo—a feeling as though his inner ear had been decalibrated—had taken hold of him the moment he had stepped ashore. The ground seemed unsteady and not to be trusted. It was as though being ashore made him seasick.

A band took the stage. It consisted of five guys in matching dove-gray suits and cowboy hats. Cheerful music began blaring from the speakers. Strung between the lampposts were garishly painted papier-mâché skeletons, jaguars, eagles, and snakes. Locals in their Sunday best milled around the food and drink stalls. The women carried toys and orange marigolds and crosses and rosaries. As for the men, Finn distinguished two sorts. The first, the drunken majority, wore guayaberas like his, were short and broad-shouldered and looked like men who worked—farmers and fishermen. The second, the sober minority, were slighter and looked meaner. They were scattered around the square in groups of two or three, present but not participating in the festival. Some of them wore black pants and silky button-downs. Others wore police uniforms. And on all their necks, visible above their collars, were tattooed crucifixes. Finn thought of Perez. A man in a yellow-and-black skull mask appeared suddenly in his field of vision, startling him, then disappeared just as suddenly. He felt twitchy. The beer he'd yet to taste was cold in his hand, but the rest of him was overheating. Here he was, deep in the Caballeros' territory, just three weeks after shooting dead one of their soldiers and intercepting one of their boats. What would they do to him if they found out who he was? He was surrounded by members of the bloodiest, most impenetrable and spectacularly successful of Mexico's narco-gangs, infamous for their wacko blend of medieval, martial Catholicism—Finn remembered hearing that the gang's leader, nicknamed the Craziest One, had even published some kind of doctrinal book—and a savagery that exceeded the already excessive violence of their rivals. The Knights moved billions of dollars' worth of cocaine across the border every year, then set up rehabs for their drug addicts. Their lieutenants wouldn't smuggle drugs on holy days, but the rest of the time they gladly beheaded uncooperative mayors and left their heads on spikes outside town halls. These were the people he was supposed to interdict. These were the people whose crimes he had dedicated his career to stopping.

Not just him. Mona always said that the people she represented and fought for weren't the criminals. They were just pawns in the game, human beings stuck in a broken system that accorded them little human dignity, that treated them as disposable. They were called "cheap" labor, "undocumented" migrants, "unauthorized" entrants—and that was just in the respectable, mainstream media. They were the people without status. The criminals, Finn remembered her saying, were the gangs who actually ran the game, who "taxed" the migrants and who murdered the ones who couldn't or wouldn't pay and buried them in shallow graves along the border. The gangsters had plenty of status, she said. They had songs written about them. They murdered everyone who opposed them, always brutally and often spectacularly, and because they got away with it, she said, they were feared and respected. These were the people he was now working with, thought Finn. Mona would be so proud.

He felt the darkness creeping up on him. He didn't want to think about Mona. He turned to Linda.

"You ever been to one of these before?" she said.

He shook his head. "What are they celebrating?"

"Anyone who died recently."

He laughed. "Diego would like that."

Finally, he took a swig of beer. The cold needles pricked his throat and then he was watching himself drink as though from above. The vertigo that had plagued him since setting foot on land began to slip away. The knot in the base of his neck was unbound. He drank some more. He was glad Mona couldn't see him, and he was glad he hadn't tried to contact her. He became aware of Linda trying to say something to him.

"I said, I'm glad you're here," she said, smiling, showing little teeth.

Finn smiled back at her. The music—loud, cheerful, and mournful all at once—never flagged. He quickly drained his bottle dry and bought another.

"What's the band singing about?" he said.

"How great the Caballeros are."

He made trip after trip to the stall, taking shots of tequila at the bar and chasing them with beers, drinking until Mona's voice was so small, he could no longer hear it. The gangsters were still there, but he stopped being aware of them. An hour passed. His shirt, soaked through with sweat, clung to him. He saw rings of light around the streetlamps that hadn't been there before; his hearing dimmed, as though he were underwater; and when he danced with Linda, he pulled her closer and she didn't mind. He buried his face in her long tresses, breathed deep her tangerine scent, and was aroused by the way she had of resisting and enticing him at the same time. When his hand pressed against the small of her warm and damp back, he sensed in her the same sputtering tension between the polarities of recklessness and self-control that he had been battling all his life. They were both pushing themselves drink by drink to the point of no return. He tried to kiss her and she let him brush his mouth across hers without it quite becoming a kiss, like a stray electrical current searching for the ground. She smiled and told him to turn around, and when he did he realized that the music had stopped. He looked up at the stage and saw that the band had given way to a black-suited man, a sash across his suit and a mustache across his lip, saying a few nervous words into the mic.

"There's going to be a play," said Linda, translating for him, slipping her hand into his.

"What's the play about?"

"The little angels."

"Who?"

"Dead children."

Finn looked up at the clouds. "It's going to rain," he said. And then: "Want another drink?"

"Yes."

He went to the stall and bought more alcohol. When he got back, the mayor, if that's what he was, was stepping off the stage. The lights went out. Linda clasped Finn's hand again. Something had shifted in her mood, and she seemed nervous now, frightened, like she had been back on the *Belle* when she told him about Cutts. He squeezed back.

A blue spotlight lit up an impressive Aztec step pyramid. A couple of men dressed head to toe in white stood on one side of the stage playing pan pipes, the notes flitting across the square like nervous birds. Finn drank some more. An offstage narrator said some things through the sound system, things that Linda didn't bother translating. Then a group of children wrapped in white robes entered from the side of the stage farthest from Finn's position, their hair glistening in the blue light. They shuffled to the foot of the pyramid, the light following them. Someone started banging a drum. The kids looked up. The blue spotlight gave way to a red one, which tracked to the top of the pyramid. The narration stopped. The spotlight settled on an actor in a huge feather headdress, his eyes heavily lined with black, an animal skin draped over his shoulders, a garland of bones hanging around his neck, shells hanging from his clothes. He had what looked like a big feather in his right hand, and through the legs of the altar painted gray to look like stone, Finn saw more feathers attached to a band tied around his right calf. Some kind of shaman, he figured. He had his hand on Linda's hip now, and hers was around his waist. Somewhere along the line they'd traded up from beer to mescal, the smoky flavor lingering in his mouth, the alcohol wormholing through his brain.

The actor who played the shaman glowered at the crowd, his eyes so wide that Finn could see the whites of them. The drummer let loose and hammered the skins. The shaman raised his hands and was about to speak when, as if on cue, a great bolt of lightning ripped through the sky behind him. There was a collective gasp from the crowd. Thunder cracked down upon the square and all the people in it. The shaman looked up at the sky, hesitated, then continued with the play. He started chanting, slowly at first, then accelerating the tempo and increasing the volume, his voice competing with the screech of pan pipes and the thump and thwack of skin drums and click-clack of hollow-log drums.

The spot with the red gel now lit up the kids from below. They looked like the comic-grim decorations hanging from the lines, the light hollowing their eye sockets and making their little faces seem scrawny. The shaman stamped his feet, shaking the bells on his ankle, and waved his big feather around.

Two adult actors led one of the kids, a girl, to the top of the pyramid and up three little steps onto the altar. They laid her down on her back. The shaman raised his feather. Except, Finn realized, it wasn't a feather: it was a chiseled stone. The shaman held it above his head against the black sky about to burst. The crowd pressed forward. The shaman chanted deliriously.

Two more great bolts of lightning flashed behind the stage, much closer now; the thunderclaps were instantaneous. Then the clouds broke and the rain came down, hard. The spotlight made a crackling sound and went out. All the streetlamps flickered into blackness.

It was a catastrophe; it was spectacular. Adrenaline pumped through Finn; the water streamed down the sides of his face and soaked through his shirt, already drenched with sweat. He whooped and hollered, saying incoherent things. He knew he sounded foolish but he was too drunk to care.

Linda was still staring at the blacked-out stage, her hair plastered down the sides of her terrorized face. Finn followed her gaze. Up on the pyramid, silhouetted against the flash of lightning, he saw the little girl still on the altar, the shaman still looming over her, the stone blade glinting in his hand.

Finn understood. He shouted in Linda's ear, "Hey! It's just make-believe. That's not Lucy, you hear?"

He took her head in his hands and wiped the wet hair off her face. Then he leaned down and kissed her. A tiny voice in his head whispered, *This is a bad idea.* He pulled away a little. Linda opened her eyes and in the faint, wet light released a volley of green and gold shards.

"Don't stop," she said, her breath hot against his damp cheek.

He put his arm around her and cleared a way through the crowd to the stall, where he made the stall-holder sell him an entire bottle of mescal. Then, to a boy under the hotel's overhang, water streaming off it in sheets, he paid ten times the going rate for two masks. Linda laughed and slipped one on: a lavishly decorated skull face garlanded with paper flowers.

In the lobby, the storm had cut the power and the hotel staff was lighting candles. A boy with a hurricane lamp led them up to their room. Finn tipped him, followed Linda into the room, and slipped on his mask.

CHAPTER TWENTY-THREE

Finn woke drenched with sweat. He felt like he'd stirred an angry swarm of stinging insects behind his eyes. He cracked open his cruddy eyes and saw the blades of the ceiling fan not turning. He raised his head and saw daylight stalking around the edges of the curtains. Linda wasn't in the bed with him. He glanced through the open bathroom door—no sign of her in there, either.

He sat upright and quickly realized that he'd made a mistake. Last night's beer and mescal came heaving up his gullet. He threw up on the carpet by the bed, then fell back on the mattress and closed his eyes.

When he felt a little better, he peeled himself out of the bed, slowly this time. A note from Linda was propped against the lamp on the night table: "Meet at boat at noon." She'd underlined *noon* three times. No explanation about where she'd gone.

Finn stumbled into the bathroom, turned the shower on as hot as he could bear, then a little hotter. It scalded his blotched and waxy skin when he got under the stream, but he made himself take it. He turned his face up and gargled the hot water, chasing out the sharp tang in his mouth. Then he turned off the hot tap and left the cold running. The sudden drop in temperature kicked the breath out of him, and all the muscles in his torso twitched. He turned off the water, stepped out of the shower, and mustered the courage to look in the mirror.

Finn saw his father staring back at him: the same deserting blue eyes and liquor-distended skin, the same thin mouth curled in disappointment.

Water dripped off his body and pooled on the tiles around his feet. His father had been caught smuggling narcotics into Long Beach. Finn thought, *Like father, like son.*

With a whip-quick jab of his right fist, he shattered the mirror; shards tinkled into the porcelain sink and onto the floor.

He stepped over the glass, wrapped a towel around his waist, and opened the curtains. The rain clouds had cleared and the light had a post-rain sparkle to it, making the world seem fresh and clean. He slid open the glass door and stepped onto the balcony.

From across the road rose the pleasing sound of children laughing. The orphans had gotten hold of Day of the Dead masks; Finn watched pint-size skull-faces chasing one another around the yard. A girl of around nine or ten was sitting alone on a step leading up to a shaded arcade on the far side of the yard. She looked very serious, sitting very still with her hands in her lap, watching the other children without enthusiasm. Behind her, partially hidden from view, stood a pair of adults in conversation. Finn watched the little girl; she seemed familiar to him. After a moment, the adults stepped from the shade and the little girl stood as though to receive instructions.

Finn instinctively stepped back from the rail.

One of the adults was Linda Blake.

The hotel room came with an electric kettle and easy-pour packets of Folgers instant coffee. Finn made himself a three-packet cup and sat on the edge of the bed to drink it. Whatever business Linda had at the orphanage, he thought, she'd chosen not to tell him about it. He looked at the bed's crumpled sheets. She'd liked the game with the masks, he recalled. She'd said something to the effect that she could be herself wearing the mask. All he'd been able to see through the eyeholes were her crocodile eyes. That, and her naked body. The skull mask he'd worn lay discarded on the floor by the bedside table. He wondered what Linda had seen when he'd worn it. Probably she'd preferred looking at a cheap plastic devil rather than his beat-up face, he thought.

He glanced at the shattered glass on the bathroom floor and knew *he* did.

He took another sip of coffee and gazed through the balcony door at the blue sky. He told himself, *I'm doing what I'm doing for a greater good.* He was only smuggling narcotics, he reminded himself, in order to save Linda's daughter from the ruthless criminal who was holding her hostage—a situation for which he, Finn, was at least partially responsible.

Once the child had been returned, he would be free to exact justice from Diego's killers.

Finn reached the bottom of the mug, where the undiluted instant-coffee granules had formed a muddy brown paste. He remembered Mrs. Gavrilia that day at the Self Help, the old lady filling the little room with her cigarette smoke and tapping her ashes into Mona's Folgers mug. He remembered her telling him about her cousin's son, Felipe, and the missing boys, how they'd disappeared from Puerto Escondido, gone to sea on *La Catrina,* and never been heard from again. He remembered her mural of the Aztec god devouring all the people. He remembered the play last night, the altar and the shaman with the knife.

Finn stood up. He wanted to know what Linda was doing at the orphanage. And he wanted to know why she hadn't told him.

He dressed, headed out of the hotel, and picked his way through the detritus of last night's festivities to the orphanage. A big sign next to the door had ORFANATO JESÚS MALVERDE painted on it. Finn rang the bell.

A black-haired woman opened the door.

"I'm looking for a friend," he said in English. "Linda Blake? An American woman?"

The woman shook her head and gave him an uncomprehending look.

Hell, thought Finn. *What's Spanish for "woman"?*

"*Un mujer americano?* Linda?" he said tentatively.

The woman shook her head some more and said something impatiently in Spanish. She glanced fearfully around the square before slamming the door in his face.

Finn stepped back, turned around. Some workers were disassembling the stage from last night and loading it onto a truck. A couple of men in police uniforms stood near their car. A group of sharply dressed men sat at a plastic table at a café across the square, drinking coffee. Finn had the distinct impression that every single person in the square was watching him.

Time to get the hell out of Escondido.

Down at the dock, Finn was happy to see that the fishermen were back. The Day of the Dead had been a holiday for everyone, he figured: fishermen and gangsters alike.

He went aboard the *Pacific Belle* and saw that Linda wasn't back yet. It was eleven thirty. He grabbed the water jug and binoculars and went back out on deck. He'd keep a lookout for Linda. The sooner they got out of there, the better.

While he waited, he leaned against the bow rail and watched the fishermen work. Down on the beach, the smaller boats unloaded whatever they had managed to hook on their lines. Finn looked through the binoculars to see what they'd brought in: a few wahoo and yellowfin, some sea bass and dorado. He put down the binoculars and turned his attention to the shrimpers on the dock. There were five of them, none of them over thirty feet long. The men were unloading white plastic buckets laden with the morning's catch onto the dock. The buckets had the names of the boats they belonged to painted on their sides. Finn was taken aback when he saw that one of the boats was called *La Abuelita*. He put the binoculars back in the wheelhouse and wandered down the dock. When he got closer, he saw DUEÑO: FELIPE GAVRILIA painted on the stern of the boat, followed by what looked like a license number.

He didn't know what *dueño* meant, but he knew that Mrs. Gavrilia was known by the nickname La Abuelita. And he remembered how she'd said her fisherman-cousin was named Felipe.

He approached the man unloading shrimp. He was a thin, wiry man in a dirty blue Adidas T-shirt, probably in his sixties, with deep wrinkles and skin darkened by the sun. He looked like a man who'd worked hard all his life.

"Señor Gavrilia?" Finn tried.

The guy ignored him and kept working.

Finn really wished he'd made more of an effort to learn Spanish at Saint Augustine. He just wasn't good in classrooms.

"I'm a friend of La Abuelita? In Los Angeles? Your cousin?"

Nothing from the guy.

"She told me about your son? The one who disappeared?"

Still nothing. The man kept working, as though Finn weren't there.

"I'm the man who stopped the boat you said your son went on. I'm with *la migra* up in California. Do you remember the boat? *La Catrina?*"

As soon as Finn said the name, the man stopped in his tracks. He looked long and hard at Finn. Then he turned and let his eyes linger on a building on the shore, as though drawing Finn's attention to it. Finn followed his gaze. The man was looking at a boatyard. It was a ramshackle affair. Several boats in various states of disrepair sat on the beach outside a large shed with a high corrugated roof. The boats didn't look like they were going anywhere anytime soon. There was no ramp into the water, just a trailer on a cable system to haul boats up the beach and into the shed. Finn turned to thank Felipe Gavrilia, but the old fisherman had already turned away.

He walked down the beach to the boatyard. The big sliding door into the shed was open. Finn saw a small shrimper sitting on a cradle, her rudder off. He heard the crackle of a gas welder from the back of the shed and recognized the pungent, ozone smell that welders give off.

He walked deeper into the shed, past the trawler, toward a workbench at the back. A man in gray coveralls was busy working on something hidden from Finn's view.

"Hello," said Finn loudly.

The man wheeled around, looked at Finn through the dark rectangle of glass in his helmet. He killed the burn on his welder and flipped up the visor. He looked unhappy to see Finn.

"*Sí?*" he said.

"*La Catrina*. Know it?"

The guy looked at him steadily. Shifting his weight from one leg to the other.

Finn noticed what was on the workbench. It was a fire extinguisher. The top had been cut off and was now being welded back on, its dome clamped into place over the cylinder, weld marks along the join. His mind flashed back to the fire in *La Catrina's* engine bay. He remembered how the extinguisher he'd found aboard had failed. He looked to his right and saw dozens of fire extinguishers standing in the corner—some cut open, some welded back together but with their red paint missing and their weld marks visible, some with their weld marks ground down but yet to be painted, and some that looked like ordinary fire extinguishers.

He marveled at the simplicity of it: fire extinguishers were so ubiquitous aboard boats as to be invisible.

Out of the corner of his eye, he caught sight of the welder flipping his mask back down. The torch switched on with a blinding flash of light.

Oxyacetylene burns at six thousand degrees. The mechanic would've seared off Finn's face if he hadn't scurried back in the nick of time. Finn kept scurrying and the mechanic kept coming at him until the hoses from the tanks feeding his torch were fully extended. Then the guy hesitated, unsure what to do next. Finn didn't—he turned and ran out of the shed.

Outside, a police car was pulling up at the road leading to the dock, and for a microsecond Finn was relieved. Then he remembered that Perez had been a cop.

He pirouetted and ran back into the shed, where the mechanic had ditched his mask and traded his torch for a heavy riveting mallet.

For a few short seconds, Finn and the mechanic danced around each other, each waiting for the other to make the first move. Then the mechanic swung double-handed at Finn's head. That was a mistake. Finn ducked the swing and the weight of the mallet pulled the mechanic off-balance, giving Finn time to deliver a four-shot combo, two body blows to the kidneys, then two hard uppercuts, one-two-one-two, like that. The mallet flew out of the guy's hands and with a clang hit the trawler's hull, and the guy stumbled back from the force of Finn's hits. This time, Finn took the offensive and glided in on light feet and finished him with a single, perfect neck-snapping jab. The mechanic crumpled and lay still.

Finn heard the policemen's voices outside getting nearer. His eyes searched the shed for another exit and found none.

He looked at the shrimper, picked up the mechanic's body, lifted him high like a lucha libre fighter, and flung him into the boat, making sure he was out of sight behind the freeboard. Then he ran back to the bench, pulled the welding mask over his face, his heavy breathing fogging up the glass, and switched on the torch.

A second later, he heard the cops walk in. Finn turned to face them. There were three of them. One of the cops was pushing a wheelbarrow. The other two had AR-15s slung over their shoulders.

Acting like he wasn't surprised to see them, Finn went back to his work and focused on welding the dome back onto the cylinder.

The cops walked up and said something to him in Spanish. He nodded and hoped to God it was just banter and they would go about their business.

The cop with the wheelbarrow pulled up and started unloading bricks of plastic-wrapped narcotics onto the workbench. He said something to Finn that made the other cops laugh.

Finn nodded vaguely, kept welding, kept breathing deeply beneath his mask, trying to slow his heart and the release of cortisol in his brain.

Once they'd unloaded all the bricks from the wheelbarrow, the cops heaved four of the finished extinguishers onto it.

Finn kept welding.

Two of the cops started moving toward the exit.

The third one, a guy with buck teeth who made spitting sounds when he spoke, kept speaking at Finn. He was getting impatient, like he was expecting an answer.

Finn steeled himself.

The cop motioned to Finn to take off his mask. Finn didn't move. Then, when the cop started raising his gun, Finn rammed the welding torch into the cop's face. The sickening smell of burned flesh filled his nostrils and the cop's brutalized scream echoed around the boat shed. Finn dropped the torch, grabbed the barrel of the AR-15, and kicked the screaming cop away.

He flipped the gun around so that the business end was pointed at the two remaining cops. The one with the wheelbarrow was frozen to the spot. The one with the other AR-15 already had its stock to his shoulder. Finn dropped to a knee.

The cop fired first but fired high—a quick burst, *rat-tat-tat*, the weapon spitting shells, the shells clattering to the ground, rounds ricocheting off the wall above Finn.

Finn pulled the trigger and the cop's chest exploded red. He immediately swung the weapon onto the third cop, who had abandoned the wheelbarrow and was scrambling for his holstered weapon. Finn looked at him along his barrel and shook his head. It should've been obvious to the cop that he was never going to beat Finn. What he should've done was drop his handgun and put up his hands. Instead, he went for his weapon. He died with a surprised look on his face.

All three cops lay still. Finn realized he was still wearing the welder's mask. He took it off now and looked around. His heart was racing. The oxyacetylene cylinders gave him an idea. First, he turned off the valves on both cylinders and unscrewed the regulators. Then he hauled the two tanks up the rolling steps, dumped them on their sides in the trawler's small cabin, and opened their valves to full. Then he closed the door, sealing the cabin, and hustled out of there.

He quickly patted down the pockets of the dead gangsters for spare clips for the two AR-15s, flung both weapons on top of the extinguishers in the wheelbarrow, took the third cop's handgun, then pushed the wheelbarrow hard to the exit, stopping only to pull the sliding door shut behind him.

"Fuck you, Caballeros," he said to no one in particular. He pushed the wheelbarrow as fast as he could down the beach, past the cop car, past the shrimpers on the pier, back to the *Pacific Belle*. All the fishermen, he noticed, had disappeared.

At the far end of the dock, he saw Linda walking up the gangplank, leading the little girl from the orphanage by the hand. The two of them turned and gave him astonished looks.

That's when he felt the heat and the force of the boatyard exploding behind him.

CHAPTER TWENTY-FOUR

Finn pushed west, away from Escondido, at top speed—fourteen knots. The *Belle* wasn't comfortable with it. Her engine thumped angrily and her hull pitched and rolled at every opportunity, but Finn didn't care. He wanted to get as far away as he could from Escondido as quickly as possible. From his position at the wheel, he glanced through the rear window every now and then at the column of black smoke rising from where the boatyard had been, keeping a watch for any craft putting to sea from the beach or the dock.

He knew that he'd stirred up a hornet's nest behind them, and he didn't like what he was seeing ahead, either. The wind had picked up and veered to the southwest, blowing strong onshore and sending white horses scudding across the outer bay. It wasn't a good sign: the wind hardly ever blew from that direction at this time of year or any other. He tried to get a weather update on the radio, but of course he was too far south to receive the NOAA's weather bulletins, and he wouldn't have been able to understand the Mexican equivalent even if he had known where to find it on the dial.

One of the AR-15s was hanging by its strap from his shoulder. Linda had put the extinguishers in their appropriate cradles: two in the engine room, one in the cabin, one in the wheelhouse. *Let's hope we don't have an actual fire aboard,* thought Finn.

He looked at Linda and the child she had brought with her, the two of them sitting on the bench by the chart table, the kid staring at Finn and Linda staring at the kid like she was the second coming. The girl was swamped in a raggedy, adult-size green sweatshirt that Linda had pulled out of somewhere. She'd also found the time to spread peanut butter and jelly on two white slices and put them on a plate in front of the kid, along with some cookies and a glass of long-life milk.

Finn watched the kid eat. She had long black hair parted right down the middle. She was small and slender. Her large, dark eyes looked out from her copper face at Finn with such placid incuriosity that he felt abashed by his own post-firefight, adrenaline-charged twitchiness. She ate everything slowly and deliberately. He figured she was no more than nine or ten years old. He had the feeling he'd seen her somewhere before. Linda stroked her hair.

"You know her name?" he said.

"Navidad," said Linda.

"What happened to her parents?"

"The Caballeros set up the orphanage for their enemies' children."

Finn suppressed a laugh. The Knights of Christ, princes of charity.

"Is that why you went down there this morning? To find her?"

"The way the Aztecs sacrifice children to their gods . . . it's so barbaric," said Linda. "You can imagine what the Caballeros do with girls like her. I wanted to help her. As a kind of restitution, you know? For all the harm I've done trying to save Lucy."

No, thought Finn, *I don't know.* He looked at Navidad again, thinking how familiar she seemed. Then it clicked. "That was her last night in the play," he said.

Linda nodded. He tried an awkward smile on the child. She stared at him impassively, chewing on her sandwich.

"She speak English?" he said.

Linda shook her head.

"I gotta be straight with you, Linda. You bring some poor kid into the middle of all this . . . on a whim? I just don't get it," he said.

"You're not a parent. I don't think you *can* get it."

"You're probably right, but try me anyway."

Linda lit a cigarette. "Last night, when I was watching the children on the stage, I kept thinking of Lucy. Lucy might be sick, but she has me. She has a *mother,* a *parent,* and that makes her lucky, you know? Doesn't matter if she's sick, I'm there to look after her, me and her aunt. Both of us, we would do anything for Lucy. Rhonda doesn't have any children of her own, so she adores her. But these children in the orphanage, they've got no one. Navidad's got no one. That play last night? It may've been make-believe, but it broke my heart. I thought, *The Caballeros will sacrifice her eventually.* Not on an altar to the gods, but in some brothel on the border. I wanted to save her from that. I thought, if I can do something, I should. And then this morning, sitting on the balcony watching the kids, I saw her sitting quietly in the yard all on her own, and it hit me: I *can* do something. So I went down there and I bought her."

"You *bought* her?"

"On paper, I adopted her. But that's the lie. Money changed hands."

Finn took a deep breath. Then he said, "You're out of your fucking mind."

Linda tapped ash into her ashtray and looked at him defiantly. "Like I said, you can't understand. You're not a parent."

He ground his teeth. "I don't need to have kids to know you're out of your mind. We've got a boat full of cocaine. Gangsters are trying to kill us. The cops are after me. Your own daughter has been *kidnapped,* for Christ's sake. You figure now's a good time to adopt a kid?"

"Lucy would understand. I mean, she will. This is what she'd want me to do. Anyway, it's too late now. We can't go back—you made sure of that."

"You should've told me about this. After last night."

"Why? You think last night meant something?"

Finn thought it had.

"It was make-believe, Finn. A smokescreen. I fucked you to block out everything else in my life for a few hours. To forget that Cutts has threatened to kill my sick daughter. To forget the crimes I've committed trying to save her life."

She put out her cigarette and quickly lit another.

"And if you had any balls, you'd admit you did, too. You fucked me the way you did for the same reason you drink the way you do: to blank out that shadow you carry around with you everywhere, to take a break from yourself even for just a few hours. You wore the mask. The minute we get back, we both know you're going straight back to your wife."

Finn didn't say anything to that.

"So, what, Lucy's got a sister now?" he said.

"She's always wanted one."

Finn tapped a cigarette out of Linda's pack for himself. He was done talking. *Woman's fucking insane,* he thought. She was right about one thing, however: there was no going back.

By nightfall, the weather had worsened to the point where it was no longer possible to travel at fourteen knots without risking the boat. Finn slowed down reluctantly. They lost speed but at least the ship's motion wasn't unbearable.

Navidad became seasick and Linda was upset about it. *What did she expect?* thought Finn. It was almost certainly the first time the kid had been to sea. Linda took her below to put her to bed in one of the crew bunks.

Finn said to Linda, "Get some sleep, too. I'll take both shifts tonight."

Linda didn't object.

Finn sat alone, listening to the wind strengthening almost to a whistle outside. He wedged himself between the stool and the bottom of the steering column—riding a nervous sea was like driving on shot springs down a corrugated dirt track, and it was easy to get thrown.

The worsening weather worried him. He figured that news of his blowing the boatyard narcotics operation sky-high would've reached the cartel bosses by now, and that worried him, too. If the Caballeros were as crazy as their reputation indicated, they'd be out looking for the *Pacific Belle* in go-fasts, storm or no storm. Finn leaned forward and set the *Belle*'s radar to sound an alarm if it picked up anything coming toward them. Then he lit one of Linda's cigarettes and scrutinized the horizon. From the look of it, last night's storm had been just the undercard; the main event was coming, and it was packing more punch than the *Belle* could take.

He considered finding a haven and waiting out the storm. Of course, that would increase the chances of the Caballeros tracking them down (they owned this coast, and he had no doubt they had spotters all along it). Even worse, they would lose precious time and miss their rendezvous with Cutts, and then Lucy would die and it all would've been for nothing.

On the other hand, if they all drowned trying to make the rendezvous, Lucy would die anyway.

He went over to the chart table and scrutinized the Baja coast, looking for safe havens. They were about 150 miles east of Cabo. Once they got around the headland, the next bay that afforded any sort of protection was San Carlos, 190 miles north and almost a day's sail away, by which time the storm would be well and truly upon them.

Finn rubbed his chin and considered. Cabo was a big town—someone from the cartel was bound to spot them there. Either they put into Cabo and waited out the storm but risked another battle with the Caballeros, or they kept putting distance between the *Belle* and the cartel but risked being run down by the storm.

Finn was too experienced a mariner to underestimate the storm. He remembered his father's words about the world not caring, and he knew a storm could break the *Belle* to bits and send them all to the bottom of the sea. But of the two, Finn preferred the weather. At least it was indifferent to them, whereas the Caballeros wanted them dead.

Finn set a course for San Carlos, leaned back into the chair, and listened to the distant rumble of thunder.

CHAPTER TWENTY-FIVE

Finn stayed at the helm throughout the night. The sea got steadily worse. At Cabo he rounded the headland and bore northwest.

At first light on the morning of November 3, he turned on the electric kettle wedged into a corner next to the chart table, then went out onto the stern deck for some air.

A gust ripped the door out of his hand. The moment he fixed his eyes on the colossal black clouds bearing down on them out of the southwest, he realized he'd made a big mistake. Finn had spent most of his life at sea, and this was the biggest thunderhead he'd ever seen. The cross sea had built to the point where he could no longer distinguish the usual, south-moving swell from the wind-driven, north-moving surface water.

Navidad emerged from the cabin below. She was wearing Linda's green sweater with the sleeves rolled up, the wind whipping her hair across her face. She looked like a gust would carry her away.

Finn went over to her and clasped her hand to the railing. "Always hold on, you hear?" he shouted.

Right then, lightning flashed below the cloud bank and a moment later a great crack of thunder rumbled over them. Finn pointed at the roiling sea. Then he pointed at the orange life preserver by the door to the cabin.

"If you go into the water, I throw this to you. Understand? You hold on to it and it will save your life. *Comprende?*" He mimicked throwing the life preserver over the rail.

Navidad nodded. Finn smiled. That he'd made himself understood was gratifying.

Linda appeared from below deck. She was wearing jeans and her green slicker. She looked anxiously at the storm clouds.

"She shouldn't be up here," said Finn, shouting over the howl of the wind.

Linda nodded and grabbed Navidad by the hand. The two of them disappeared into the cabin.

Finn made his way back into the wheelhouse, fighting the wind all the way. Inside, he heard a constant high-pitched sound, like a whistle. Thinking it was the kettle, he went over to deal with it, only to discover that it had switched itself off after reaching a boil. He looked around the wheelhouse and realized that the sound was coming from the navigation system.

He scrambled over to the screen and saw two green dots no more than three miles away, traveling fast from the direction of Cabo, directly at the *Belle*. He switched off the radar alarm he'd set and thought, *You have to hand it to the Caballeros: they've got balls.*

He took the AR-15 from the locker where he'd stowed it and stuffed the spare clips into his pockets. Then he picked up the binoculars and peered out the window on the side he expected to see the boats. For the time being, all he could see was the wind-whipped, foaming sea. The boats were low and still under the horizon, but the radar was telling him that they were traveling fast. The storm, meanwhile, was also moving up fast. Here were his choices, starkly narrowed: the Knights of Christ or the wrath of God.

Finn pulled back on the throttle, slowing the boat. The door opened and wind punched through the cabin. Linda scrambled in and pulled the door shut behind her.

"Why we slowing down?" she said, holding fast to the edge of the table and wiping the hair out of her eyes.

He pointed at the radar screen. "We got company. Two of them. I want the storm to catch us first."

He peered through the binoculars through the salt-streaked starboard window again. He could make out the boats now—two red hulls speeding off the crests of waves, spending more time in the air than on the surface. They were no more than a mile away.

Again he looked out the back windows—the dark, rain-filled cloud mass was maybe two miles behind them.

"Crazy fuckers," he said.

Two minutes later, the boats were within range, careening at them out of the east. He heard a faint popping sound, like corn popping in another room, and realized that they'd opened fire. The boats came flying off the crest of a wave and suddenly they were right alongside the *Belle*'s starboard bow, two long, sleek, fiberglass hulls. It was ludicrous to come out in a sea like this in boats as flimsy as that, thought Finn. He was sitting in forty feet of rugged steel and didn't feel safe; what chance did they have in hulls built to be as light as possible?

One of the go-fasts went around the *Belle*'s stern, the whine of her inboards just discernible over the cry of the wind, while the other shot ahead, then looped back into the sea and bore down on her. Finn peered through the binoculars and saw a man leaning a weapon atop the go-fast's windshield. He heard the metallic hammering of bullets ricocheting off of the *Belle*'s thick steel hull.

"Get your head down," he shouted. Linda dropped below the level of the windows. Finn stayed upright. He needed to be able to see.

The storm was much closer, but still not close enough. He looked to his right and saw the second boat running alongside them, a few feet off their starboard side, the gunman not shooting. He was fumbling with something with both hands. Finn's stomach lurched into his throat.

"Grenade!" he shouted.

He turned the wheel full-tilt to starboard, and the *Belle* leaned heavily into the turn. The lean gave the gunman on the first boat a line of sight onto the *Belle*'s deck, and bullets started hammering off the superstructure, throwing sparks. Finn ignored them and looked back at the second boat in time to see the grenade come over the rail and land on the foredeck, no more than ten feet from the wheelhouse.

His heart in his throat, he watched it roll down the deck's steep lean and miraculously disappear through a scupper. He didn't see or hear an explosion, which meant it was underwater by the time it detonated, and the density of the water would've slowed the velocity of its shrapnel. The guy hadn't cooked it off long enough before flinging it at them. Finn released his breath. He knew it was a lucky break.

He kept the *Belle* in her tight turn. The sea was on her beam now—the worst place it could be—and the boat rolled so severely that he had to grip the wheel to stop himself from falling. Still he kept the wheel on full lock, straightening only when she had turned 180 degrees and was heading the way she had come. In other words, straight into the eye of the storm.

The two gunboats circled the *Belle*, firing round after round, concentrating their fire on the wheelhouse. They got lucky with one volley and shattered one of the starboard windows, flinging glass all over the floor, the bullets ricocheting off the ceiling. Wind and rain came raging through the cabin, stinging Finn's face. He was literally wedged into the high chair now, his legs braced against the footrest, his hands clasped to the wheel. He looked over at Linda—she was holding on to the edge of the chart table for dear life.

"Take the wheel," he shouted.

She looked up at him, nodded, her mouth open, and felt her way over to him. They swapped places.

"Head straight into that," he shouted, pointing at the black wall of cloud ahead before bolting for the door. The gale almost knocked him flat the moment he opened it. Legs spread wide, leaning forward into the wind, he made his way over to the port rail, got down on his knees, rested the AR-15 on it, and started firing in the general direction of the go-fast, just letting it rip in full automatic mode. He wasn't hitting anything and he knew it: the gun wasn't known for its accuracy on firm ground and he was firing from a heaving, rolling platform at another through fierce wind. The only upside was that it was the same for them. He emptied an entire clip. While he was reaching for another, he kept his eyes on the two gunboats. One pulled ahead and disappeared from sight. A moment later, he heard a clang and saw another grenade rolling along the deck toward him. His heart banged like a kettle drum. He dived for cover behind the elevated fish-hold hatch.

The explosion was tremendous—Finn worried that his eardrums had burst. Something sharp cut his cheek and he thought he'd caught some shrapnel. Only when he opened his eyes did he realize that it was glass from the wheelhouse rear window, knocked out by the shockwave. He checked himself: apart from the cut on his cheek, he was unscathed. The *Belle*'s solid construction had saved him— the shrapnel hadn't made it through the raised steel sides of the fish-hold hatch. He got to his feet and looked over the starboard rail at one of the go-fasts—the guy in the passenger seat was working the pin out of a third grenade.

Finn set the barrel of the AR-15 on the rail, tilted it down to compensate for the *Belle*'s upward heave, peered down the sight, and pulled the trigger, firing at least twenty rounds. He stopped and looked over the go-fast. He hadn't hit a damn thing.

But he *had* made the two men in the boat duck for cover. The one handling the grenades was crouched down in an awkward position, his elbows tight against his ribs. He pulled the pin and held the grenade for a second, cooking it off. Then both boats hit a big wave. The impact was bigger for the lightweight go-fast. It knocked the grenade from the man's hand. Finn watched him scramble on the floor between the boat's bucket seats. *Too late,* he thought. He ducked his head beneath the rail. The blast was tremendous. He popped his head up over the rail again. The go-fast's hull was careening ahead with no one at the helm, its windshield gone and its fiberglass superstructure blasted to pieces. The hull kept going till it hit an oncoming wave, pitchpoled, and came to a rest upside down, propeller shafts poking up, blades spinning to a stop. Finn scanned back over its track and saw with savage pleasure a man's torso being tossed about on the stormy sea, the foam around it crimson.

He heard more gunfire from the other side of the *Belle,* more bullets zinging off her hull. The second go-fast. He was scrambling across the deck to deal it, clasping the AR-15 in both hands, when everything went eerily dark.

He'd forgotten about the storm. The colossal bank of clouds was right on them now. *Colossal* was an inadequate word to describe the size of the thing; from where he was, the cloud mass was on a cosmic scale—like the annihilating face of a hammer belonging to some merciless, Aztec god. Towering cracks of lightning shattered the sky, their terrific thunder deafeningly close and making the grenade's explosion seem like the sound of a bubble popping. Finn's senses were working at their highest level, the way a prey animal, sensing movement in the grass, watches not just with its eyes but with every hair on its vulnerable body. It had been dark before, but only in the southern half the sky; now they were enveloped in darkness, and through it Finn could barely make out the candy red–hulled go-fast still tracking along their starboard side. Hailstones started crashing into the *Belle,* hitting rather than falling on her at an almost horizontal angle. Stones the size of baseballs rolled around the deck. Finn ran for cover in the wheelhouse. He found Linda at the wheel, the wind and water blasting through the missing windows, the hailstones jackhammering into the wheelhouse roof, the uproar interrupted only by the frequent, terrifying cracks of thunder.

She didn't answer when he called her name and asked if she was okay. At first he thought she hadn't heard him through the din, but when he followed her frozen gaze, he understood.

"Oh my god," he said.

Coming at them was a wave.

More accurately, coming at them was a towering wall of water the size of a warship traveling at the speed of sports car.

The *Belle* began to yaw. Linda, paralyzed at the wheel, did nothing. They were losing steerage. If they didn't take the wave head-on, they would broach, no question. Even a boat as solid as the *Belle*, a wave that size on her quarter would flip her like a toy.

Finn threw his gun onto the bench, shoved Linda aside, and grabbed the wheel. He had only one job now: to keep the wave from destroying them. Out of the corner of his eye, he glimpsed the go-fast right alongside the *Belle*, scudding along the crests of the waves that preceded the monster. They'd stopped firing. Finn figured they had seen the wave by now. They must've realized their fate.

He focused on bringing the *Belle*'s head back on track. So far, the rogue wave had held its shape, but it appeared impossibly top-heavy. Finn turned the wheel to full-lock and the *Belle* slowly came up again, regained steerage, and even picked up a little speed, crashing over the front waves of the set. He kept his eyes fixed on the monster's crest, his whole body tense as a mainstay, his forearms aching from holding the wheel so tightly. Then, to his horror, he saw the top of the wall of water lurch forward, saw the crest curl and break, foam flying off it like snow being whipped from a mountain.

Linda started to scream. The *Pacific Belle* started falling away, exposing her beam to the breaking monster. Finn heaved on the wheel with everything he had, locking the rudder all the way over,

but still she kept falling away. When he looked up, instead of seeing sky, he saw nothing but seawater and realized there was nothing more he could do.

"Hold on!" he screamed.

For three long seconds, the *Pacific Belle* heaved up the side of the
wave. Then there was an eerie, standstill moment, and Finn allowed
himself to believe, to hope, that the wave was going to pass beneath
her keel. The din died down, leaving Finn and Linda in an uncanny
quiet, as though they could speak at normal conversational volume.

Then the stillness gave way to a world of indescribable violence.

Through the space where the rear window had been, Finn saw
the top half of the wave collapse under its own weight, and then
the starboard side of the *Belle* disappeared underwater and she began to roll. Everything inside the wheelhouse that wasn't bolted
down—plastic water bottles, charts, pens, sunglasses, coffee mugs,
the electric kettle on its power cord, the radio mic on its coil, the
AR-15—fell through the air toward the water rushing in the starboard window. Finn held on to the wheel, his right leg dangling free,
his left one jammed against the base of the high chair. The whole
cabin rolled past ninety degrees. He thought of Mona, of never seeing her again. He thought of his father, of seeing him soon. He heard
a scream and watched in horror as Linda slid away from the table,
her hands grasping at nothing, and fell through the hole where the
starboard window had been. He reached out for her with one hand,
but missed, and she disappeared into the torrent of water rushing
along the inside of the gunwale. Finn clung for his life, unable to
do anything except wait, wait, wait. Water filled the cabin.

And then, unbelievably, he felt it: the *Pacific Belle* slowly, wearily started coming right again, like an old automobile struggling
up a hill. The noise was deafening—not just the deep and loud thump
of the wave collapsing, but the torrential rush of water flooding over
the rails and through the scuppers. Somehow, they had survived;
somehow, Finn had managed to give the *Belle* just enough way to

get her over the crest, and now, instead of being rolled under its breaking face, they were heaving down its back.

With the *Belle* returned to more or less level (a relative term), Finn turned his attention to the inundated stern deck. Linda was nowhere to be seen. He thought she'd been swept over with the receding water. He called out her name—nothing.

Then he saw an arm sticking out of the water. He half ran, half swam across the shifting deck, clawing his way against the buffeting wind, seawater up to his thighs, rain stinging his face. His soaked-through clothes weighed him down. He found her wrapped around one of the steel legs of the cable drum. She wasn't moving at all. He reached under her arms and pulled her up. The wind thrust her into his arms. He shepherded her to the wheelhouse, holding her shivering body against his.

He brought her in, sat her on the bench, held her face cupped in one hand and slapped it hard with the other, and shouted her name in her ear. She coughed, opened her eyes, vomited water, swallowed great gulps of air, and grabbed hold of his arms with bruising strength. Suddenly she peeled back from him and stared into his eyes in horror.

"My girl!" she shouted. She tore herself away from him and before he could stop her dashed outside and opened the door to the below-deck cabin.

"Wait!" he said, but she was gone.

He made his way back to the wheel. The main thing was that Linda was alive and still aboard. They had survived the rogue wave, and the sea was smaller now—waves no taller than twice the height of the boat—but he knew there could be more monsters in the wake of the one that had nearly ended them. What was more, the sea had turned them all the way around, so the storm-driven waves were slamming into the *Belle*'s stern, making her yaw again. He was soaked to the bone, the wound on his arm smarted, blood was streaming from his cheek, and he felt a huge bruise growing on his shin where he'd hit the edge of something. But none of that mattered. What mattered was keeping the *Belle* afloat in this watery hell.

Finn checked the dials—the engine, miraculously, was still running. He put his hands on the wheel, closed his eyes, and took a long breath. He felt what the *Belle* was doing through his hands and through the soles of his feet. She was jerking this way and that, like a fly trying to find its way through a windowpane. He filtered out the storm's raging shrieks and listened through his hands to where she wanted to go. She felt heavy by the stern, and he realized that the weight of all the water still caught on the stern deck and rushing from the scuppers had pressed her down a fraction, pushing her screw deeper into the sea, giving her traction. They had way. He opened his eyes and pushed the throttle forward.

But then a following wave raised her stern, tilting her forward at an angle so steep that Finn had to lock his arms to stop from falling into the instruments. His stomach lurched, and he felt her bow start to come around. Hand over hand, he counterturned the wheel and set her right again. The wave passed beneath her and now she tilted over the crest, and instead of roiling water, he found himself staring through the rain-whipped window at the blackened sky, so close that he felt he could almost touch it.

He realized, exhilarated, that this heavy boat was actually surfing the waves and that as long as he kept her moving, he had a degree of control over her heading. The *Belle* careened down the slope and slammed into the trough with a jarring shock. Finn lunged forward and caught the wheel painfully in his ribs. The *Belle*'s bow disappeared into the water, her stern lifted, and her blades cleared the water. He had lost traction again, and again her head started turning to port, her starboard side dipping. He glanced back, saw another huge wave approaching. He pushed the throttle to full speed and desperately counter-steered, his hands flying over each other until at last she obeyed, tilted back to center, and started bearing back to where Finn wanted her to go.

The next wave lifted her at an astonishing speed from the eerie quiet of the hollow to the crest, where the shriek of the wind was at its most fierce. And then the wave moved on, and they slid down toward the next trough. Finn screamed for joy and told the *Belle* he loved her. He was elated; he wasn't beating the storm, exactly, but he felt as if the *Belle* were rewarding his commitment, and that together they were colluding against the chaos engulfing them. All he had to do was stay with her and give her his full attention through the gale, no matter how long it lasted.

CHAPTER TWENTY-SIX

For forty eight hours and six hundred and fifty nautical miles, Finn didn't leave the wheelhouse or the deck—not to eat, not to sleep, not to piss, not to throw up. When he had to piss or throw up, he did it over the side. Linda brought him food and drink but otherwise stayed sheltered below with the girl. The Caballeros had shot out both the stern and starboard windows of the wheelhouse, and the rain and cold swept into Finn's bones.

At some point during the ordeal—the relentlessly pelting rain so distended the passage of time that he lost any useful sense of it—he changed into dry clothes and wet-weather gear that Linda brought him. She also brought him oatmeal cookies, and once, when the raging swell seemed to have lulled a little, she brought him a mug of something hot, which he never got to taste—a wave hit the moment she walked through the door, and the mug's contents ended up all over the floor.

Forty eight hours had passed, but he knew this only from the clock in the corner of the display screen; the quantity and quality of light in the world surrounding him no longer followed the logic of the Earth's rotation. The storm had engulfed them on the morning of November 3, and by noon it had been so dark that it could've been night. Then, by late afternoon, he had become so used to the darkness that when a hole appeared in the clouds and everything was bright again, it took him by surprise. And then the real night fell and plunged them into real darkness. The storm clouds blanketed out the stars and the moon, and the only lights visible from the *Belle,* apart from her own, were the cracks of lightning ahead of them, for the storm had overtaken them and they were in its tail now. It was the morning of November 5. It had taken everything he had, but his gamble had paid off. They were heading for Two Harbors. He was six hundred and fifty nautical miles closer to setting everything right.

Linda appeared with a Thermos and more cookies.

"Thank you," he said, reaching for the coffee.

She flipped off her waterproof hoodie, shook out her hair, and leaned against the chart table. She seemed lively and alert—fired up, he presumed, at the prospect of being reunited with her daughter.

"How's the kid?" he mumbled through a mouthful of cookie.

"She looks green."

"Understandable."

"She hasn't complained once."

"Well, she'll learn how to do that in America."

No response from Linda.

The sea had dropped. The swell was getting closer to a normal size, without the confusing and dangerous cross sea that Finn had spent so many hours tackling. At long last, he could let himself relax. His head drooped and he could barely keep his eyes open.

"That was a joke," he said.

"I know," said Linda's silhouette.

"You think she'll be a match for Lucy?" he said.

It took a moment for Linda to answer. "I hope so," she said, her voice so soft that he barely heard her.

"Me too," said Finn, "I like her."

"Who?"

The question surprised him. He reached for another cookie. "Both of them. Navidad and Lucy."

Linda fell silent and Finn, too tired to push the conversation, did, too.

"You need to sleep, Finn," she said finally. "I can take it in from here."

He shook his head. "I'm fine. Got to keep an eye out for patrols."

"I'll wake you if anything shows up on the radar. You're dead on your feet."

Finn yawned. "Maybe I will sit down for a bit."

"Go below. It's warm and dry down there," said Linda.

"No. I'll just stay here. I'm fine, really."

He stumbled over to the bench by the chart table, sat down, tucked his hands into his armpits, and closed his eyes. He planned to rest with his eyes closed, keeping his ears open for the radar alarm.

But within a minute he was fast asleep.

He dreamed he was in bed with Mona. She smiled and said, *"Cinq à sept?"* and gently put her hands over his eyes. When she took them away, he found himself staring at walls made of dirt and a rectangle of blue sky, like he was lying in a hole. Diego's face appeared cut out against the sky.

"Hey. Get out of *my* grave," he said. He reached an impossibly long arm down to Finn and pulled him out. Now Finn saw that they were in the cemetery and Diego was in full dress uniform. In the center of a row of mourners sat Mona in black, holding a folded Stars and Stripes on her lap.

"I want my pipes and drums," said Diego. There was a black-edged entry wound in his forehead. Finn, frightened, turned away in time to see the honor guard lowering their rifles at him.

"Please, no," he said.

He heard the order to fire, and all twenty-one guns erupted.

He woke to the sound of insistent beeping and instinctively jumped to his feet. The dream evaporated and the military part of his mind noted that it was night—he'd slept through the entire day. Linda was staring at the electronic display. Finn hustled over and looked over her shoulder. The weather was throwing up a lot of clutter, but there was nothing ambiguous about the green dot traveling in a straight line at twenty knots directly toward them from San Diego. His heart sank. A boat that fast, at this time of night, heading in that direction, could only be a CBP Interceptor.

"You think they're coming for us?" said Linda.

"Their patrol zone extends to about here," he said, pointing at an area twenty miles east of their position. "If they get to the end and turn back, they're on routine patrol. If they cross it, then it means they've spotted us and want to know who we are."

He saw Linda bite her lower lip, her face lit by the display's glow. Finn rubbed his eyes with the backs of his hands, then looked at the screen again. The *Pacific Belle* was about twenty miles off the southern tip of San Clemente, an island the navy used as a ship-to-shore firing range. The waters around San Clemente were a no-go zone. The course they'd plotted to Two Harbors took them up San Clemente's eastern side, clear of the island. But if they stuck close to its western shore, he realized, its mass would block them from the Interceptor's radar.

"Set a new course," he said, pointing at the ocean side of San Clemente.

"We'll be in the no-go zone," she said.

"Exactly."

"The navy won't like it," she said.

"We've just come through a goddamn hurricane. If anyone asks questions, we say it blew us off course."

Linda nodded. One thing about Linda, he didn't have to explain things twice. She adjusted their course and pushed down the throttle. The engine's rumble, so ubiquitous that Finn's ears had tuned it out, increased in pitch, and the *Belle* picked up a knot and hit her top speed of fourteen, bashing awkwardly through the waves.

Now all they could do was wait until they reached the island. Finn lay back down on the bench.

He woke of his own accord. Or rather, in his sleep, he noted the change in the boat's rhythm, and woke to check it out. He got to his feet and looked at the display. They were running north half a mile off the western shore of San Clemente. The island was refracting the swell, changing its direction, which was why Finn had noticed the change in the roll of the hull.

He peered into the darkness to starboard and just made out the lights of a radio tower high on the island. He checked that the VHF was on channel 16. The navy would want to talk to them; it was important that they could.

"What happened with the Interceptor?" he asked.

"We got around the point before they got to the end of their sector, so I didn't get to see."

He nodded.

A voice crackled through the VHF: "Unidentified vessel, unidentified vessel, this is U.S. Navy calling, identify yourself, over."

Finn turned up the volume and picked up the transmitter. "U.S. Navy, U.S. Navy, this is fishing vessel *High Hope*, over."

"*High Hope, High Hope,* you are in a restricted zone, repeat, restricted zone."

"U.S. Navy, acknowledge we are in a restricted zone. We were blown off course by the storm; we have an injured crew and are returning to home port of San Pedro, over."

A moment passed. Finn held his breath.

"*High Hope,* do you require assistance, over."

Finn laughed and said, "U.S. Navy, no, thank you."

"*High Hope,* try to exit the restricted zone as soon as possible, over."

"U.S. Navy, wilco, over and out."

By ten, they had cleared the northern point of San Clemente. They were on schedule to make their midnight rendezvous with Cutts at Two Harbors.

Finn went out on deck. They were well out of the storm now and for the first time in two days Finn could see stars and the waning moon. He went below and found Navidad sitting up in a bunk.

"You all right, kid?" said Finn.

She looked at him without reacting. *Fucking Linda, with her big heart,* he thought. What if Cutts double-crossed them and killed them both? What would happen to Navidad then? He smiled at the child, and she smiled back. At least that didn't need translation, he thought.

He went into the galley, opened two fifteen-ounce cans of chili, and heated the contents in a pot on the stove. He filled a bowl and devoured it with six slices of bread. He'd had no idea how hungry he was until he started eating. He grabbed a can of Coke and took it with him back up to the wheelhouse.

Linda was at the helm. Finn checked the screen: they were halfway across the stretch of water between San Clemente and Santa Catalina. There was a lot of chatter on the radio—more than there should have been at this time of night. Finn turned up the volume.

They were talking about a suspicious boat. He leaned forward and listened carefully until there was no doubt.

"They're looking for us," he said.

"What's this *Bertholf* they keep talking about?" Linda asked.

"The *Bertholf* is a big coast guard cutter, four hundred twenty feet long with a 57-mm gun on her foredeck. A warship, basically."

Linda looked at the radar screen. "Where is she? I don't see her."

She sounded surprisingly calm. Finn wasn't. While the *Belle* could never outrun an Interceptor, she could certainly outrange one—Interceptors burned fuel like they owned their own oil fields. But the *Bertholf* was another matter; the cutter could travel at twice the *Belle's* top speed and, compared to the *Belle*, her range was limitless. If the *Bertholf* started after them, they would never make it to their rendezvous.

He pointed at San Clemente. "She must be in the lee of the island. We won't see her. . ."

"Till she comes out of the radar shadow. Okay."

Linda pulled back the throttle, taking all the way off the boat. "Let's go fishing," she said.

Finn had no idea what she was talking about. "Linda, if she finds us, that's it. We can't outrun her. We'll never make it to Two Harbors, not unless we make ourselves invisible."

"Exactly."

Finn followed her out onto the deck. Linda switched on the high-intensity lamp on top of the mast, flooding the deck with white light. She opened the fish-hold hatch and told Finn to steer the gantry crane over the hold. Once the crane was in place, Linda grabbed the hook and told him to lower the block into the hold. She climbed in with it.

"All right, bring it up," she shouted from below. He hit the rubber-encased Lift button and watched the roll of black neoprene he'd found when he'd searched the *Belle* rise out of the hold. Linda climbed out and wrangled it over the edge of the fish-hold cover.

"What is it?" he said.

She grinned. "An invisibility cloak."

"What?"

"See those diamond-shaped tiles? They're carbon black. The same stuff the air force covers their Stealth fighters with. We set it just like a seine, except out of the water instead of in it." Linda was obviously enjoying Finn's amazement. "You'll see. Bring it over to starboard," she said.

Finn maneuvered the boom over, following Linda's hand gestures, until the roll was hanging over the starboard rail. She signaled for him to hold it there, then ran a line through a series of eyelets along the bottom edge of the material and back through a block at the stern before tying it off. Finn looked on in astonishment. Linda took the crane's control unit from him and expertly hoisted the pole until it was level, then swung it aft. Like a bullfighter's cape billowing out in slow motion, the black material swathed the *Belle*'s superstructure and hull down to about four feet off the water, all the way around her stern from one bow to the other.

Linda switched off the masthead light and made the *Belle* dark again. Finn followed her back into the wheelhouse. He looked at the speedometer. They were doing just three knots. Linda explained that they had to go this slowly on account of the sea jumping up and tugging at the *Belle*'s skirt. Any faster and the sea could yank it off.

"But it makes our radar profile so faint, no one notices us. Like we're hidden behind a mask."

Finn could only shake his head in wonder. He looked through the forward window. The skirt blocked their lateral and rear views of the water, but they could still see the narrow track directly ahead of them through the gap between where the skirt began and ended at the bow.

"Where'd you get it?" he said.

"It used to belong to the navy," she said. "Cutts got hold of it, he says from a materiel guy down in San Diego. Calls it his 'modesty skirt.'"

Finn had to admit, he was impressed. When he looked at the radar screen, however, he knew that the biggest test of the "modesty skirt" was quickly closing in on them. Linda had made it clear that she'd never encountered the *Bertholf* before. The cutter was the coast guard's newest flagship. Finn knew from talk around the Air and Marine Station that she was equipped with all the latest technology. She had emerged from the lee of the island and was bearing down on them from their stern quarter. Linda had turned off all the navigation and interior lights. The only light in the wheelhouse now came from the navigation-system screen. Finn and Linda stood side by side, watching the green dot get closer. Compared to the *Belle,* the *Bertholf* was racing across the sea, even though she was ten times the *Belle*'s size. In no time, she was within a half mile. Had it been daylight, they would've been able to read each other's numbers. Linda dimmed the screens and killed the engine. Its steady throb disappeared and gave way to the sound of the sea slapping at the Belle's hull. Finn stood next to Linda in the dark, listening. She reached for his hand. They drifted together. For two long minutes, all he heard was the sound of his own breath. Then there was the slow crashing of the *Bertholf*'s huge bow heaving down on the sea, shouldering it aside. Finn held his breath, as if that were enough to give them away. The four-hundred-foot cutter couldn't have been more than a couple of hundred feet away. And it was getting closer.

Another minute passed. Linda's hand became clammy. He couldn't hear her breathing, and figured she was holding her breath also.

Finally, he heard the regular sound of a ship's twin screws turning. If they could hear the screws, they were behind the boat; the *Bertholf* had passed by the *Pacific Belle*. He whistled. The coast guard's newest, first-in-class cutter had passed within maybe a hundred feet and hadn't looked twice. He thought about Diego, about what he'd have to say about that. He let go of Linda's hand.

"So you're the phantom."

"What?"

Finn rubbed his chin. "That night. Diego and I were looking for a phantom."

After a moment, she said, "I'm sorry, Nick."

Finn was struck; she'd never used his first name before.

She stroked his cheek. "I'm sorry for Diego. For everything. I'm sorry for the whole nightmare." She put her arms around him.

"I'm sorry, too. But it's almost over," he said.

She rested her cheek on his chest. "Yes," she said, "Yes, I suppose it is."

CHAPTER TWENTY-SEVEN

By eleven thirty, when they were within sighting distance of Catalina, Finn and Linda brought in the radar-absorbing skirt. It had done its job getting them past the *Bertholf.* Now it was just slowing them down.

Finn couldn't see the shore in the dark, but he sensed it from the way the sea behaved differently, and anyway it was right there on the radar screen, a sharp green line against the inky background. He brought the *Belle* in as close to the invisible white cliffs as he dared. It was dangerous, but being spotted by an Interceptor would be worse, he figured. He would use the cliffs for cover.

Two Harbors is just that: an isthmus a few hundred feet across, with harbors on either side. At eleven fifty, Finn and Linda reached the headlands guarding the bay on the southern side. They anchored just outside, in about forty feet of water, in the lee of a promontory called Lobster Point.

Linda went below to check on Navidad and to tell her that under no circumstances was she to leave the cabin. While she was gone, Finn took the AR-15 from the locker, loaded it with a fresh clip, went out on deck, and tucked it beneath the edge of the fish hold. He wanted it somewhere he could get to easily, in case things went wrong during the handover. He had the handgun he'd taken from the cop in Escondido tucked into the back of his trousers. Cutts had Lucy, which meant he was calling the shots. Finn wouldn't make a move against Cutts until he was sure the girl—both girls—were safe.

Still, he'd be damned if he was going into this thing with nothing up his sleeve.

Midnight.

Finn and Linda stood in the wheelhouse, peering into the darkness, waiting for Cutts to appear. Linda chain-smoked. Finn sipped a cup of coffee. He thought about how it had all begun when he and Diego had found the floater in the water on the northern side of the isthmus. *No, that's not right,* he thought. It had begun before that, when they'd intercepted *La Catrina,* again just a mile or so offshore on the leeward side; when he'd shot and killed Rafael Aparición Perez. Now here he was at Two Harbors again, coming in from the ocean side, closing the circle.

Linda had set up a rope ladder on the *Belle*'s lee side, ready to be thrown over. Just then, Finn saw something moving toward them from the harbor.

"There," he said.

Linda stepped out of the wheelhouse and flashed the spotlight three times. The approaching boat replied with three flashes. Finn felt a tension in his neck. Two minutes later, the boat came under the *Belle*'s lee, and Linda switched on the masthead light. Finn went out on deck, grabbed the line that someone on the other boat flung over the bow rail, and attached it to a cleat. He did the same with a line that came over the stern. Then he dropped the rope ladder over the side to the boat below.

"God damn," he said.

The boat was one of the sleekest cigarette boats he'd ever seen—a millionaire's toy. Its long bow jutted out aggressively from a luxurious-looking cockpit in cream trim. Whatever was in the engine bay was growling angrily, as if traveling at less than fifty knots was an insult. It was a beautiful, luxury version of his own beloved Midnight Express Interceptor.

He saw only Serpil in the cockpit, holding a spotlight and dressed in a thick pea coat with the collar up. No sign of Lucy. No sign of Cutts.

"Get that light out of my face," shouted Finn.

Serpil dipped his light.

"Where's the girl?" shouted Finn.

Serpil pointed at the forward hatch. "She's in here, nice and dry. You have the product?" he shouted back.

Finn wanted to see the girl alive. And he wanted to know why he was talking to this guy and not the Irishman.

"Where's Cutts?" he said.

"He got sick, had to go back to the hospital," shouted Serpil.

Finn scanned the boat again. Something wasn't right. "Show me the girl," he said.

Serpil hesitated before he shouted, "Where is Linda?"

It was a good question. Finn glanced back at the wheelhouse and saw her walking toward him.

"It's Serpil. He says he has Lucy below. He says Cutts is in the hospital. He wants—"

Lacerating pain seared through his thigh before he could finish his sentence. He looked down, saw the needle in Linda's hand, her thumb all the way down on the plunger. He looked up, saw tears streaming down her face.

"Goddammit, Linda!" he said.

"I'm sorry, Finn. He said if I didn't . . ." She dropped the syringe to the ground, ran to the rail, and waved at Serpil. Then she turned and stared back at Finn.

Finn reached for the handgun in the small of his back, black rage snaking its way through his bloodstream along with the drug. He saw the top of the rope ladder tauten and then Serpil appeared over the side and stepped onto the deck. The smug look disappeared from his face the moment he saw the gun in Finn's hand.

"He has a gun!" shouted Serpil.

"I didn't know, I swear!" shouted Linda.

Finn raised the pistol, the barrel wavering unsteadily between Linda and Serpil, his eyes seeing double. Whatever had been in the syringe was affecting him already: his arm felt heavy and his aim was completely off. He yelled at Linda to move out of the way, then fired off his clip.

Every round went high.

The empty pistol fell from his hand and clattered across the metal deck. Finn charged Serpil. He threw a right hook, but missed.

Serpil laughed, toying with Finn now. "You know why propofol is my favorite sedative?" he said.

Finn swung again, a left hook this time, but all he caught was air. He felt like every punch he threw was in slow motion. He started edging toward the fish hold, where he'd left the AR-15.

"It's so *fast*," said Serpil. "Forty seconds and the patient's yours."

Finn turned unsteadily toward Linda and saw her standing at the rail, staring at him.

"Help me," he said.

She sobbed and turned her head away.

His vision blurred. His mind darkened.

Forty seconds, he thought. He had no time to get to the rifle, let alone use it. He turned and lunged one last time at Serpil, who laughed and stepped easily out of the way. Finn let the momentum carry him across the deck. He kept going all the way to the starboard rail.

He threw himself over and fell into the cold black sea.

The water temperature shocked him awake. He couldn't see a thing, but he knew instinctively he had to find cover. He dived deep, did a tuck turn, and swam under the hull.

He swam with big sweeps of his arms, kicking hard with his legs. He scraped the backs of his hands against the *Belle*'s barnacled hull. He was trying to make it all the way under her to the other side, but he had come up short. He felt the involuntary panic that kicks in when the body can't get the air it wants. *Keep going,* he thought. He pushed off the hull with both legs and forced himself on.

At last he made it to the bow and broke through the surface. He'd swum some fifty feet underwater, fully clothed, in the dark, with a powerful hypnotic pumping through his bloodstream. He felt dizzy. He gasped for air. Then he heard steps on the deck above and saw a beam of light trailing along the *Pacific Belle*'s waterline. Serpil, sweeping the handheld spotlight around the hull. Finn took a deep breath and dived, hauling himself under the hull again, pulling himself along the barnacles like an upside-down rock climber reaching for holds, the barnacles cutting the flesh in his hands.

He got to the deepest part of the hull and started counting, "one Mississippi, two Mississippi," determined to wait ninety seconds underwater, in the cold and dark, long enough to convince Serpil he'd drowned. He got to ninety and made his way back to the surface, his lungs burning. He was shivering, almost out of control. He was on the verge of blacking out. Moving at all demanded great effort. When he could take it no more, he found his way back to the surface and broke through for the second time. He tried to breathe quietly, but his lungs gulped loudly for air, like after intense exercise. It took everything he had to quiet his breathing. He kept scanning for signs of movement from the deck high above his head. He couldn't see any spotlight, and he couldn't hear any voices.

A moment later, he heard the growl of the cigarette boat's engine and saw her bow appear around the *Belle*'s stern, the spotlight shining from the console. Serpil was circling the *Belle,* looking for him. Finn dived deep. He held on to the *Belle*'s keel with numb hands and started counting. When he got to thirty, he heard the muffled sound of the *Belle*'s diesel engine starting up. He broke his count and made his way back to the surface. He heard the windlass grinding and saw the anchor chain going up. The hull started moving forward. They were leaving, he thought. He had to move *now*—if the hull didn't crush him, the *Belle*'s blades would slice him to pieces. Climbing back aboard wasn't possible—the *Belle*'s sides were sheer. He couldn't see the cigarette boat. The hull kept moving forward, bringing her propeller ever closer to his legs. He knew that once the anchor was off the bottom, Linda would kick the boat into gear and the blades would start turning. He kicked hard against the hull and swam into the darkness.

He took ten strokes, stopped, and turned, utterly exhausted. He was shocked to see how far the *Belle* had traveled away from him in such a short time—he'd never make it back to her. The propofol had muddled his mind. He had no idea in which direction the island lay. He swallowed water. His body started to shake uncontrollably.

Then he saw the lone figure of a girl on the stern deck, silhouetted against the light spilling out of the wheelhouse. Lucy or Navidad, he couldn't tell. He shouted feebly. He used all his strength to wave an arm. He didn't know whether the kid could see or hear him across the night-covered sea. She didn't wave back. But a moment later, he saw her step forward, out of the light. Then he saw something fly off the *Belle*'s stern and into her wake.

Finn swam toward it. His body was at the very edge of failure. He'd fought for his life, fought the propofol for several long minutes, fought the cold, but he felt himself succumbing now. He didn't think he was going to make it. He imagined the very worst. He imagined himself drowning, then being found floating in the channel, two stumps where his legs had been. He reached the spot where he thought he'd seen the object splash into the sea and found nothing but more water. He stopped swimming. Water washed over his head. He had barely enough strength left to keep his mouth above the waterline.

Out of the corner of his eye, he glimpsed a flash of orange behind a wave. His heart leaped. With one last effort, he splashed on,
swallowing water, until he reached the life preserver that he had
shown Navidad how to throw to someone in the water. He clambered on, hung his arms over the sides, and wedged himself in so
that he'd remain afloat when he passed out, which he knew he was
about to do. He watched the *Pacific Belle*'s navigation lights dim and
then go out completely. He resisted wave after wave of drowsiness
until he had no resistance left.

He woke with his teeth chattering and could not stop them no
matter how willfully he tried to clench his jaw. The effort it took to
move his arms shocked him. Movements he would normally make
unconsciously demanded his complete attention. After what he per-
ceived as hours but could only have been seconds, he finally managed to lift his hands, which he could no longer feel, out of the
water. His fingertips were blue, which surprised him, since he no
longer actually felt the cold. When he felt compelled to peel off his
clothes, he remembered learning during his navy training of a
symptom of hypothermia called "paradoxical undressing"—his
brain was trying to convince him that his body was overheating.

He was grateful, at least, to still be in the life preserver. He stared
at his blue fingertips. He knew the color meant he was hypother-
mic. Soon he'd lose his motor skills, then his memory; his pulse and
breathing would slow down, his organs would begin to fail, and then
he would die. His navy training had been meticulous about the
details.

He kept staring at his fingertips until it registered on him that
he could actually *see* his fingertips. It was dawn, which meant he'd
been in the water for six and a half hours. He looked up and saw the
slate-dark sea stretching away before him, and a curtain of darkness
dropping to the horizon. But the sky directly above him was purple-

gray. He realized he was facing southwest. He turned around, his movements clumsy, until he was facing east and saw first light spilling over the hilltops and brown-gray cliffs of Santa Catalina Island. He didn't recognize the stretch of coast, but he knew it could only be Catalina. The current had obviously carried him south from Two Harbors. He was no more than half a mile from land. He wanted to scream with joy, but his throat was too swollen from the salt. He began paddling toward the island. His progress was excruciatingly slow. His arms felt as though they had sandbags lashed to them, and his legs dangling underwater below the ring made him the least seaworthy vessel he could imagine. He stopped paddling and, with great effort, shifted his position so that his torso lay atop the ring, as though he were on a boogie board. That way, his legs were free to kick behind him.

Through salt-dried eyes, Finn noted the spot where the cliffs fell away into a little bay. He'd never seen it before, but he was willing to gamble that there was a beach within it, or someplace shallow where he could get out of the water. He looked at the coast south of his position (he could only go with the current) and saw no other option. It had to be the little bay. He started kicking and paddling toward it. If the exercise was insufficient to reverse the hypothermia, at least he felt that it was impeding its progress. The effort got his circulation going. The sun was rising and the world was getting warmer.

He'd been paddling for ten minutes when he felt his leg brush against something. His heart skipped a beat. He peered into the water immediately around him until his eyes adjusted to see through its surface. He saw giant, dark leaves swaying in the dark green water a few feet below and realized he'd swum into a kelp forest.

He started to paddle again, putting everything he could into it, trying to stay focused on the little bay between the cliffs ahead and not what lay beneath him. A few feet in front of him, a school of inch-long silverside fish leaped as one from the water and stippled its surface. Then he heard another splash to his left. He turned to look, but whatever had broken through was already gone, leaving behind a little patch of foam. He redoubled his efforts.

The island was closer now, its crumbling palisades looming high. He was almost at the edge of the long shadows they cast as the sun rose beyond them. He fluttered his legs hard and kept paddling.

When he was no more than a hundred feet from the mouth of the little bay, a large gray fin broke through the surface some twenty feet to his right. Finn felt a rush of nausea. His vision tunneled and he felt the urge to urinate. The fin slowly cruised around him. Then he heard another splash to his right. He turned his head and saw another fin. Sharks corralling him. His heart beat like a kettledrum.

He closed his eyes, took a deep breath, then opened them again and looked for the closest access to shore. He was just outside the mouth of the bay, but the rocks at either side were too sheer to scale. His only real hope was the little beach he saw at the far end of the bay. He had trouble gauging how far it was. Was it two hundred feet or less than that? He kicked and paddled and ignored his thumping heart. He started humming "Swing Low, Sweet Chariot."

Something dense collided into his legs.

"God help me," he said for the first time in his life. He urinated involuntarily. When he tried to look back, he upset his balance and fell off the life preserver. His head sank underwater. Too frightened to shut his eyes, he saw prowling through the shifting bluish green light a shark the size of a car. He had no idea how big the one he couldn't see was. He scrambled back onto the ring and gasped for air. *Keep going*, he told himself. He was in the bay now. The beach was right there. He could hear little waves lapping at its shore.

The water felt warmer, which meant it was getting shallower. He was so close. He looked left and right to see where the fins were. The one on the left was still there, but the one on the right, the bigger one, had disappeared.

Instinctively, he turned and saw the fin directly behind him. The shark was tracking him directly now. Coming in to strike.

Nick Finn stopped swimming and praying. There was nothing more he could do. He understood that now. Somewhere deep in the stillest part of his brain, beneath its roiling surface of emotion and beneath the complicated machinery of language that occupied its middle depths, Finn realized that he was powerless over whatever happened next. He knew it to be an irrefutable truth, and accepting it gave him a focus he had never before known. He felt sharp, calm, and alert. He saw the approaching fin, the mouth of the bay, the rock faces framing it, and the lightening sky doming it all with acute clarity. He floated in the water, facing out to sea, and waited for the mouth of the shark.

The thick, gray-black fin drew near, water streaming off its broad dorsal surface. Finn noticed that the tip of the tail fin was several feet beyond the dorsal, and from sheer curiosity he tried to calculate the overall length of the shark. He figured it was no less than twelve feet long. He saw its long, gray snout. The shark came within touching distance, then changed course a point, tilted slightly, and glided slowly past to Finn's left, just below the surface of the water. The predator seemed as large as his Tacoma. Finn saw the jagged teeth the size of keys in its giant, slightly open mouth, its white underside, its black, fathomless eye watching him. He saw its fluttering gills, its pectoral fin, the slow, lazy undulations of its tail fin. He reached out and ran his fingertips over the shark's sandpaperlike skin. With a quiet splash, the shark turned and dived into deeper water, and its fins disappeared from the surface. He looked to his left—the other fin had also gone. The last ripples petered out and the water's surface was smooth again. Finn climbed back onto his life preserver.

The first time his foot hit the sand, he thought it was the other shark. Then his other foot hit the ground and he knew he was in the shallows. He half walked, half swam the rest of the way. He crawled over the cold, wet sand until he reached the dry stuff beyond the reach of the tide. He collapsed onto his back, shivering uncontrollably, not from fear but from exhaustion and cold. He heard the sounds of water lapping at the shore and of his teeth chattering. Soon after, the sun rose clear of the hilltops and blanketed the bay in its warmth. He breathed deeply and long and, before letting himself pass out, resolved never to forget the truth he had grasped in that moment when he had stopped struggling and had turned to face the shark.

CHAPTER TWENTY-EIGHT

Finn opened his eyes. The sky had turned purple and red, and the sun was setting over the sea. He tried to sit up but a severe cramp in his gut made him collapse back onto the sand. The wounds in his arm and cheek smarted. His tongue had swollen so much, it felt like he had a rag stuffed in his mouth, and he had to breathe with his jaw wide open. He felt dizzy to the point of fainting. He closed his eyes and saw a kind of static on the back of his eyelids. His heartbeat was fast and shallow.

He heard a voice say "Drink."

It took him a moment to regain his focus, but when he did he saw a face with a long gray beard, blue eyes, and long gray hair. He tried to speak, but his throat was bone-dry.

"Drink," the man said again. He tilted a tattered plastic water bottle to Finn's lips.

Finn felt cool, fresh water on his tongue. It was the most exquisite thing he had ever tasted. He drank like a newborn calf at its mother's teat.

The man brushed away Finn's hand. "Drink slowly," he said.

Then he carefully put the empty bottle away in a small, threadbare backpack sitting on the sand next to Finn. He wore dirty yellow board shorts and an old frayed T-shirt. He slung the pack over his shoulder, then sat back on his heels, waiting.

Finn started to feel marginally better. The man put his hands under his arms and helped him to his feet. His legs felt wobbly. His body felt anemic. The man helped him up the beach. The sun-warmed sand beneath Finn's bare feet gave way to cooler earth, and soon they were walking through scrub. Sweat pearled on Finn's forehead. He felt like he was burning up, yet his teeth were chattering. Soon the soil underfoot gave way to rock, and Finn found himself being led up a precipitous goat track along the side of the cliff, the man still at his side, guiding him, one strong, thick-veined hand clasped to Finn's arm, standing between him and the void.

At the top of the track was a cave in the cliff face. By the entrance, Finn saw three fish that had been run through their gills hanging from a branch over a firepit, the rock wall behind it smoke-blackened. A grill was leaning up against the wall, a couple of pots sitting on the dirt next to it, a plastic deck chair next to that. Inside the cave was an old, filthy sleeping bag spread on the ground. Next to it was a pile of wood and a cluster of plastic bottles that looked like they'd washed up on the shore. All were full. The man grabbed one and handed it to Finn.

"Drink, but drink slowly," he said.

Finn lifted his trembling arm and drank. He wiped the sweat from his forehead. The old man walked back into the deepest part of the cave, where he pulled back a tarpaulin and revealed hundreds of books piled high, as well as all kinds of flotsam—Finn saw an old paraffin lamp, various clothes, a boat barbecue, a kayak paddle, piles of rope, a windsurfing wishbone, flip-flops, and an old boogie board with its plastic bottom peeling off. The man rummaged around until he found another sleeping bag.

He laid it down near the fireplace. "Rest," he said.

Finn didn't need to be asked twice. He collapsed onto the sleeping bag. It had the acrid smell of stale sweat, but he didn't care.

It was dark when he woke. The first thing he noticed was the smell of burning wood. He saw the man standing over the firepit, placing a pot on its hot coals. Finn lay back and watched the shadows play on the cave walls. He still felt weak and feverish.

After a few minutes, the man took the pot off the fire and set it on the ground. He dipped a mug into the pot and filled it with what turned out to be boiling water. Then he rummaged through his old backpack and pulled out a bunch of leaves. He broke these up in his hands, rolled them together, then put them in the mug.

He walked over and handed it to Finn. "Tree mallow," he said, "It'll help with the fever."

Finn propped himself up on an elbow and drank. It tasted bitter.

Then the old man handed Finn a handful of huckleberries. "You should eat," he said.

Finn put a berry into his mouth. It tasted sweet and delicious—the nicest huckleberry he'd ever eaten—and it must've shown on his face.

"Never had a wild huckleberry before?" said the man, but not in a way that expected an answer. He unhooked a whole, desiccated fish from the pole and handed it to Finn. "Here, try this."

Finn tore strips off with his fingers. It tasted of woodsmoke and brine. The more of it he ate, the hungrier he realized he was. Soon there was nothing left but fish bones.

The man took the carcass from him. "I use the bones for fish-hooks," he said, putting it away in an old plastic bag.

Finn wiped his hands on his salt-stiffened trousers. He felt stronger now. His mind was clearing. He looked at the old man by the firelight, taking stock of him. His weathered skin was covered in wrinkles so deep, it reminded Finn of a relief map of the ocean floor. He was barefoot, his feet covered in calluses, the nails as thick as oyster shells.

"You live here?" said Finn.

The man nodded.

"How long have you been here?" said Finn.

The man thought for a moment. "Since 1985," he said.

"Thirty years," said Finn. The old man gazed into the fire. A long silence ensued. Finally, to break it, Finn said, "My name's Finn."

The guy kept staring at the fire. He seemed not to care what Finn's name was. He didn't offer his own in return.

"You haven't asked how I got here to your beach," said Finn.

The man pointed at Finn's orange life ring leaning against the wall. "I watched you paddle in," he said. "You finished with it?"

Finn almost laughed. "Yes," he said.

"Something like that would be mighty useful out over the reef," said the old man.

"You can have it. It's yours." said Finn.

The man nodded.

More silence.

"You fish the reef?" said Finn eventually.

The man nodded.

"What about the sharks?" said Finn.

"I leave them alone."

Finn absorbed that. Then: "You ever go to the mainland?"

"Nope."

"Anyone ever visit you out here?"

The man shrugged. "Hikers and campers sometimes. Yachts anchor in the bay in summer. Rangers know me, let me be, mostly."

"You don't get lonely?" said Finn.

The man took his time before answering, giving the question some thought. "I miss my wife sometimes," he said finally.

"What's her name?"

"Dovie Mae. I called her Mae. She died."

"When?" said Finn.

"Nineteen eighty-five."

Finn looked down. "I have a wife. Her name's Ximena. I call her Mona."

The man nodded. "You miss her?"

"Yes," said Finn.

The old man was quiet for a while. Finally he said, "Then I'll help you return to her." He got up, fetched a pair of old, worn-thin flip-flops from his pile of things that looked as though he'd found them washed up on the beach, and dropped them next to Finn. "When the fever dies down and you feel better, I'll show you the trail to Two Harbors. It's about seven miles, so you'll need those. From there you can take the ferry back to the mainland. That's where you're from, I assume?"

"Yes. Thank you," said Finn, meaning it.

"Don't thank me, they're not mine. They washed up on the beach like everything else here. Except the books. I brought those with me."

It wasn't just the flip-flops Finn was thanking him for, but he let it go.

The old man stretched out on his sleeping bag. Finn lay down on his, on the opposite side, and watched the play of the shadows cast by the fire on the roof of the cave. His thoughts turned to Mona. He whispered her name. On the *Belle,* he'd tried to think back to when things had started to go bad for him. First, he'd traced it back to when he and Diego had found the floater off Two Harbors. Then he'd thought, no, it had started before that, when he'd shot Perez. Lying there in the cave now, Finn realized that he'd been wrong in both cases. His life had gone off the rails the moment he'd taken that first drink in Bonito's. Everything else, he was equipped to deal with. The consequences of shooting Perez had been difficult, but he'd had Mona on his side, and together they would've gotten through it. Finding Espendoza's shark-eaten body had unnerved him, but he'd seen worse things and put them behind him. He could deal with everything life threw at him except alcohol. He had no defense against that.

Neither had his father, he realized. Finn had hated the man for taking what he'd always considered the coward's way out. He'd spent years hating his father for teaching him that the world was cold and uncaring, then leaving him alone in it. But now it seemed to him that his father had been wrong about the world, that he'd made a mistake in leaving it. Finn understood that it was the drink that had taken his father at the end. Once the drink had him, he'd done what every alcoholic eventually does one way or another: he'd given it everything that mattered in his life. And then he'd given it his life.

That night in Bonito's, when the darkness had occupied his mind and he had taken that drink against it, Finn had started down the same road. He was no better than his father; he was just luckier. He was lucky because he was still alive (although only just, he had to admit). And he was lucky, he realized, because he was stone-cold sober. He hadn't taken a drink since the Day of the Dead. He was back among the living.

He thought about Mona, how much he loved her. He closed his eyes and pictured her in her straw hat down by the water's edge, laughing.

Just then, as though reading his thoughts, the old man broke the silence: "You're lucky. It's good to have a wife."

Finn's ordeal had weakened him physically far more than he realized. Even after two days, the old man didn't think he had recovered enough strength to walk the seven miles to Two Harbors, but Finn insisted on leaving. He wanted to get back to the mainland as soon as possible. He wanted to make sure Linda, Lucy, and Navidad were safe. He wanted to bring Diego's killers to justice. And he wanted to put things right with Mona.

The old man gave him a couple of handfuls of wild berries and

two bottles of water for his journey. He went through his pile of flotsam and fished out a faded canvas tote bag to carry the water bottles in, as well as an old Dodgers cap and a long-sleeve T-shirt. "Sun
can be fierce, even this time of year," he said. Finally, he gave Finn
a handful of cash. "For the ferry," he said. When Finn tried to pro-
test that it was way too much, the old man shrugged it off.

"It's not my money," he said. "It washed up on the beach, a wad
of it wrapped in plastic. Personally, I hate the stuff."

He nodded toward the trail leading north.

"Two Harbors's that way," he said.

Clambering up the steep goat track out of the bay, Finn found out
the hard way that the old man had been right about his diminished strength. Despite the food and water and the two days' rest,
his legs felt like they were running on empty, and he had to take
frequent breaks.

Finn turned things over in his mind while he walked. He'd expected Cutts to try something, he just hadn't expected it to come
through Linda. He should've known better, of course. She was a desperate parent. Someone had told him a story once of a woman who
had lifted a car clean off her child—how she'd developed superhu-
man strength to save her child. In Finn's mind, Linda was like that
woman. She'd go to any lengths, that was clear. She'd said herself
that she was prepared to do anything to save her daughter. Even if
"anything" meant leaving him for dead in the sea. What had happened between them at Escondido made no difference.

After an hour, the slope began to lessen and he emerged at the
bottom of a pasture that rose to the crest of the hill. He vaguely noticed a large boulder on the crest. He paused again, wiped away the
sweat streaming down his face with his sleeve, and looked west, out
over the Pacific. A gentle onshore breeze was blowing, cooling him.
Countless silver pinpricks glinted on the surface of the sea. He saw

the dark patch of the kelp bed he had swum through and the mouth of the little bay far below, the water there greener than that beyond its mouth. He saw the white triangles of several sailboats a few miles offshore. They looked immobile.

A loud snort behind him made him wheel around. A huge bull bison was sitting on top of the rise. Finn had been so focused on recovering his breath, he'd mistaken it for a boulder. The animal turned its massive, horned and bearded head toward him. Finn remembered the sharks down in the bay, and in the bison's eye he saw the same fixed, inscrutable look he'd seen in the sharks'.

He gave the animal time to see him. He let his shoulders drop. After a long minute, he started walking slowly up the hill, arcing around the colossal beast. The bison let out a loud snort. Flies buzzed around its eyes. Finn reached the crest and found the rest of the herd grazing on the green slope. Far beyond it, to the north, he saw a few buildings crammed into a narrow isthmus and a few yachts bobbing silently on their moorings on either side.

Two Harbors.

Three hours later, Finn walked into town. A handful of off-season day-trippers wandered about in Crocs and breezy tans. Normal people doing normal things. Finn, despite his worn flip-flops and weariness, felt returned to the land of the living.

He went into the public restroom at the ferry pier, cupped his hands under the faucet, and washed his face in the cool, soft water. Then he checked his appearance in the mirror. Sweat had bleached the underarms of his shirt. His eyes and skin were red, and he hadn't shaved since he'd left the hotel in Escondido. He splashed more water on his face and did his best to untangle his hair. Then he refilled his water bottles and made his way to the visitors-information board. The ferry was due in an hour. He bought a ticket from the kiosk and asked for a handful of quarters. He dropped four of them into the pay phone by the kiosk.

"Hello?" said Mona. Hearing her voice, his heart skipped a beat.

"It's me. Don't hang up," said Finn.

A long silence, but no click.

"Where are you?" she said.

"I'm on my way home. Listen, I know who killed Diego. It was a man called Diarmud Cutts, who owns a bar called Bonito's down in San Pedro. Him and his associate, Serpil. They killed Diego because we connected the floater we found out in the channel to the *Pacific Belle*. Cutts uses the *Belle* to smuggle narcotics in from Mexico. The skipper is a woman called Linda Blake. Cutts kidnapped her nine-year-old daughter, Lucy, and threatened to kill her if Linda doesn't do what he wants. Hello? Are you still there?"

After a moment's silence, Mona said, "The police have issued a warrant for your arrest."

Finn pulled the bill of his cap down lower. "Arrest for what?"

He knew the answer before she said it.

"For murdering Diego."

He heard a stifled sob.

"Mona, listen to me. I didn't do it. I swear to God, I didn't do it."

"For God's sake, Nick. I know you didn't kill Diego. But they have your gun. They say the ballistics match. Every cop in California is looking for you."

Finn's shoulders bunched up around his neck. He instinctively looked up from the pay phone.

"Cutts set me up. That night I drank, when you went to Sacramento? Cutts mugged me and took my gun. He killed Diego with it so that the cops would have a culprit. Listen to me, Mona: Cutts killed Diego and set me up because he wanted to get rid of us *both* after we found out about the *Pacific Belle*."

"Where are you?" she said.

"I'm coming back. I need help. Can you meet me?"

A beat. He waited for her reaction.

"Where?" she said.

His heart leaped. He told her he'd be at the San Pedro ferry wharf at 8:00 P.M.

CHAPTER TWENTY-NINE

Mona's RAV4 pulled up outside the ferry terminal. Finn got in. He had the bill of his cap down low. She pulled away from the curb and merged into northbound traffic on Harbor Boulevard.

Mona was also wearing a baseball cap. Hers was in USC Trojans' colors, cardinal red on gold. She'd been on the soccer team as an undergrad, including the year they'd won the national championship. On the sideboard in the living room of their house was a framed photo of Mona and her team holding up the trophy.

The sight of his estranged wife gladdened Finn's heart. She'd lost weight since he'd seen her last, but she still looked beautiful to him. She seemed much more composed than she'd sounded over the phone when he'd called her from Two Harbors.

She looked him over and said, "You look like a vagrant."

Finn rubbed a hand over his gaunt, bruised, scarred, and bearded face. He couldn't argue with that. He'd slept the last two nights in a cave. Before that, he'd spent the night adrift at sea. Before *that*, he'd stayed awake for forty-eight hours. He'd done some hard drinking in Mexico. He'd been badly beaten up. He'd killed four men and watched four others die. The last time he'd seen Mona was when she'd packed her bags and moved to her parents' house. It felt like a lifetime ago.

Finn started talking. He told Mona how, after she'd left, he'd gone back to the *Pacific Belle* and confronted Linda Blake; he told her how Linda had broken down and confessed that she'd been running narcotics for Cutts, who'd loaned her the money she needed to pay for her daughter's medical treatment, and who'd taken a share in the *Belle* as collateral, through his company Muir Holdings.

Finn told Mona how Cutts had lured her brother down to San Pedro, and how Serpil had killed Diego with Finn's stolen gun; he told her how Cutts had then kidnapped Lucy and threatened to kill her unless Finn helped Linda smuggle in another load of narcotics aboard the *Belle*.

He told her about Escondido and the Caballeros, about La Abuelita's fisherman cousin, and about the cocaine hidden in the fire extinguishers. He told her about Navidad. He told her about the storm and the *Bertholf* off San Clemente. He told her how Linda had betrayed him at Two Harbors, and how he'd washed up in the cove where the old man had saved him.

He told her the whole story except the part about what had happened between Linda and him on the Day of the Dead. What had happened in Escondido now seemed unreal to Finn, like a feverish dream that dissolves with wakefulness. He saw no reason to hurt Mona with an incident as hazy as that. He never wanted to hurt her again.

They were on the freeway now. They drove on awhile, Mona not saying anything, absorbing it all.

Finally, Finn said, "I wasn't sure you'd even talk to me, let alone help me."

"The detectives investigating Diego's murder came around asking questions about you," she said. She shook her head slowly. "You've got a lot of problems, Nick, but I know you didn't kill my brother. I know I didn't marry a murderer. I asked them what motive they thought you had, and when they said to stop Diego from testifying against you for shooting Perez, I knew for certain they had it all wrong. I told them Diego had given a sworn statement supporting your account of what happened on *La Catrina*. They said they had a different story. They said Diego was ready to write an affidavit stating that you were emotionally unstable when you shot Perez. They seemed pretty sure of themselves. They said that it fit with your history of violence. Then they told me that they had your gun and how the ballistics matched. For them, that sealed it, they said. I told them they weren't as smart as they thought they were if they believed that rubbish. They wanted to know if I knew where you were or where you might've gone. I said I had no idea."

She glanced at Finn.

"After the police left, I tried to call you, but you didn't answer. I knew you were still looking for Diego's killer and I knew you were suspicious about the *Pacific Belle*. So I went down to San Pedro and asked a fisherman there which one she was. The guy told me she'd put to sea. He couldn't tell me where she'd gone or when she was due back or how to get in touch with her. All he knew was that she'd left on the morning of the twenty-eighth—right when you disappeared. I took an educated guess and figured that you were aboard.

"Then I thought, Why would he go to sea without telling *me*? We were supposed to be working together. Something wasn't right. I had to figure out a way to get in touch with you without alerting the CBP or the port police or coast guard or anything like that. So I went to this private investigator we use sometimes to find people. He tried contacting the *Belle* through VHF radio, but you didn't answer. He said you were probably out of range. But I had a bad feeling. I asked him to keep the port under surveillance and let me know when the boat came back in. Then the big storm hit Baja—it was all over the news how all these boats were destroyed—and I got really worried. Finally, two days ago the PI called to say the *Pacific Belle* was back in port, but that you weren't aboard. When he told me that, I imagined the worst. That's why I was so emotional when you called."

Finn stared out the passenger-side window awhile, at the millions of city lights latticed across the darkness. Then he said, "What happened with your bill? In Sacramento?"

"The bill? The committee passed it without amendment. They're sending it to the floor to vote."

Finn felt a surge of pride. A lot of people talked about making a difference. Mona made it.

He went back to staring out the window. He was trying to formulate a way of telling Mona how much he loved her. How he wanted to come back to her a better man.

"Mona . . ."

"Nick, please, don't. I'm glad you're okay, but that doesn't mean I want to go back to before. I'm helping you because so long as the police believe you killed Diego, then they're not looking for the real killer. The person who really killed my brother is still free and the police aren't doing anything about it. *That's* the reason I came down to pick you up. Let's not make this about anything else."

It was a sound enough reason, thought Finn. Still, he knew the risks Mona was taking to help him—risking not just her career but her liberty. Her composure, her matter-of-factness, seemed put on. He could hardly blame her for holding back from him, after everything he'd put her through, bringing his drinking and its chaos into their marriage.

"I was just going to say, congratulations on getting the bill through the committee," he said. "That's really great."

"Thanks. You said on the phone you needed help."

Mona in strictly business mode. Smart and efficient.

When Finn had left for Escondido aboard the *Belle,* he'd vowed to kill Cutts and Serpil when he got back, then kill himself. But after his moment of clarity in the cove, he now imagined a different future. He no longer wanted to check out of this life the way his father had. He wanted to live. Preferably with Mona, but even without her, he wanted to live.

"I need a car," he said.

She waited for more.

"That's it?" she said.

"That's it."

"Are you serious? You think I'm going to sit on the sidelines? You think you're what, my *champion*? Do you even know me a little bit?"

"These are really dangerous people, Mona. I don't want you to get hurt."

"Oh, please. Have you seen your face? Anyway, look in the glove compartment."

He opened the compartment and found a semiautomatic. "Jesus. When did you get this?" he said.

"My father got it for me. After what happened to Diego."

Finn took it out. It was a Heckler & Koch P7—a powerful, reliable, and easily concealed 9-mm. He popped the clip.

"Here, I've got more of those," said Mona. She took a hand off the wheel and used it to rummage around in her handbag. The car veered alarmingly. She dumped three more magazines into his lap and straightened the wheel.

"We're a team, right?" she said.

"Seems that way," he said.

"So you take the gun. You know how to use it better than I do. Now, tell me your plan."

There were two parts to Finn's plan. First, he said, they had to find Linda, her daughter, and Navidad and take them somewhere safe, after which they had to persuade Linda to testify against Cutts. Second, Finn planned to find Cutts. This time, Cutts wouldn't be expecting him.

Mona asked if Finn knew a safe place, and he said no.

"I know a place," she said. "A safe house up in Inglewood, where we take women trying to escape their traffickers."

Finn said that to persuade Linda to testify, they would have to satisfy her that Lucy was safe from Cutts and Serpil. They'd also have to reassure her that she wouldn't do any prison time because that would separate her from Lucy and Navidad.

"That's going to be hard," said Mona.

"Why?"

"Because it's not true."

"All the crimes she did, she was coerced into doing. Cutts took her daughter."

"Only after you showed up. Before that, all those trips to Mexico? No one forced her to do that."

"But her daughter, the treatment costs . . ."

"There are plenty of people in this country without health care, Nick. They don't all become drug smugglers."

Headlights from a car in the opposite lane lit up Finn's face.

"You really fell for her, didn't you?" said Mona.

"I felt sorry for her daughter, that's all."

"Uh-huh. Look, I'm sorry for her daughter, too. But my brother is dead and Linda Blake is partly to blame. If the prosecution thinks her testimony will help them get first-degree-murder convictions against Cutts or Serpil or both, then yes, maybe she can cut a deal. But she did a bad thing and we shouldn't pretend she didn't. I'm surprised at you for not seeing that."

"I'll talk to her, make the legal situation clear."

"I'm the lawyer. It's better if she hears it from me," said Mona.

Finn didn't think so. "She doesn't know you," he said. "She trusts me."

"Maybe, but I don't trust her. She left you for dead in the sea, Nick."

Finn couldn't see a way out of it.

"You said she lives with her sister?" said Mona.

"In Palos Verdes," he said.

Mona took the next exit.

CHAPTER THIRTY

Finn pressed the doorbell by the front door of Linda's sister's house.

He stood next to Mona on the front step in the pool of light that a motion sensor had switched on when they'd walked up the path. Linda's white Tahoe was parked in the driveway in front of the garage door.

The front door opened. Linda Blake was wearing an olive hoodie over jeans and sneakers. She had her hair back. Her face went white when she saw Finn.

"Oh my god," she said. Tears welled in her eyes. She threw her arms around him and drew him in. Finn looked awkwardly at Mona over Linda's shoulder. Mona just looked bemused. Finn felt Linda's hand brush against the semiautomatic he'd tucked into the back of his trousers. After a long moment, she broke her embrace and stepped back. Finn and Mona followed her into a dimly lit hallway. Mona closed the front door behind her. In the hallway, Finn noted two doors on the right and one on the left, all of them closed. The end of the hallway opened into what looked like a living room.

"Who else is here?" he said.

Linda wiped her cheeks with the back of her hand. "Just Lucy. She's asleep."

"Where?"

Linda went to the second door on the right and slowly turned the door knob so as not to make any noise. Finn peered in. In the wedge of light that spilled through the open door, he saw a cabinet with dolls arrayed neatly on one shelf and picture books on the next; pinned to a corkboard on the wall were myriad artworks drawn by a child's hand; glow-in-the-dark stars were stuck across the ceiling; along the far wall was a child's bed; under a duvet with little pink ponies on it, Finn just made out a small form shifting in her sleep.

Linda put her finger to her lips and quietly closed the door.

"Come in here, I don't want to wake her," she said.

Mona and Finn followed Linda to the living room at the end of the corridor. Someone had decorated it in a Mexican theme—walls painted the color of yellow clay, tassels hanging from lampshades, an ocher textile draped over the back of the couch, folk masks hooked to the walls. On the coffee table, Finn noticed two dolls like the ones he'd seen on the reception counter in the hotel in Escondido, the ones Linda had called Catrinas: skeletons wearing dresses and headpieces, one pastel green and the other crimson, both holding bouquets. He looked up and saw Mona and Linda staring at each other. Mona still had her Trojans cap on.

"You must be Finn's wife," said Linda. "He talked about you on the boat."

Mona gave her the hard smile that Finn knew she reserved for people she didn't like. "This is your sister's house?" she said.

Linda nodded.

"Where is she now?"

"She should be home soon. Her shift ended a half hour ago."

Mona's gaze was unflinching.

Linda turned to Finn. "I'm so, so sorry for what I did," she said. "But you have to believe me, I didn't have a choice—Cutts said if I didn't knock you out, he'd kill Lucy."

Her hands were trembling. Finn was surprised to see a slight curl at the corner of Mona's mouth, almost a sneer.

"We'll talk about that later," he said. "Right now, we've got to get you and the girls out of here. We're taking you to a safe house where he'll never—"

"You had a choice," Mona cut in. "Don't say you didn't."

Linda turned to face her. "I'm sorry?"

"Nick told me the things you did. You had a choice. There are other ways to get medical treatment than paying for it with drug money."

"But the insurance company . . ."

"The sector I work in, I meet a lot of people without insurance. They work hard, they find ways. They don't become criminals."

Linda's eyes were dry now. She looked at Mona defiantly. "Are you a parent?" she said.

"No."

"So who are you to judge me?" she said.

"You killed my brother," said Mona.

The puff went out of Linda's chest. "That wasn't me. It was Cutts or Serpil."

"They might've pulled the trigger, but you set him up," said Mona.

Linda looked from Mona to Finn and back again. "I swear, I didn't know they were going to kill him. I was so *scared*. You have no idea what kind of monster Cutts is. You have no idea!"

Linda realized she'd raised her voice and glanced anxiously in the direction of Lucy's bedroom.

"Maybe we can talk about this later," said Finn, looking at Mona emphatically. "Right now, we need to round everybody up and get going."

Then it occurred to him. "Where's Navidad?"

Linda collapsed onto the sofa, covered her face, and started sobbing into her hands. Eventually, her tears subsided enough for her to take her hands away from her face and look up at Finn with tear-reddened eyes.

"Cutts took her," she said.

Finn's mind reeled. "What are you talking about?"

"He's a monster, Finn. I told you. You have no idea who you're dealing with."

She plucked a Kleenex from a box on the coffee table and waved a finger at Mona and Finn. "You want me to testify against him, right? That's why you're both here?"

"We want to bring my brother's killers to justice," said Mona.

"And that means you need me to testify, otherwise you've got nothing on Cutts. That's why you came to me first, rather than going directly after him. That's how smart he is. He doesn't leave any traces, anything that implicates him in his crimes. It's amazing that you're still alive, Finn. Believe me, he's ruthless."

"What happened to Navidad?" said Mona.

Linda reached for the pack of cigarettes on the coffee table. She held her husband's Zippo in two shaking hands.

"Is she dead?" said Finn.

"No. But she will be soon," said Linda. "You want me to testify, fine. But you should know what you're dealing with first. You might want to sit down, the both of you, to hear this."

"I'm fine standing," said Mona. Finn stayed standing, too.

Linda shrugged and dragged on her cigarette. "Suit yourselves," she said. She waved her cigarette at Finn. "The narcotics we picked up in Puerto Escondido? That's only part of it. Cutts and Serpil are running another racket. Something . . . unspeakable."

She paused and sucked so hard on her cigarette that Finn heard it burning.

"They steal people's organs and sell them."

Mona sat down after all, in the armchair on the other side of the coffee table, facing Linda. She stared at Linda for a moment. Then she calmly took her smartphone out of her handbag, started the voice-recorder app, and placed it on the coffee table in front of Linda.

"Start talking," she said.

Linda paused as though to collect her thoughts. Then she looked at Finn and said, "You know Cutts was in the IRA back in Ireland, right? He was an enforcer, he said. That's the word he used: *enforcer.* But then something went wrong, he didn't tell me what exactly, except that he upset the wrong people and had to disappear. He ended up in the French Foreign Legion, serving in Kosovo during the war there. That's where he met Serpil."

Linda took another long, slow drag on her cigarette.

"Either of you ever heard of the Yellow House?" she said.

Neither Mona nor Finn said anything.

"The Yellow House was a farmhouse out in the boondocks of Albania. A group of soldiers from the KLA, the Kosovo Liberation Army, took prisoners there. Serbs, mostly. Anyway, that's where Serpil comes into it. He's a doctor, from Turkey originally. I don't know what he was doing in Albania, but he was there. He started the racket with those KLA soldiers. Cutts got involved. Cutts's job was to find the buyers. As soon as he found a buyer—someone in Europe or the Middle East or Russia who needed an organ—Serpil would go to the Yellow House. They'd set up a crude little operating theater there. The KLA would bring him a prisoner. Serpil cut out the organ he needed, usually while the patient was still alive. The organ lasts longer that way. And then"—Linda put two fingers to her temple—"*bang!* The soldiers put a bullet through the poor man's head."

Finn and Mona stared at Linda in horror.

"Cutts told you all this?" said Mona.

Linda dragged on her cigarette and nodded.

"Why? Why would he trust you with all these details?"

Linda lit a fresh cigarette with the burning end of her last one. "To make it clear what would happen to my daughter if I didn't cooperate."

She held Mona's gaze; neither woman blinked. Finally, Linda turned her attention to the ashtray and continued her story.

"The war ended and the KLA ran out of prisoners. On top of that, word got out. The UN started investigating. They were onto Serpil. Cutts helped him get out of Albania, first to France and then here."

Mona shook her head. "There's no way Cutts could've qualified for a green card," she said. "A known member of the IRA? A designated terrorist group?"

"You think Cutts is his real name? He was a legionnaire, remember. You join the French Foreign Legion under any name you want. Afterwards, they give you a French passport in the name you joined up. Whoever you were before joining the Legion no longer exists."

All the time Linda was talking, a sort of hollowness had been spreading in Finn's stomach. He remembered the way Linda had reacted so violently to the play in Escondido on the Day of the Dead, when the shaman had been about to cut open Navidad on the altar. He saw the scene played out again now in his mind's eye. Now he understood the horror she'd felt. He remembered what the coroner had told him, about Espendoza's missing kidney. His eyes searched out Linda's.

"Espendoza . . ." he said.

She nodded. "Yes. Him, too."

Finn thought of the young men from Escondido who'd gone aboard *La Catrina* and had never been seen again. He looked at Mona. From the look of horror on her face, he surmised that she was thinking the same thing as he was.

"What happened to all the bodies? Where are they buried?" Mona asked.

"They're 'buried' at sea, if you want to call it that," said Linda, making air quotes around *buried*. Finn thought of all the shark sightings off Two Harbors. Linda turned her attention back to Finn and said, "You were supposed to be next. Cutts was furious that we lost you overboard. He wanted to carve you up bit by bit."

A chill ran through Finn. He was surprised at how calmly his wife was taking this. She had on her thinking face.

"Talk me through how they do it," said Mona.

"What do you mean?" said Linda.

"Talk me through the whole operation, step by step: where they get the organs, who removes them, and where. And how they get transplanted into patients. Surely you can't just walk into a hospital with a human organ in an icebox and say, 'Here, put this in me.' There have to be protocols."

"Sure, there are protocols, but these guys are professionals, remember. They did it all before in Kosovo. They've got it all worked out. The victims are sourced from Caballeros country down in Mexico. Mostly from rural towns in Sinaloa. Cutts pays the cartel a set fee per head. They're smuggled north, to Serpil's operating theater at Two Harbors. After they're . . . they're harvested, the organs are brought across to the mainland—"

"How?" said Mona.

Linda took a long while to answer. "Aboard the *Pacific Belle*."

Mona could barely disguise the expression of loathing on her face. Linda looked at the floor.

"Then what happens?" Mona asked.

"Once they're on the mainland, Cutts has a contact at the hospital who gets them into the system."

"Which hospital? What's the name of his contact?"

"A guy called Dr. Brian Wilson in the transplant program over at Pacific Memorial. He's the organ-procurement director there. He whitewashes the stolen organs. Then he makes sure that the organs are allocated to the people who paid for them."

"'Whitewashes them'—what does that mean?" said Mona.

"There's a centralized organ-allocation system. You need an organ, your name goes on the list, and you wait. When a consenting organ donor dies, his doctors flag his organs in the system. Dr. Wilson makes the stolen organs appear in the computer records like they came from legitimate sources. And he also makes sure the client gets it. Usually, when an organ becomes available, the computer uses a secret algorithm to determine who gets it. They keep the algorithm secret so that no one tries to game the system by pretending to be sicker or younger or whatever, stack the odds in their favor. But Dr. Wilson can game the system. He has access."

"Why would he?" said Mona.

"You know how much you can get for a healthy adult kidney these days?" said Linda. She sucked on her cigarette and answered her own question: "A half million dollars."

A black thought crossed Finn's mind. "So, Navidad . . ." he said.

Linda shook her head sadly. "Cutts says children are worth twice as much."

Finn had heard enough. "Where is he now?" he said.

"You want to hear the definition of irony?" said Linda acidly. "He's back in the hospital. Turns out he needed an organ himself. Both his kidneys failed. So last month, he stole one. Espendoza's, actually. That's why he killed your brother, Mona. When Diego and your brother came around asking questions about the *Belle,* he let slip that he and Finn had found Espendoza's body—*to the very person who'd killed him.* Cutts had a part of Espendoza right there inside of him. If Diego hadn't mentioned Espendoza to Cutts, he'd still be alive today, and Finn wouldn't be framed for murder."

She gave another bitter laugh before continuing. "That's why Cutts has lived as long as he has, he says—he *always* covers his tracks. Anyway, it looks like his luck might have finally failed him. His body started rejecting the kidney, which is why he's back in the hospital. I wouldn't feel too sorry for him, though—Pacific Memorial has the top-rated transplant team in the state. Cutts is getting the best care that money can buy. No doubt Dr. Wilson will find a fresh kidney for him any day now."

"Do you know where Navidad is?" Mona said.

Linda shook her head. "I have no idea." She started sobbing again.

Finn turned to Mona. "Can I talk to you for a minute?"

They walked into the corridor, out of Linda's hearing. Mona spoke first.

"You believe her?" she asked.

"It adds up," said Finn. "The coroner said Espendoza was missing a kidney. Cutts didn't look well that night Diego and I went to see him about Espendoza. We asked what was wrong, he said he'd just been operated on. He didn't like the questions we asked. And what about what La Abuelita told us, about all those young men from Escondido, who disappeared? And then, the sharks . . ."

"What sharks?"

Finn rubbed his face with his hand. Over Mona's shoulder, he watched Linda light yet another cigarette. At the rate she smoked, she'd need a lung transplant soon herself.

"A lot of sharks are being sighted off of Two Harbors. Way more than usual. All those bodies . . ." From the look of horror dawning on Mona's face, he saw that he didn't need to complete that sentence. "I think she's telling the truth," he said.

Mona studied his face for a moment. "She's in deep," she said. "She could spend the rest of her life in prison. Why's she telling us?"

"You see how frightened she is? She doesn't want to go to prison, be separated from her daughter. Her husband's dead, all she has is her daughter. It's all she talks about. She knows that we need her testimony. She's coming clean to us now, making it clear she's on our side."

Mona nodded. "Okay. So then we should call the police, tell them to pick up Cutts at the hospital."

Finn shook his head. "There's not enough time. You heard what she said about Navidad. You want the police to do anything, then you have to convince them first. You have to get Linda to repeat everything she just told us. Doesn't matter if you've recorded it—they'll need to hear it. And she's not going to do that until she feels Lucy is absolutely safe and she has a guarantee she's not going to prison. Navidad will be dead by then."

"So what do you want to do?"

"You take Linda and her daughter to the safe house. Get them settled in, make her understand that Cutts will never hurt her again. Then call the police from there. Meanwhile, I'll go to the hospital and find out where Cutts is keeping Navidad."

"What if he won't cooperate?" said Mona.

Finn's eyes went cold. "He will," he said.

CHAPTER THIRTY-ONE

Finn drove Linda's Tahoe to the hospital. Along with her car keys, he'd relieved her of her cell phone, with which he planned to stay in touch with Mona. He also wanted to make sure Linda didn't change her mind again and use it to call Cutts. He wanted to see the surprise on Cutts's face when he walked in.

Pulling into the parking lot, he recognized the hospital as the one he'd tailed Linda to, where her sister worked. The car started beeping at him when he backed into a parking space. He put the car into park and killed the ignition. In the center console he noticed an employee swipe card on a lanyard. It had the same logo on it as the big neon one over the hospital's entrance. He figured it was a spare card belonging to Linda's sister. Finn slipped the lanyard over his neck. It was ten at night. Visiting hours were long over. A swipe card around his neck would open doors, literally.

He walked into the hospital. Ansel Adams prints decorated the walls. Nurses and doctors in blue smocks and white coats walked purposefully along the linoleum floor. A huge oil painting of Ronald Reagan hung on a wall. It was one of those paintings where the eyes follow the viewer, and it left Finn feeling found out, as though the Gipper, with his wily smile, was looking right through his shirt at the semiautomatic pressing into the small of his back. He scanned the big hospital-directory board nearby until he found what he was looking for: nephrology, seventh floor.

In the elevator, he needed the swipe card to get access to the seventh floor. The doors opened onto a long corridor, the floor lined with the same linoleum as on the ground level. A waist-high roll of heavy-duty rubber matting covered the walls, protection against gurneys banging into them. No black-and-white landscapes of mountain peaks and lakes here. Instead, Finn walked past a poster with a caption that read: DIABETES—KNOW THE WARNING SIGNS.

A ward nurse was talking on the phone at her station by the elevator. Finn gave her a friendly smile and walked purposefully past her, like he knew where he was going. She nodded, glanced at the card around his neck, and continued her conversation. He walked down the corridor, glancing into each room he passed. Toward the end, he heard a pair of TV sportscasters calling a football game. The 49ers at Seattle. Something dark and thick and nameless mushroomed in his heart.

Cutts was lying on a hospital bed, above the sheets. The arms of his hospital gown were too short, and decades-old, coarsened tattoos snaked down from his shoulders to above his wrists. The top half of the bed was tilted up. The white hair on the back of his head was pressed flat against a pillow. Clear liquid dripped through a tube from a plastic bag on a stand, through a machine and into Cutts's left arm. There was an adjustable-height table on the other side of the bed with a tray and cell phone on it, a glass and a pitcher of water on the tray. Cutts was watching the football game, the TV attached high on the wall opposite the bed.

There was no one else in the room.

Finn shut the door behind him. He pointed the P7 at Cutts's head. It was a small room: a mere six feet separated the barrel of his gun from the space between Cutts's eyes. Finn put his fingers to his lips. He took a moment to let the blackness in his heart ebb and to enjoy the dumbfounded look on Cutts's ravaged face. Then he said, "Call for help and you're dead. Understand?"

Cutts nodded.

"Navidad. Where is she?" Finn said.

"Who?" Cutts looked genuinely surprised.

Finn couldn't believe it. The guy was playing games even now. He kept the gun pointed at Cutts's head while he moved around the bed to the IV stand.

"I got to hand it to you, Cutts, you're pragmatic. You're confronted with a problem, you don't dawdle, do you? You get the job done. Professional. I'm the same way myself. That's why I couldn't figure out why you stuck by Linda. An amateur like her, cracking under pressure, crying all the time? I mean, she almost brought you down once already, telling me about Diego."

Finn tilted his head to read the name of the drug in the bag hanging on the stand. " 'Zenapax.' Sounds serious. What's it for?"

"It's an immunosuppressant," said Cutts in a low voice. His face was very pale.

"Huh," said Finn, his tone conversational. "So anyway, that's what I asked myself: why is Cutts sticking with Linda? Then I get it: *he thinks she's the perfect cover.* She's a woman, a veteran, a widow, a mother. Everything a smuggler's not, basically. Even if the *Belle* does get intercepted, she's not going to raise any red flags. But maybe you also realize, after she tells me about Diego, she's unstable. She's not thinking clearly. So you decide you need to reassert control. Really get into her head, make it clear to her what her priorities are. And how do you do that?"

Cutts looked like he was about to speak, so Finn shook his head and said, "That was a rhetorical question, Cutts. I know damn well how you did it. You take her most precious thing. You kidnap her daughter."

With his spare hand, Finn started toying with the plastic tube that ran into the cannula in Cutts's arm. "An immunosuppressant. That's a drug that shuts down your immune system, right?"

Cutts nodded wearily. "What do you want, Finn?"

"Let me finish my story," said Finn. "We head south, we get you your narcotics. But Linda's mental state is fragile. She's on the brink. We get to Escondido, they're celebrating the Day of the Dead. She sees this kid being pretend-sacrificed in this folk play, and she comes apart, mentally. She 'rescues' the girl from the orphanage, ranting about how Aztecs sacrifice children—I mean, just outright crazy talk. I could see she was going out of her mind, but what could I do? It wasn't like we could take the kid back to Escondido."

Finn yanked the tube out of the cannula. Cutts gave a little cry. The machine started beeping. Finn found the volume knob and turned it all the way down.

"You noticed how everything beeps at you these days? Bugs the hell out of me."

Finn held up the end of the tube. Liquid dripped from it.

"Linda told me you took Navidad from her. She's somewhere safe now, her and her daughter, somewhere you'll never find them. No one knows I'm here. Serpil won't be coming through that door with a gun behind my back. It's just you and me, and, I suppose, a piece of Espendoza."

He poked the barrel of his gun into Cutts's side. Cutts arched his back in pain.

"Where's Navidad?" said Finn.

Cutts clenched his fist. Sweat filmed his forehead. "I'm telling you, I don't fucking know, Finn."

Finn jabbed him in the side again. Not particularly hard, but more than Cutts could stand. The Irishman's eyes bulged. He looked twenty years older. Spittle appeared at the corner of his mouth.

"Jesus Christ, Finn, if you're going to kill me with that thing, just shoot me and get it over with."

At exactly that moment, the 49ers scored a touchdown. The roar of the crowd blared from the TV. Finn grabbed the remote and turned it up. Then he leaned over Cutts and pointed the gun right between Cutts's eyes.

"Last week, you gave me a choice, then you counted down till I decided," said Finn. "Now it's your turn. Five . . ."

"Jesus Christ, Finn! I don't know where the girl is!"

"Four . . ."

"I never even laid eyes on her! Linda has her!"

"Three . . ."

"I swear to God, Finn!"

"Two . . ."

"Her daughter is sick! Lucy! She's right here in the hospital!"

"One . . ."

"Linda *bought* the child from the Caballeros because her own daughter needs a kidney!"

Finn's mind did a hand-brake turn and spun wild. "What are you talking about?" he said.

Cutts's breathing was short and shallow. "Just what I said. Linda's daughter is dying, renal failure, like me. She's here in the hospital, waiting for a transplant. That Mexican girl . . . what'd you call her?"

"Navidad."

"Navidad. *She's* the donor. Get it? Linda's been screening for her for months."

Finn bristled. He waved the gun at Cutts. "You better start making sense very soon, Cutts."

Cutts sat up and raised both hands defensively. "Just hear me out, okay? I'll tell you everything. Just take it easy with that thing."

Finn dropped his arm but kept the pistol in his hand.

Cutts settled back into the pillows.

"They diagnosed me with kidney disease just after the New Year," he said. "Both of them failing. They put me on the organ-donor list. Then they tell me I have to attend the support group here at the hospital.

"I walk in, sit down, and this woman starts staring at my tattoos. When it's her turn to talk, I find out she's not a patient: she's there for her little girl. The counselors tell us we should have faith and live in the day. But I know I'm going to die if I don't get an organ, lad. Linda knows it, too, about Lucy. The kid has less chance than me, even. It's depressing. I never go back.

"Then one night a few weeks later, Linda walks into my bar. She says she knows a way of getting us both donors, but she needs my help." Cutts laughed an ugly laugh. He had Finn's full attention now. "She says she knows a doctor living in France who can help us. Trouble is, she can't get him into the country because Homeland Security has him on a list. She thought maybe, with my IRA background, I could help."

"How could she have known you were in the IRA?" asked Finn.

Cutts pointed at the tattoos of the Kalashnikov and the Celtic knot on his arm. "You make a statement like that when you're young, you're still making it fifty years later."

"Linda tells me her plan," Cutts went on. "She says she knows where to get donors. She says her sister's a nurse here at the hospital, she can get the kidneys into the organ network and make sure they're allocated to us, as well as to whoever else is willing to pay."

At the mention of Linda's sister, Finn automatically reached for the security swipe card hanging around his neck. He took it off and put it in his pocket.

"The only thing she needs is someone to harvest them from the donors," Cutts continued. "I still have a few contacts from the old days. I call some people I know, Serpil arrives. We set him up on Catalina because we figured no one patrols the island—not you guys in the CBP and not the coast guard. Perez brings up the donors and the product in *La Catrina* and takes them to Serpil at Two Harbors. Serpil harvests what he needs. Then Linda brings the narcotics and the organs across, and dumps the bodies in the channel."

Finn's stomach churned.

"But the donors Perez is bringing up, they're unscreened. None of them are a match for Lucy. Turns out, the kid has a rare blood type. She can only have a kidney from another kid with that exact same blood type. Meanwhile, she's deteriorating fast. That's when her mother comes up with the malaria idea."

"Malaria idea?"

"Linda sets up a charity at an orphanage down there to screen kids for malaria. Testing their blood."

Finn's eyebrow twitched. He remembered Linda's visit to the orphanage. "You're making this up, Cutts. I just saw Lucy, asleep in her bed."

But even as he said it, the seed of doubt germinated in his mind. What had he seen, really? A shape under a duvet?

Cutts shrugged. "I'm telling you, lad, Linda's kid is right here in the hospital, in the children's ward on the fifth floor. Go see for yourself."

Finn took several hard, shallow breaths through his nose.

Mona.

With his spare hand, he pulled out Linda's cell and dialed Mona's number.

Straight to voice mail.

He raised his gun again at Cutts's head. "This is a bunch of bullshit, Cutts. You're trying to save yourself. You kidnapped Lucy and terrorized Linda into submission. I was there. I saw it myself."

"Pure fucking theater, lad, for an audience of one. Open your eyes. What we should've done, after you found Espendoza, we should've laid low and waited for things to die down. But that's not what Linda did. She had to put to sea. And she duped you into helping her."

"Why? Why would she do that?"

"The same week you found Espendoza, she got word from the orphanage that they'd found a compatible donor. Right age, right blood, everything. She said she couldn't afford to wait for things to die down. *Lucy* couldn't afford to wait. I pointed out that Perez was dead and *La Catrina* impounded, and she said she'd just have to go down herself on the *Belle*. I told her, you and Diego in the bar, you'd mentioned the *Pacific Belle* specifically. I said CBP Interceptors would be on the lookout for her. She said she'd just have to take extra precautions."

Cutts gave Finn a piercing look.

"It had taken her months to find that donor. Lucy had weeks to live. Linda knew she *had* to get through. You and Diego, you were a threat. So she waited for you outside the bar with a couple of fishermen friends of hers. It was Linda who took your gun and sent that text to Diego."

All the time Cutts was talking, Finn was holding a gun on him with one hand and frantically redialing Mona's number with the other.

"Who pulled the trigger?"

Cutts sniffed. "Linda," he said.

Finn wanted to throw something through the window.

"Why just Diego? Why not me, too?"

"She wanted insurance—someone to take the fall if she got busted. That's you, Finn. Her husband was a drunk, too, so she recognized it in you. She figured she could play you, and she was right. Did you even hear what her sister said to her on the phone that night? For all you know, she was giving her a recipe for cake. The whole thing was staged, lad. All that wailing around on the ground—all of it. The child was asleep at home, in her aunt's care, next to her fucking teddy bear, probably.

"Once Linda got the Mexican girl across the line, she didn't need you anymore. You stopped being insurance and became a liability. She decided to make you disappear the same way she'd made all the others disappear. Open your goddamn eyes."

In his mind's eye, Finn saw a dark vision. He saw Linda holding Navidad, stroking her hair. Almost as an afterthought, his voice soft, he said, "You killed Espendoza and stole his kidney."

Cutts shrugged wearily. "It's a cannibal world we've fashioned for ourselves, Finn. If you're not eating others, you're getting eaten.

For what it's worth, I bought his kidney, I didn't steal it. I paid him a small fortune. He wasn't supposed to die. Serpil stitched him up. But he's forgotten how to keep patients alive. The wound got infected. Espendoza died out there on the island, a few days after my operation."

Mona's phone kept going straight to voice mail. A terrible sense of dread took hold of Finn. *Stay calm*, he told himself. *Do what you have to do, one task at a time, and focus on that.* He stopped dialing, pulled out the handcuffs, and slapped one onto the old man's left wrist. He closed the other around one of the bars of the safety rail on the side of the bed. Then he pulled the IV stand closer to the bed, within Cutts's reach. But the old man just lay there, not bothering to reinsert the tube into his arm. An uncharacteristic expression had slipped onto his face: remorse. He looked at Finn, his eyes old, rheumy, contrite.

"You don't want your medicine?" said Finn.

Cutts shook his head. "I spent the eighties fighting the British army," he said, a tremor in his voice. "In the nineties, I saw things in Central Africa and in Kosovo that no one should ever see. I spent a decade running guns into Mexico. I've met some bad people in my time, Finn, but Linda Blake . . ." He turned away, his sentence unfinished.

"I'm tired of this world. I'm ready to go," he said to his reflection in the window.

CHAPTER THIRTY-TWO

Finn left Cutts's room feeling polluted to his very core. In the corridor, nothing seemed real. The linoleum floor, the fluorescent lights, and the posters encouraging people to "know the signs" felt sketchy, and if the walls and ceiling had suddenly disappeared to reveal a vast and hostile sky, he wouldn't have been surprised. He went to the nurses' station. It was empty. He glanced both ways down the corridor, then hurried around the counter and sat down in front of the computer. He toggled to the hospital's patient-management system, typed "Lucy Blake" into the search tab, then selected the "search by patient" filter.

A new window popped up.

Name: Blake, Lucy
Sex: F
DOB: 12/27/2005
Blood type: O-
Diagnosis summary: end-stage renal disease
Treatment: Kidney transplantation
Scheduled: 11:00, November 10

Just two days away.
Next to the word *donor*, Finn read: "dead, unrelated."

For a moment, all he saw were those two words. He refocused, then toggled to the staff directory and typed in "Rhonda Blake."

Rhonda Blake, RN
Transplantation Services
Transplantation Procurement Coordinator

The woman in the picture was the woman he'd seen wearing a nurse's uniform outside the house in Palos Verdes, strapping Lucy into the car. He typed "Brian Wilson," the name Linda had given him, into the staff directory. The message read: "This search has zero results. Try again?"

Finn breathed hard and fast through his nose and remembered his father's words: *The world doesn't care if you live or die.*

But that wasn't true, thought Finn.

He cared.

He cared about Mona.

He cared about Navidad.

Navidad had saved his life that night in Two Harbors. Time to return the favor. He made a mental note of Lucy's room number. In the elevator, he swiped Rhonda's card and he pressed the button for the fifth floor—pediatrics.

The children's ward was decorated in a nautical theme. The linoleum floor was an underwater-green-blue color covered with stylized sea creatures. Finn walked over a friendly-looking octopus, a dopey-looking turtle, and a shark with a surprisingly menacing smile. Desert islands with palm trees and treasure chests decorated the walls. Between two of them, someone had painted a cloud with a human face, his cheeks puffed like balloons, blowing a sailboat across the surface of the sea. A couple of nurses were busy talking to each other at their station.

"Visiting hours are over," said one in an irritated tone.

"I'm here to see my daughter, Lucy Blake? Room 517. She's being operated on day after tomorrow. I just want . . . I just want to sit with her for half an hour, if you don't mind."

The nurse's expression changed. Now she gave him the earnest half smile that people reserve for those facing tragic life circumstances.

"Of course, Mr. Blake. I'm sure Lucy will be happy to see you."

Like all the doors on the children's ward, Lucy's had been left open. The child lay in the bed, asleep. Finn went over to her. The room was softly lit. Her face was turned toward the window, through which could be seen the sky glow thrown up by the city's innumerable lights. Lucy's dirty-blond hair was fanned out on the pillow around her heart-shaped face.

A tall, white machine—taller than she was—stood by her bed. It had a screen at the top and a sort of control pad lined with dials and buttons. It looked like the square, primitive robots Finn had seen on TV as a boy. His eyes followed the tube snaking out of it and into Lucy's arm. He shook his head. *No goddamn justice in this world,* he thought.

Linda's phone rang, catching him off-guard. His heart leaped when he recognized Mona's number on the screen, the number he'd just called two dozen times.

"Thank god. I've been trying to reach you. Where are you? Are you all right?" he said.

Finn thought he heard someone snigger.

"You mean me, or your wife?" said Linda's voice.

Finn's throat constricted. "If you've hurt her . . ."

"Relax. She's alive."

"Let me talk to her."

"I'm afraid that's not possible."

"Why not."

"I dosed her with propofol."

Finn took a breath. "Where is she?"

Linda ignored his question. "I just called the hospital to see how Lucy is," she said. "Imagine my surprise when they told me her father was visiting! You're fond of her, aren't you, Finn?"

"You hurt Mona, Linda, and I swear I'll kill you."

"Do you know much about the human kidney, Finn?" said Linda, carrying on as though he hadn't said a word. "It's a hardworking organ that does several things at once. It filters all the waste from our blood. It absorbs glucose and amino acids, and it produces hormones. It's a crucial organ, which is why nature gives us two of them. If they both fail, you die."

Lucy turned her head in her sleep and made a soft, plaintive sound.

"Both Lucy's kidneys are failing," said Linda. "She was born with polycystic kidney disease. You ever heard of that? It means she has to have regular dialysis just to stay alive. But six weeks ago her fistula got infected, Finn. She almost died. They can't use it anymore. Now they have to perform the dialysis through a catheter. Lucy can't live like that, Finn. Look at her. She's just a child. She needs a new kidney. A healthy one."

"Where is Mona?"

"Approximately six thousand Americans die a year waiting for a suitable donor. For someone like Lucy, with type O-negative blood, the chances are . . . You know what the doctor told me when I asked her what Lucy's chances were? She said it would be like winning the lottery. You ever met anyone who's won the lottery, Finn?"

Finn said nothing.

"Neither have I," said the voice on the phone. "She's beautiful, don't you think?"

Finn glanced at the child. He saw in her face her mother's arched eyebrows and full lips. There was no denying it: she *was* beautiful.

"The worldwide shortage of suitable organs creates a market," said

Linda. "In Egypt, people sell their kidneys on the Internet. In
Kosovo . . . well, I already told you about that. In Iran, the organ
trade is legal. There's no waiting list in Iran. The Chinese harvest
theirs from their executed prisoners. The Chinese executed almost
two thousand people last year. That would've made up almost a third
of the supply shortage here, if there weren't so many Chinese who
needed organs themselves. Why should it be any different here? Lucy
needs a kidney, but there's no market in America, even though we're
supposed to be the home of the free market. So you see, I *had* to
steal it, Finn. You understand? I had no choice.

"I've been thinking about how markets work," she went on. "I've
given it a lot of thought. You've heard those guys on CNBC say
how the market determines the price of a commodity, right? So
let's say you need a commodity like a child-size kidney, blood
type O-negative. You'd think something rare like that would be
expensive. It turns out in Mexico, it's just five thousand dollars.
And apparently in Egypt, they're even cheaper. Other places, too.
Bangladesh, Africa . . . It's funny how the market decides things
like that. What people are worth according to where they're born."

She hesitated for a moment, then said, "But *funny* isn't quite the
right word, is it?"

"If you hurt Mona . . ."

"Have you ever thought about how our lives are determined by
the smallest things, Finn? Look at Lucy. If her father and I hadn't
both been carrying the same gene, she'd be a healthy little girl. And
if she had any other kind of blood type, then I could've given her a
kidney myself, and maybe she'd be in school right now, instead of
dying in a hospital bed."

Finn heard something that sounded almost like a sob.

"Anyway, what are the odds of you and Diego stumbling across
Espendoza's body like that? In all the vast sea, you happen to drift
into the exact tiny patch where the sharks were feeding on Espendoza. I mean, what are the odds?"

Finn's throat constricted. "Tell that to the jury," he said.

"Oh, Finn, please. Don't be naïve. They have the murder weapon and it belongs to you, not me. I'm just a widow with a sick child. Who do you think they're going to believe?"

He thought of the confession that Mona had recorded on her phone.

The same phone Linda was calling him from now.

"Listen, Linda. I understand why you did what you did. Any parent would've done the same. No one can blame you. But Mona can't help you. Hurting Mona can't help you. So what we need to do is, we need to come to an arrangement."

There was a pause on the line.

"What are you proposing? A deal?"

"That's right. A deal."

"What could you possibly have that I want?"

Finn looked down at the sleeping child. "Give me Mona and I won't harm Lucy."

Linda laughed. "You're not going to hurt Lucy, Finn, and you know it. Not even to save your wife. You don't have what it takes for that kind of . . . that kind of ruthless action. You have scruples, Finn. I've seen them."

Lucy asleep looked like the most peaceful thing in the world and Finn knew that Linda was right.

"I'm sorry about your wife," said Linda. "It's obvious you really love her, and that's a rare thing. But I can't let her live—not now. We'll be in Two Harbors before dawn. I promise she won't feel a thing. I promise you that. And, of course, I won't breathe a word to her about us. Oh, Finn. I'm sorry it had to end this way. But we'll always have Escondido."

Murderous rage surged through him. "You even touch Mona, I'll hunt you down to the end of the earth and kill you. You understand?"

"I'm so glad we had this little chat, Finn," said Linda. "They should be arriving any minute now."

"Who?"

"When the nurse told me that my husband was visiting Lucy, I made a point of telling her that my husband died in 2010. She sounded as shocked as I did. She promised she'd call the police right away. That was ten minutes ago. I also called 911 myself, just to be sure. I told them I'd seen you in the hospital, that I'd recognized your photo from the TV—that border agent who the police were looking for, the one who shot his partner? They said you were very dangerous and that I shouldn't approach you under any circumstances. I'm going to heed their advice. Good-bye, Finn."

The phone clicked off.

Finn let out a roar from the darkest depth of him.

Lucy opened her eyes.

"Mommy?" she said.

CHAPTER THIRTY-THREE

There was pandemonium in the corridor. Nurses were shepherding bawling kids to the elevators. Finn went against the flow of the crowd, heading toward the fire escape, but when an LAPD SWAT team member in a balaclava and black body armor emerged from it, he turned a quick 180 and hustled back toward the elevators.

"You! Stop!" screamed the officer. Finn, his heart pumping, made like he hadn't heard. He saw the red dot of the guy's laser site tracing along the wall next to him. He kept walking. A kid to his left looked up at him. A nurse yanked the kid away.

Finn got to the end of the corridor, drew his gun, ducked to the right, and bolted toward the elevators. In his way was a male nurse standing by a child lying on a gurney, the nurse frantically pushing the elevator-call button. The nurse turned, saw Finn, and screamed; the elevator door opened; Finn shoved him aside, swiped his card, and hit the Close button. The elevator started speaking, telling him it was going down. Goddamn elevator, doors taking forever to close. The LAPD marksman poked his gun around the corner. The doors finally started closing. Just as the doors met, Finn saw the muzzle flash and heard the shot ring out, and the mirror on the back wall right behind his head exploded. Shards flew everywhere.

The elevator went down, skipped the fourth floor, and stopped at the third. He pressed the button for the ground floor, then stepped out into an empty third-floor corridor, breathing hard. "Going down," said the elevator.

The third floor had been cleared. He figured the SWAT guys had worked their way up the fire escape, clearing each floor as they reached it. The guy on the fifth floor would've radioed down, letting them know that Finn was in the elevator. They would've seen it stop on the third floor. Finn knew he had only seconds to find a way out before the gunmen came swarming in. He knew the adrenaline pumping through him was helping keep his mind keen and his choices stark; he had three simple steps to follow: first, look and determine his options; second, decide which one is best; third, do it.

There was no time to hesitate.

Finn scanned the corridor and saw a metal box with a handle recessed into the wall, the size of a laundry basket. He pulled back the tilt tray, peered in, and estimated that he would fit down the chute, but not through the tilt tray. He tucked the semiautomatic into his waistband, took hold of the tray with both hands, put one foot against the wall, and yanked hard. The panel came free with a tearing sound. He flung it to the ground and climbed into the chute, feet first. The aluminum sides creaked under the pressure, the noise echoing down the tube like an elevated train passing overhead. Finn wedged himself against the sides to stop from falling, then lowered himself down bit by bit. Sweat dripped from his chin and fell onto the pile of laundry he saw far, far below. He kept shuffling down, aiming to reach a height from which he could let himself fall onto the pile of bedding with a reasonable chance of not breaking anything. He must've been some twenty-five feet from the basket when his sweat-covered hands slipped off the aluminum.

The landing was far softer than he had expected. He lay there for a second, then jumped out of the trolley and scanned the room.

It was a vast laundry, the size of a hangar except with a low ceiling cluttered with ventilation ducts. It had been evacuated—Finn was alone. A long row of industrial washing machines occupied one wall. Half a dozen giant flatwork finishers took up the middle of the room. To the right were dozens of Dumpster-size laundry carts, piled with sheets and hospital wear. Beyond them was a long table with plastic-wrapping machines, where the laundry staff must've wrapped clean clothes before sending them back up into the wards. Finn spotted a set of double swing doors at the far end of the room.

He ran to the piles of clean clothes. The hospital scrubs were sorted by color and size and arranged in piles. He quickly found an XL set of blue scrubs and put them on over his own clothes. At the end of the table, he saw three cardboard boxes full of operating-room garb. He slipped a set of overshoes over his shoes, a scrub cap over his hair, and a mask over his mouth. He pulled the mask down halfway, so that it partially covered his face, making it look as though he'd just stepped out of an operating theater. Then he stuffed the gun under his blue shirt, calmed his breathing, and walked out of the laundry and up some service stairs to the ground floor.

Hospital workers were streaming out of the elevators and stairwells, headed to the green exit signs. Finn slipped in behind a couple of orderlies. But before he had even reached the lobby, he heard the sound of military boots running across the linoleum floors ahead. He darted into the nearest room. A fat man sat in a wheelchair, a drip bag on a hook next to him.

"Where the hell did everybody go?" he said, his unshaved jowls wobbling when he spoke.

Finn pulled down his face mask and glanced at the name on the hospital ID tag on the man's wrist.

"We haven't forgotten you, sir," he said. He unscrewed the tube from the cannula taped into the crook of the man's elbow. Then he released the brake on the chair.

"What's going on!" said the man.

Finn pushed him out of the room and into the corridor. "Fire drill," he said.

"I can walk, goddammit!"

"I have to push you, sir. Regulations."

"*Stop!*" screamed a SWAT team officer from the end of the corridor.

Finn stopped pushing and put up his hands. His heart thudded against the inside of his chest like a man buried alive trying to get out.

Three black-clad, body-armored men ran to him, rifles up. Two of them kept going past Finn and the old man toward the laundry. The third stopped, looked at Finn, and said through his balaclava: "You see anyone come out of the laundry?"

"No. We were just told to get out. I was taking Mr. Maxwell to the assembly point."

"You need to exit the building right now. I'll go with you."

Finn pushed Mr. Maxwell along the corridor, scrambling to keep up with the officer. The officer took them all the way to the exit. He held the door for Finn to push the wheelchair through.

"Thanks," said Finn.

Outside, Finn pushed the old man past the line of police cars and SWAT team vans lined up parallel to the hospital, their blue lights spinning, toward the crowd of hospital workers and patients clustered in the parking lot. He spun the chair around so that Mr. Maxwell could watch the action in the hospital.

"That wasn't a fire drill. And Maxwell's my first name, not my last name. Max Fishman. That's me," said the guy in the wheelchair.

The old man looked around and realized that he was talking to himself.

CHAPTER THIRTY-FOUR

Finn reached the San Pedro quay and got out of Linda's Tahoe. The stench of fish prevailed. The quay was deserted. Even the gulls were gone, to wherever San Pedro gulls went to roost at night. He saw the empty space where the *Pacific Belle* usually docked and felt the hollowness gaining in his chest.

He peered into the eel-black night. He thought, but wasn't sure, that he could just make out a set of green and red navigation lights on a boat heading out on the quiet sea, bearing toward Catalina. He figured the *Belle,* if that's who she was, was no more than a mile and a half away, two at most. He wasn't that far behind. All he needed was a boat.

Finn got back into the car and sped down the empty road to the San Pedro Yacht Club. He abandoned the car in front of the impassable boom gate to the parking lot and walked down to the docks, where he scanned the pleasure craft for something easy to steal.

He picked a thirtysomething-foot Bayliner, an older model, the name *Slip Aweigh* written in fading letters across her stern. Boats with pun names pointed to owners with cavalier attitudes. He glanced around the dock, saw that he was alone, and climbed aboard. He had a brief moment of compunction about stealing someone else's boat. Then he thought about Mona and Navidad and his compunction evaporated.

He walked across the deck to the cabin. The sliding door was locked but the locker next to it wasn't. He opened it and found a set of keys hanging there on a little hook. He tried the keys one by one until he found the one that unlocked the door to the cabin. He went through to the helm and tried the keys again until he found the ignition key. But when he turned it in the ignition, nothing happened. Someone had isolated the battery. Finn examined three switches on the dashboard. Their function labels had worn off long ago. He didn't know what they controlled, so he flipped all three and tried the ignition again. Bingo. The inboard fired up and the navigation lights went on. He waited for the fuel gauge to power up. She was more than three-quarters full. Bingo again. He had no idea how big her tank was, but he could tell from the size of the boat and the fact that she had berths and a galley that this particular model was a weekender, which meant she had the range to reach Catalina and back.

He went outside, stepped across a kayak fastened to the foredeck, and untied the boat. Then he went back into the cabin, helmed her out of the berth, and motored through the channel leading to the sea.

Finn pushed the *Slip Aweigh* as fast as she could go, but of course the Bayliner was strictly a pleasure craft, which meant she was slow, steady, safe—another man's idea of pleasure—and had nothing on the Interceptor's exhilarating speed. Terrifying images of Mona lying on an operating table, Serpil standing over her, intruded into his thoughts. He kept his hand on the throttle, the throttle pressed all the way down, and his eyes on the sea, as though by will alone he could urge the boat to travel faster. But the speedometer's needle stubbornly refused to go past twenty knots. Slowly, the adrenaline dissipated from his system. He began to notice the cold and searched the cabin for clothes. In a locker beneath a bench, he found a yellow sou'wester, along with a paddle for the kayak. He put on the jacket and laid the paddle on the bench, then went back to the helm. The Bayliner puttered along. Finn stared out the window at the glassy black sea and at the stars reflected in it, gleaming like teeth in the mouth of a shark. He remembered the sharks in the cove he'd drifted into on the south side of the island. He'd never been into that cove before, hadn't even known of its existence. He told himself he'd have to look it up on the chart sometime, see if someone had given it a name.

Finn tried to figure out what kind of sharks he had encountered. He knew that the family of sharks most often accused of being man-eaters had been designated "requiem sharks." Not that they had tried to eat him. On the contrary, they had done nothing more than swim peacefully alongside. "I leave them alone," the old man had said, when Finn had asked him how he dealt with them. Finn liked the restful sound of that word: *requiem*. He thought of the peaceful look on Lucy's face, asleep in her hospital bed.

It was past midnight, the early hours of November 9. There wasn't much left of the moon. A month had passed since he had intercepted *La Catrina* here in the Devil's Triangle. The moon had been waning then, too. Out there in the darkness was the phantom with his wife aboard.

"Mona."

Saying her name out loud reassured him. He said it again. And then he looked up to the stars and prayed to God she was alive.

When he was done, he realized that it was the second time he had prayed in a week. In fact, it was the second time he had prayed in his entire life. He wondered if it was habit-forming.

He set Mona's Heckler & Koch P7 on the dash above the wheel, where it glinted in the starlight. It took some of the piety out of his prayer, he thought. The stars and sea and darkness didn't seem so sacred anymore. He asked himself, if he got to Two Harbors and Mona was alive, would he still spare Linda? What about Serpil?

He didn't need to ask himself what he would do if Mona was already dead. That wasn't an unanswered question.

Conscious that he couldn't make the *Slip Aweigh* go any faster, Finn set the helm on autopilot and went out on deck. Sunk deep in the part of his mind that made sense of the world taxonomically—that found its bearings by classifying the smells and sights and sounds surrounding him—the smell of the water along a shore was indexed as sharp and sulfurous. Ebbing tides exposed tiny creatures that lived in the muddy shallows to ever-hungry gulls and waders. Waves tossed seaweed ashore and left great clumps of it there to die. Plankton clung to rocks in layer upon layer and decomposed. Finn associated the shore with decay.

But out here on the open water, where the ocean's shallows moved in endless motion over its ever-darkening depths and the air slipping over them eddied and curled in on itself in constant self-renewal, wind and water integrated in an uninterrupted cycle as old as the ocean itself, their dual rhythms broken by no inert, jagged shore. Finn knew he was in a place where, with nowhere for decay to cling to, life appeared and disappeared abruptly: a sea lion's whiskered head popped up, peered about, then disappeared without a trace; a whale fluked and then was gone; a rustle appeared suddenly on the water's surface when a school of fish rose, and then evaporated; a fin sliced through the water before submerging. The air moving across all this shoreless water was charged with a quality Finn classified as the opposite of decay; as buoyant, palliative, and vivifying, and he sucked it in now deep into his body, one big breath after another, remembering the pleasure of being alone on a boat in the middle of a gentle, night-veiled sea.

And that was when he knew what he would do in Two Harbors.

The island's black mass blocked out the stars closest to the horizon. Finn had blacked out the boat. The only illumination aboard was the small blue glow of the little light above the ignition, the only sound the low throb of the sound-insulated inboard engine and the occasional splash of water displaced by the bow.

None of the few boats moored in the harbor had its lights on. The only light he saw was on the pole atop the kiosk at the end of the jetty, where he'd bought his ferry ticket. He didn't see too many lights in the village beyond the bay, either. It felt like a ghost town.

Finn motored in slowly, keeping the engine revs down. As soon as he saw the *Pacific Belle*—even at a distance, he immediately recognized her stern in the starlight—he steered for the nearest mooring and cut the motor, letting the boat drift onto the buoy. He scooped it up with the gaff and made fast the boat, working as quietly as possible.

Linda had anchored beyond the last row of moorings, in the deeper water, no more than a couple of hundred feet from the *Slip Aweigh*. Finn watched steadily for two minutes but didn't see any movement on deck. Then he looked to shore and saw movement on the dark beach. He heard the whine of a small outboard.

Back on the *Belle,* someone switched on a light. The door to the wheelhouse opened, and silhouetted against the light spilling from it stood the figure of a woman. The whining got louder. A small Zodiac approached through the moorings, the starlight revealing its thin wake, hoary white against the oil-dark water. The boat arced around to the *Belle*'s stern. The figure at the tiller—Finn figured it had to be Serpil—put it into Neutral and the outboard's whine faded to a coughing murmur; there was movement at the *Pacific Belle*'s stern; he saw the outlines of two women lowering a third down into the Zodiac. One of the figures got into the dinghy, and one went back into the *Belle*'s cabin, only to return a moment later leading a child by the hand. She shepherded the child into the Zodiac, then got in herself. The outboard kicked into gear again, working hard with the extra weight of the passengers, and the inflatable boat slowly headed back to shore.

Working quickly and quietly, Finn unfastened the kayak from the foredeck. He carried it to the stern, slipped it soundlessly into the water, then climbed down the stern ladder with the paddle in one hand. His jacket sagged with the weight of the P7 and the extra clips in its pocket.

He settled into the molded plastic seat, breathed deeply, pushed away from the boat, and made for shore.

CHAPTER THIRTY-FIVE

Finn pulled hard through the moored boats. The Zodiac landed on the beach and killed her outboard, and suddenly Finn's paddling was exposed and sounded incredibly loud. He held the paddle clear of the water and let himself glide ahead on the momentum he already had.

He saw silhouettes getting out of the boat. The sound of pebbles crunching beneath their feet carried across the bay. One figure hauled the Zodiac a little way up the beach. Linda's voice drifted across the water, asking someone to help her with "the woman." Finn saw two figures drag a third up the beach and disappear into a stand of palm trees. A fourth figure walked behind them, holding a child by the hand. He heard an automobile engine turn over and saw a set of headlights come on. Finn started paddling hard for the beach. He kept his eyes on the car's red brake lights, tracking it as it headed north, up a hill through the darkness. It wasn't difficult—it was the only car on what he knew was the only road. By the time Finn had reached the shore, the car had reached its destination—he saw the lights stop moving and then go out at a spot high on the hill overlooking the bay. He watched until he saw a rectangle of light appear, then disappear—a door opening and closing.

Finn beached the kayak, found the road, and started hiking fast toward the house on the hill.

The road was paved only through the village. Once he'd passed the last of the bungalows, the bitumen gave way to packed dirt. He hiked on. It was so quiet, every rustle from the surrounding brush made him turn his head. Once an animal, either a small fox or a large squirrel, scurried across the road ahead, making him reach for his gun. He took a deep breath and carried on.

After a steep, twenty-minute hike through the darkness, he came to a gate. He climbed over and followed two wheel ruts through a field. A loud and abrupt snort from his right startled him. This time he whipped out his gun, his heart in his throat. He squinted until he could make out a herd of bison standing on the side of the hill. He heard one swish its tail. He kept his gun in his hand and kept walking up the hill.

Five minutes later, he reached the house. His eyes, now well adjusted to the starlit night, made out a single-story, ranch-style structure standing on its own on the side of the hill facing southeast. He saw soft yellow light slipping through the cracks of the drawn curtains and shadows moving within. The ground beneath the house was sloped, and its front section was propped up on stilts. Three steps led to a small stoop in front of the door. A Cherokee was parked off to one side. It was cold out, and Finn heard the Jeep's exhaust manifold still ticking.

He walked past the Cherokee and around to the back of the house, holding the gun in both hands, a finger on the trigger. Behind the house, he saw a large plastic rainwater tank, the pipe that connected it to the roof bisecting the starry sky. Light spilled out a curtainless window set in the back door. Finn sidled up to it.

He held up the gun, took a deep breath, and glanced through the corner of the window into what turned out to be the kitchen. He saw Navidad sitting on a high-backed wooden chair at a wooden table in the center of the room, eating cookies off a plate. She had on the gray sweater that Linda had given her. A glass of milk stood by her hand. Her last meal, figured Finn, feeling sick in his stomach. There was a sink on one side of the room, a cooker with a kettle on it on the other, a thin plume of steam rising from the kettle's spout. Through another door at the back of the kitchen, he saw what he figured was the living room, and in that room he saw another door next to a curtained window, which he figured was the front door, the one that opened onto the stoop he had seen out front. He didn't see Mona, and he didn't see Linda or Serpil or Rhonda Blake, assuming she was the other woman, but he saw shadows moving against the living-room curtains. He took his left hand off the gun and, with the fleshy part of his fingers rather than his nails, gently tapped on the glass. Navidad looked up and met his gaze. He put his index finger to his lips. She nodded. He lowered his hand and tried the handle—the door wasn't locked. He turned it slowly.

The moment Finn stepped into the kitchen, the kettle on the cooker started to whistle. A fraction of a second later, Serpil walked in from the living room. He was wearing hospital scrubs with bloodstains on them. He stopped dead and looked directly at Finn, mouth open, eyes wide, astonished. They stood ten feet apart, staring at each other for a fraction of a second. Serpil started to raise his hands. One part of Finn's brain noted that he was unarmed. But still he centered his weapon squarely at Serpil's chest and fired.

Twice.

The sound of the shots in the confined space was shocking, the force of the impact at such short range more shocking still. The two shots lifted Serpil off his feet and sent him flying back into the front room, almost to the front door, before he crashed onto his back and a dark patch began to bloom from the center of his blue smock. In the living room, a woman screamed. Finn hustled past Navidad, who hadn't made a sound, and into the main room. He saw a lamp on a sideboard, a couch next to it, a coffee table in front of the couch. He saw a woman he assumed was Rhonda Blake furiously trying to open the front door. He put a bead on her and was about to tell her to stop when he heard a sound at the far end of the room. He swung his gun in that direction in time to see Linda pointing a gun at him. They both fired at the same time. They both missed their targets. Linda stepped back into the room behind her and slammed the door. Finn emptied his clip into it, splintering the wood. Then he took cover in the kitchen and slid a fresh clip into the P7. He looked up into the living room and saw the front door swing open. He heard the fading steps of Rhonda Blake running away. The kettle behind him was whistling furiously, rattling in its fury. The sulfurous smell of burned powder stung his nostrils. He waited.

He didn't have to wait long—a battery of shots exploded through the door behind which Linda had disappeared, splinters flying everywhere, and Finn watched the slugs blast the plaster off the living-room wall closest to him. One slug caught the lamp and the room went dark. His ears were ringing when the shooting stopped. He glanced back over his shoulder into the kitchen. Navidad had dived under the table. He pointed at the back door, waving vigorously for her to get out. She had her fingers in her ears and her eyes shut tight. He shouted at her in a hoarse whisper. She couldn't hear him. Finn dashed over to the cooker and lifted the kettle off the hotplate. The whistling stopped. He rushed back to the doorframe.

He heard Linda shouting, "I have Mona here! I have your wife!"

Finn said nothing.

"I know you're there, Finn," said Linda through the splintered door, "I know you're not dead. I heard you take the kettle off the stove."

"Fuck," said Finn under his breath.

He heard Navidad whimpering beneath the table. He turned to her, smiled, and put his fingers to his lips again. Then he pointed to the door. She stifled her sobs and shook her head. Stubborn kid.

"I'll shoot her, Finn," said Linda, shouting. "I swear to God I'll put a bullet in her head right now. Why wouldn't I? There's nothing stopping me."

"You touch her and I'll kill you," Finn shouted back.

"You'll kill me anyway, Finn. We both know that," said Linda.

"I swear to God, you let her go, I won't hurt you. I know why you did what you did, Linda. I understand. Who wouldn't do anything to save their child?"

A moment of silence made him think he might've convinced her. But then Linda said, "We're wasting time. Make up your mind."

"How do I know she's not dead already?"

A moment passed. Finn stuck his head around the corner. The far door started to open, bright white light spilling out. He put a bead on the spot where he expected Linda's head to be.

Instead, he saw Mona. She was naked. Her head drooped to one side and her arms and legs hung limply. He couldn't tell whether her eyes were open or closed. Linda had an arm under her breasts, holding her up. In her other hand, she held a gun to Mona's temple.

He tried, but he couldn't get a clear line on Linda, not at this distance with both women backlit like that, making it hard to distinguish one from the other.

"What've you done to her? Where the hell are her clothes?"

"The doctor was prepping her for surgery," said Linda. "You got here just in time, Finn. He'd already found a buyer and was all set to operate. You've saved her life."

Finn kept his gun pointed at Mona's head. Linda's was directly behind it. If only Mona would wake up, tilt her head a few inches to the right. He stepped carefully into the room, holding his gun up with both hands. The floorboard creaked beneath him.

"It's over, Linda," he said. "Serpil's dead. So is Cutts. Rhonda's gone. There's no one left."

"You know I don't give a damn about them, Finn. Cutts got his kidney. Serpil was in it for the money. I don't give a damn about money."

"You don't want to die, Linda. Think of your daughter. Think of Lucy."

Linda gave a bitter laugh. "You think I think about anything else? Lucy's *all* I think about, Finn. She's all I have."

"So put down your gun. For her."

He inched forward. Linda and Mona were framed in the door, light spilling out from behind them.

"You think this is setting a good example for her?" he said.

"That's funny. You're hilarious, Finn. Why don't you come over here, tell me some more jokes."

Finn took one agonizing step closer. "It's over, Linda. Can't you see? What can you possibly get out of this?"

"Navidad."

His throat constricted. "Not going to happen," he said.

"Navidad for your wife. It's up to you. You choose."

Something cold and black snared Finn's mind. The skin around his eye twitched and he had to make a willful effort to think straight and to keep his voice even. He kept inching slowly toward the two women.

"She's no good to you now, Linda. The doctor's dead. Who'll operate?"

"Finding the doctor's not the problem—the problem is finding the donor. It took me months to find that girl, Finn. And Lucy doesn't have any more time. You can always find another doctor if you have enough money. But Navidad is rare. I found her. She's mine. Give her back."

"There's no way that's happening, Linda. Forget it."

A beat. He moved a half a foot closer.

"Then say good-bye to your wife."

Another beat.

"I don't believe you'd let Lucy die, Finn. I saw you with her from the very start. You risked everything for her, going to Escondido. You're a *good* man."

Her words hit a nerve. Finn wasn't so sure he'd done it for Lucy. Maybe he'd done it for his own reasons; maybe he'd done it to get Diego his pipes and drums and goddamn honor guard; maybe he'd done it to prove to Mona that she could count on him to do the right thing. But right now he had only one objective. He thought he saw Mona's head move slightly.

"You had good motives, Linda. I understand that. Anybody would. But you did a bad thing. And now it has to stop."

Every second felt excruciatingly long. He took another step. Linda shuffled back into the room a little.

"Come any closer and I swear I'll shoot her," she said, her voice trembling. She sounded vulnerable and desperate, like she had that night aboard the *Belle,* when Lucy had been "kidnapped." Except this time, Finn knew it was authentic.

He steeled himself. He'd closed the gap. He was now no more than fourteen feet away. But still he didn't shoot. He had to be dead sure of his shot, and right now he wasn't.

"I care about Lucy, too, Linda," he said, "Of course I do. Why do you think I agreed to go to Escondido? I *want* to help her. But not like this. I want to help her the *right* way."

"Don't be naïve. It's too late for the right way, Finn. You think I didn't try? It's not how the world works. Lucy will be dead in days without a new kidney.

"You see, you got nothing on me, Finn. One way or another, this is the end of the road. If Lucy dies, I have nothing left. She *has* to get that kidney. So give me Navidad, or I swear to fucking Christ I'll kill your wife and you, too, if I can. We can all go to hell together."

If Hell exists, it must look a little like this, thought Finn.

"Even if I did agree, how would it work? Who puts down their weapon first?" he said.

"You do."

He shook his head slowly. "I handed you my gun once already, Linda. You should've killed me when you had the chance."

"Believe me, I don't know why I didn't."

"You made the right decision."

She laughed.

"Put down the gun, Linda. This is your last chance," he said, his voice even. He pressed a little tighter on the trigger. He breathed steadily and deliberately, tried to relax the stiffness out of his arms.

This time, he definitely saw Mona move her head a little to the side. Linda seemed not to notice.

"Now you know what it feels like," said Linda.

"Like what feels like?"

"Having to choose between two lives. We all pretend we're good people, don't we? That we wish others well. But when you're forced to choose—we all choose the same thing. We look after our own. You're just like me, Finn. We're the same."

"You're wrong, Linda. I'm nothing like you."

"You'd choose Navidad over Mona?"

"No."

"There's no other option here."

"You're not getting it, Linda. I *have* to shoot you."

Linda's eyes opened wider. "You'd sacrifice your wife to save a child who means nothing to you, not even your kin?"

"Yes."

She tilted her head to one side, a little farther away from Mona's, and for the first time Finn saw a line of light dividing Mona's head from Linda's. He had his sights lined up on Linda's face. He saw her quizzical expression.

"Why?" she said.

"Because anything else is unforgivable."

He pulled the trigger. The sound of the shot was tremendous. Linda's head snapped back. A wet, red cloud appeared in the air behind her, a splattering of airborne blood lit up in the bright light spilling out of the room.

Linda fell back, pulling Mona back with her. Finn heard the thud of both women's bodies hitting the floor together.

And then it was very quiet.

He ran over and pushed the door all the way open. It wasn't a bedroom. It was an operating theater. The white light was coming from a giant lamp on an articulated arm over an operating bed. He saw LED lights flashing from the display of a life-support machine in one corner; he saw the glint of surgical instruments laid out on a stainless steel tray next to the bed. There was a refrigerator against the wall. The room smelled of gunpowder and antiseptic. He felt queasy. He dropped to his knees, pulled Mona into his arms, and held her tight. Over the top of her head, he looked at the red-black hole he'd put in Linda's forehead. He saw the puddle of blood spreading on the floor underneath her head. Her eyes were still open. He saw her black pupils distend and absorb the gold shards in her beautiful sad green irises.

He looked down at Mona. She was coming to. He put his left hand on her cheek and said her name.

She opened her eyes.

Finn picked her up and carried her out of Serpil's operating theater.

Navidad was still cowering under the kitchen table. Mona turned her head briefly toward the child, then rested it against Finn's chest.

EPILOGUE

Finn stood at attention by Diego's casket and waited for the priest to finish speaking. Like his peers standing shoulder to shoulder with him, he wore full-dress uniform: dark blue Ike jacket with a white braided cord piped through the left epaulette. The leather strap of his felt campaign hat was digging into his chin, the hat tilted forward just so. Everyone was ready for the flag-folding ceremony: the pipes and drums had performed their piece; the honor guard had draped the Colors over the coffin; the bugler was standing by. The Star-Spangled Banner, the flag of the California Republic, and the Customs Ensign fluttered above the standard-bearers' heads.

It was a crisp, cool fall morning, the rich-blue sky scattered with clean white clouds. Finn saw Mona standing by her parents in the front row of mourners just beyond the casket. Mona was wearing a black dress, her hair neatly set beneath a small black hat, her eyes dark and wet. Her father, Carlos, stood with his hands clasped in front and his shoulders thrown back; her mother, Maria, wore an old-fashioned black veil over her hair.

Hundreds of CBP and coast guardsmen and women from stations across the state and beyond had turned out for the internment at Oceanview Cemetery, and Finn could tell from Carlos's proud posture that he was moved by the numbers, though he was too much a man of his generation to say anything.

The priest started talking about the blanket of freedom and security that Diego had died defending. Finn's mind tuned out. This was the second funeral to which he had worn full-dress uniform in two days. There had been no flag blanketed over Lucy Blake's tiny casket. No one had spoken of the sacrifices she had made for the nation's freedom and security. No one had shown up except for Finn and Mona.

After Lucy's internment, Finn had spent a restless night dreaming of sharks. He had woken in a cold sweat before dawn and seen Mona lying peacefully beside him. He had stood by the kitchen window waiting for the coffee to percolate, watching the lightening sky and trying to think of a reason for Lucy's death. There was none. But he had learned one thing, at least: meaninglessness wasn't the same thing as indifference.

He looked at Mona standing proud and upright over her kid brother's casket, her tilted hat casting a shadow over her almond eyes and down to her lips, and love filled his heart. He thought about all the hard work she'd been doing looking for a home for Navidad. The adoption process in California was prohibitively complicated, but Finn felt confident that Navidad would be okay. She had Mona in her corner.

After they'd come back from Two Harbors, there had been a week of madness, and Mona had stayed with her parents while Finn had dealt with all the different law-enforcement agencies—ICE, the LAPD, the FBI—who'd staked a claim in the case. Rhonda Blake was in jail, awaiting trial. Cutts had died in his hospital bed. After the narcotics were discovered in the extinguisher, Edsall, Luna, Cheng had abandoned their wrongful-death suit and Ruiz and Petchenko had returned to Washington. Glenn had resigned in disgrace. All charges against Finn had been dropped. The media had set up camp outside Finn and Mona's condo, but Finn hadn't granted a single interview, and now they were gradually peeling away. They still ran their stories, but all they had to go on were press releases and the usual leaks.

Amid it all, Finn had snuck out to an AA meeting. He'd met a guy there, ex-MESF like him, who'd been sober awhile. After the meeting, they'd sat down for a cup of coffee together and Finn had told the guy a little bit about himself. The guy had listened, not saying much, which Finn had appreciated. He found himself going to more meetings. He just did it without thinking too much about it. Then, one day, Mona had moved back home.

The priest finished with an Amen, closed the book, and looked down into the pit. The bugler raised his horn. In time with his five comrades, Finn raised his gloved hand in salute and listened to the long, mournful notes of taps. Hairs rose on the back of his neck; he had to keep his eyes fixed on the middle distance and his jaw clenched just to hold it together.

When it was done, Finn stepped to one end of the casket and took hold of the edges of the flag. A fellow CBP marine interdiction agent did the same at the other end. They lifted the flag, pulled it taut, and stepped to the side of the casket, where they slowly folded it lengthwise three times. Then, with measured precision, Finn began to fold it diagonally, moving a small step closer to his colleague with each somber movement. No one made a sound. A shadow fell upon him when a cloud passed in front of the sun, and then cleared when the cloud moved on. By the twelfth fold, he was toe to toe with his fellow agent.

He turned and looked at his wife, at the strength and tenderness in her big brown eyes, and held her gaze a moment longer than protocol allowed. Then he stepped forward and knelt in front of Diego's mother. In his white-gloved hands, he held out the Stars and Stripes.

"On behalf of a grateful nation . . ." he began.